THE PORT OF LONDON MURDERS

THE PORT
OF LONDON
MURDERS

JOSEPHINE BELL

With an Introduction
by Martin Edwards

Poisoned Pen
PRESS

Introduction © 2020, 2021 by Martin Edwards
The Port of London Murders © 1938 by The Estate of Josephine Bell
Cover and internal design © 2021 by Sourcebooks
Front cover image © Mary Evans Picture Library

Published by Poisoned Pen Press, in imprint of Sourcebooks, in association with the British
Library
P.O. Box 4410, Naperville, Illinois 60567-4410
(630) 961-3900
sourcebooks.com

The Port of London Murders was originally published in 1938 by Longmans, Green and Co.,
London, New York, and Toronto.

Library of Congress Cataloging-in-Publication Data

Names: Bell, Josephine, author. | Edwards, Martin, writer
    of introduction.
Title: The Port of London murders / Josephine Bell ; with an introduction
    by Martin Edwards.
Description: Naperville, Illinois : Poisoned Pen Press, [2021] | Series:
    British library crime classics | The Port of London Murders was
    originally published in 1938 by Longmans, Green and Co., London, New
    York and Toronto.
Identifiers: LCCN 2020056349 (print) | LCCN 2020056350 (ebook) | (trade paperback)
    | (epub)
Subjects: LCSH: London (England)--Fiction. | GSAFD: Detective and mystery
    stories.
Classification: LCC PR6003.A525 P67 2021 (print) | LCC PR6003.A525
    (ebook) | DDC 823/.912--dc23
LC record available at https://lccn.loc.gov/2020056349
LC ebook record available at https://lccn.loc.gov/2020056350

Printed and bound in the United States of America.
SB 10 9 8 7 6 5 4 3 2 1

INTRODUCTION

THE PORT OF LONDON MURDERS WAS FIRST PUBLISHED in 1938, shortly before the term "Golden Age" was first applied to detective fiction of the period. Today we usually associate Golden Age detection with the "Queens of Crime" who dominated the 1930s: Agatha Christie, Dorothy L. Sayers, Margery Allingham, Gladys Mitchell, and Ngaio Marsh. One might assume that Josephine Bell wrote books in much the same vein. Sometimes she did, but there is nothing cozy about this novel. No country house, no locked room puzzle, no "Great Detective" uttering enigmatic remarks prior to revealing a surprise solution to the assembled suspects.

On the contrary, this well-crafted story now reads like a precursor to the type of post-war detective fiction that was more realistic in mood than the typical interwar whodunit. Gillian Mary Hanson discusses the novel interestingly and in considerable depth in *City and Shore: The Function of Setting in the British Mystery*, but it's noteworthy that she gives the publication date as 1958, rather than twenty years earlier. This reflects the year of the book's belated appearance in the U.S., but also indicates that this is far from being a conventional old-fashioned mystery.

For a present-day reader, an important aspect of the appeal of vintage crime novels is that they are fascinating social documents. In *The Port of London Murders*, Josephine Bell provides us with a window into ordinary lives that is unusual in fiction published during the Golden Age. Her focus was on the working-class environment on the edge of the River Thames, a community she portrays with insight and compassion. An accident on the river, an apparent suicide, and a missing policeman are among the ingredients of a story which marked a departure for the author and suggested a growing confidence in her own literary talents.

Josephine Bell's real name was Doris Bell Collier (1897–1987). She was born in Manchester, and educated at Godolphin School, Salisbury, where an older pupil was Dorothy L. Sayers. She studied at Newnham College, Cambridge, and trained in medicine at University College Hospital in London. In 1923, she married a fellow doctor, Norman Dyer Ball, and the couple had four children.

I'm indebted to a member of the family, Isobel Middleton, for sharing with me extensive extracts from the as yet unpublished memoirs of Josephine Bell (for convenience, I'll use the pseudonym), which paint in details of her career that were previously unknown. Her practical approach to her craft is evident in her observation that she decided early on not "to write about my inner soul, or not exclusively… I knew I was not a literary character, merely a storyteller."

At the age of thirty-two, she wrote a book called *Corpse at the Mill*, very much in the conventional Golden Age mould, and took it to a leading literary agency (where she bumped into Hilaire Belloc, but was too shy to introduce herself), only to have it rejected. Since she later consigned it to the waste-paper bin, we will never know if it had much merit, but such abortive efforts are part and parcel of a literary apprenticeship.

Her husband, who was nicknamed "Brun," agreed to help her devise her next plot; they realized that their medical expertise gave them a particular advantage, well worth exploiting. At first, the couple wrote alternate chapters, but they found this didn't work, and Josephine decided to do all the writing herself, while consulting her husband on details of the plot. Unsurprisingly, she opted to create an amateur detective who was a doctor; thus was born Dr. David Wintringham.

The result was *Murder in Hospital*, which was published by Longman. Professional rules debarred her from using her own name, since this would have been regarded as an unethical form of advertising; her chosen pseudonym combined her own middle name (which was also her grandmother's maiden name) and a feminization of her father's first name, Joseph.

In her first three books, she avoided the conventional country house milieu while keeping to the general approach of the detective stories of the time, making use of settings she was familiar with, as well as her medical knowledge. The books were well received, but, tragically, Brun was not around to share in his wife's success. He'd been killed in a car crash which also claimed the life of Shelagh Clutton-Brock (whose husband, Alan, later wrote a detective story, *Murder at Liberty Hall*).

Josephine and Brun had practised in Greenwich, and knowing the port of London area well, she decided that should be the setting of her fourth book, her first non-series mystery. She researched the workings of the River Police, taking tea with a retired detective who in turn introduced her to the commander of the force. This led to an enjoyable visit to their riverside headquarters and a couple of hours spent "watching the patrols come in and out and talking to different officers."

By this time, she'd moved to Guildford, where she met Freeman Wills Crofts (several of whose books have been reprinted in the British Library's Crime Classics series) and his wife. The Crofts invited her to a Detection Club dinner at the Dorchester, to witness the initiation into the club of Nicholas Blake (that is, the future Poet Laureate, Cecil Day-Lewis). She loved the occasion, but when she was invited to join the club shortly thereafter, she declined, because she couldn't afford the cost of the dinners.

Originally, she had planned only to write half a dozen detective novels before venturing into mainstream fiction, but she found that her non-genre novels did not enjoy noticeably better reviews or sales. At this time, about a couple of thousand copies of each book were sold, a fairly common figure for authors who were well-regarded but not highly renowned. A wartime mainstream novel, *Alvina Foster*, did better, while another, *Compassionate Adventure*, became her "all-time bestseller," with fifteen thousand copies sold shortly after the end of the war.

Josephine Bell continued to publish novels into her eighties, and her long career illustrates the rollercoaster nature of an author's life. Twice, the publishers of her detective fiction closed their crime lists, but she remained undaunted and continued to write prolifically. In 1953, she became one of the founding members of the Crime Writers' Association;

within a few years, she had co-edited the CWA's first anthology (choosing the stories over afternoon tea at the Charing Cross Hotel, in the company of Michael Gilbert and Julian Symons) and chaired the organization, in succession to Symons. In 1954, she finally joined the Detection Club, of which she remained an enthusiastic member until her death, and she ceased to practise medicine in order to concentrate on writing. To this day her hospitality is recalled by Sheila Mitchell, widow of the former Detection Club President H. R. F. Keating. Josephine used to invite them to Sunday lunch at her home in Guildford, and Sheila describes her as "a very caring person with boundless energy."

Josephine Bell published over sixty novels, more than two thirds of them mysteries, with David Wintringham making the last of a dozen appearances in *The Seeing Eye* in 1958. Overall, hers was a literary career of quiet accomplishment which deserves to be celebrated. I've previously included a couple of her short stories in anthologies in this series, namely *Crimson Snow* and *Deep Waters*. Reader reaction has been very positive, and I'm delighted to be able to usher this novel back into print. As *The Port of London Murders* shows, she could certainly tell an entertaining tale.

—Martin Edwards
www.martinedwardsbooks.com

1

In the early afternoon of a bleak first of November, the *San Angelo*, with a mixed cargo from the East, and after a voyage remarkable in its latter part for almost continuous storm and gale, steamed thankfully into the wide mouth of Thames river.

She was British-owned, and most of her crew of eleven, including her captain, were also British. There had been moments off the coast of Spain when they had given thanks for the gale, which lessened their chance of attack from the Spanish political maniacs. But that incalculable danger passed, the increasing force of the wind menaced them across the Bay of Biscay, and followed them into the Channel, where it blew with, if anything, an added ferocity and terror. The more often they saw the English coast, spray-clouded and forbidding, looming before them, the fainter grew their hopes of ever reaching its shores in safety, and the clearer became their vision of a ship battered on the rocks and their own drowned bodies rolled up on the sand.

But the *San Angelo* survived, ploughing doggedly on,

losing some of her deck fittings, sustaining some damage to her life-boats, and some injury, in the shape of a broken wrist and a cut head, to members of her crew, but making up at last into the estuary of the Thames, where the waves sank to half their former proportions, and it began to be possible to shout audibly above decks.

She slid past the Nore and Sheerness on Sheppey. There was no fleet of brown-sailed stately barges turning out from the Medway as she passed; the weather was too much for them. But as she moved on towards Tilbury, a faint gleam of silvery winter sunlight broke through the grey clouds and shone on the huge petrol tanks above Canvey Island, making them gleam with a queer formal beauty. Then the gap in the sky closed again and the light faded swiftly and steadily.

It was nearly dark when the *San Angelo* found her appointed berth and drew alongside the wharf, ready for unloading on the following day. The routine inspections over, the crew went off for their gear, arrangements were made for the immediate transfer of the casualties to hospital, and the captain walked slowly towards his cabin.

He felt almost too tired to move; he had not had a full night's sleep since leaving Gibraltar, and for the last two days no sleep at all. But here they were, safe and sound, and no damage to speak of, considering. And the cargo hadn't shifted after all. That had been his main anxiety in the Bay. A mixed cargo, different weights and sizes, taken on in many different ports. It was a wonder they'd had no trouble. Not but what a few cases here and there would come out cracked, he didn't mind betting.

He looked out of his cabin port-hole. It was quite dark now, but lights twinkled everywhere, on shore, on the riverside, making bright paths across the black water, on the tugs and barges moving ceaselessly to and fro in an endless procession. And far away on all sides a red and orange glow covered the sky, shining steadily on the vast labyrinth of London.

The rush hour in the City was nearly over. There were still a good many discreet dark figures, attaché case in hand, making their way to the tube stations and bus stops, but it was possible now to walk against the stream without being jostled and to drive a car without being checked every few yards by the solid flow of pedestrians crossing the roads.

Interrupting the row of brightly lit shops, the steps of Lancaster House in Prince Albert Street loomed up darkly. It was a narrow entrance between stout pillars and gave no indication to the casual passer-by of the rabbit warren of offices that lay within. But at the top of the steps the walls on either side of the dark little portico were covered with boards giving the names of all the business firms or individuals who had premises inside the building. The boards went up so high on the walls that it was difficult, even on a fine day, to read who occupied the top floor. Consequently, in the dark winter months, visitors to Lancaster House, after one fruitless craning of the neck, gave up the impossible feat, and went in through the glass doors to find the commissionaire. This functionary, anticipating just such action, had made his permanent resting-place round the corner of the ground-floor corridor and well out of sight. The lift-boy, however, though usually stationed at one of the upper floors, could be summoned and questioned. So the determined visitor reached his goal without undue delay, but the helpless and the impatient and the diffident were usually to be found wandering up and down the stairs and along the corridors, papers in hand, staring at the arrows and other marks that directed them to many fascinating and obscure trades, but never to the one they wanted. And it was remarkable, though nobody, not even the lift-boy, ever noticed it, that none of these visitors ever inquired for the last room in the basement corridor, where the frosted-glass door bore in small black letters the name "M. HOLMAN. IMPORTER." Only two men ever went into this room, and one of them was the importer himself.

On this particular evening, the first of November, the commissionaire and the lift-boy, following the home-bound stream of clerks and typists, had left Lancaster House at six, and though one light still shone in the hall, all the offices on the ground floor were dark. On the upper floors of the building the offices were dark too. Only in the basement one frosted-glass door glowed in the dark corridor, showing that Mr. Holman's office was still occupied.

The importer himself sat inside. He had turned his swivel chair away from his desk and sat with his feet up on a small table which stood near the electric fire. In this way his legs stretched across the front of the fire and his calves were pleasantly warmed by it. But in spite of the cosiness of the small room and the seeming prosperity of the well-chosen modern office furniture, Mr. Holman did not appear to be enjoying himself. He was restless and ill at ease, and continually passed his fat short hand with its diamond-studded ring across the thinning hair that lay in shining black parallel lines from his forehead to the nape of his neck. Several evening newspapers were on the desk beside him. He picked them up one by one and glanced through them impatiently. What he sought was not there, however, for presently he threw them down again swearing and felt in his pocket for a cigar. When he had lit it he sat back in his chair, recrossed his feet in the opposite sense and stared morosely at the artificial flicker of the non-existent flames of his electric fire.

The telephone broke in upon his musing with a suddenness that made him jump. He snatched it up eagerly, but as he listened his face drooped into its former lines of anxiety and ill-humour.

"No, I've heard nothing yet. Why do you think I'm sitting here? Would I have waited in this God-forsaken dungeon if I'd heard any news?—Oh, all right. But it's all very well for you; you get about, you see things. I'm stuck here day after day, week after week, no air, no light but electricity, winter and summer, and then this sort of thing happens!... I don't suppose he'll phone me to-night even if she does get in later—Oh, yes, I'll let you know. Where will I ring you?... Again?—I thought there was a new attraction—Well, I am minding my own business. It seems to me I'm minding all our businesses. If it wasn't for me... Yes, they are getting impatient. They were promised the new consignment two days ago. They say they can get rubber from hundreds of firms. So they can, of course; but they get it cheaper from me. Only I don't want to upset the present arrangement. Liston swallows all I say about experiments, so I have no trouble—Yes, of course—Well, don't I know that?—Yes, I'll let you know. But I'm not stopping here more than another half-hour. I've got a date, and I'm late already. Yes, yes, I'll ring you up if I hear. Didn't I say I would? All right, all right. But I didn't make the weather, did I?"

Mr. Holman put back the receiver with a vicious bang, and taking the cigar out of his mouth, regarded it with a bitter look. He got up restlessly and took a turn across the office floor, his black eyes flickering from side to side as he tried to make up his mind on some of the difficult problems that beset him. But before he had time to arrive at any decisions the telephone rang again, and this time he pounced on it with increased excitement and a sudden swift hope.

"Yes…yes, it's Holman speaking. She has?—This afternoon? That's good. I'm very glad to hear it. I said I was very glad to hear it! I was a little anxious, with all this bad news we've been having in the papers lately—You'll have the stuff delivered on Monday. Good—Thank you. Good-night."

As he put down the receiver again, slowly and carefully this time, he sighed his relief. Things would come out all right after all. He swept the newspapers off his table into the waste-paper basket, turned out the fire, and collected his hat and coat from the peg on the back of the door. He went quietly up the stairs into the hall and stood listening. The night watchman was on the floor above, testing the doors one by one. Mr. Holman tiptoed across the hall, and softly let himself out through the swing doors. He was just in time to get out without a fuss; the posts of the movable railings were in place, but the barrier itself had not been fixed in position.

About a hundred yards farther along Prince Albert Street a woman stood looking at a shop window. As Mr. Holman paused beside her she turned away, and they walked on together. "Whatever have you been doing?" she said irritably, pulling her fur coat about her, "I was here just on half-past six, and it's nearly seven now."

"I'm sorry, Martha," replied the man. He put his hand under her elbow to guide her across the road, but she shook him off and crossed in front of him.

"It's bad enough to have to wait outside in the cold,

without you being half-an-hour late," she repeated as he caught her up on the other side. "What kept you, anyway?"

"Waiting for news of the new consignment."

"Oh, isn't it in?"

"It wasn't. I heard just before I left that it's come."

"Oh, I see. But I think you might of let me know you'd be late. I don't see why I shouldn't come to the office."

"You could if it was in the ordinary hours. But it would look a bit queer if you took to coming after hours."

"It looks a bit queer me waiting in the street. People might take me for a tart."

They might, thought Mr. Holman, regarding her with a critical eye. Her hair was very golden, escaping from her little black hat in a large roll all round her head; her make-up was lavish, and her legs plump above her smart black patent leather shoes. But he did not say what he thought, because she suited him very well, and was, moreover, indispensable to his work. Instead, he shifted his cigar to the other corner of his mouth, drew her hand over his arm, and said, soothingly,

"Where do you want to go, dear?"

"Home," replied Miss Kemp shortly, "I've been on my feet all day, not to mention standing on the pavement for the last half-hour."

She waved at a bus that had drawn in to the curb, and pulling her hand free ran awkwardly towards it and scrambled on board just as it started.

With an inward curse Mr. Holman hurled his fat body at the bus as it passed him, swayed uncertainly into the interior and sat down beside Martha Kemp, panting and glowering, with his bowler hat tipped to the back of his head.

"Heh, Tony! Turn off that bloody wireless!"

"Oh, but, Pam, I want to dance."

"There isn't room. You're always turning the place upside down. Shut it off, Tony."

"But Babs wants to dance. Don't be mean, Pam!"

"We all want to dance!"

The voices clamoured in unison, and the wireless continued to pour out a torrent of syncopated noise. Tony and the other four men near him rolled up the carpet and pushed it against the wall.

Pamela Merston watched them with fury in her dark eyes. She lay curled on a sofa, her arms held up on a pile of silk-covered cushions, and her face propped in her hands. In the half-circle formed by her body a man sat negligently, using her knees as a rest for his right elbow, and her hips as a support for his back. His left hand wandered lazily about her neck and hair. He watched her anger with a curiously amused expression and spoke lightly.

"Let them dance if they want to. It keeps them happy."

The girl called Babs came nearer to the sofa. "You invited us here, darling, didn't you?" she said sweetly. "Didn't you want a party to-night, after all? And you see," she went on, with a side glance at Tony, "we've finished all the lovely eats and all the drinks, so we haven't anything to do now unless we dance or play something."

The rest of the visitors sniggered; Pamela's face hardened.

"Nice friends I've got!" she said stonily, and dropped her chin on to the pile of cushions. "Go on! Do what the hell you like. Don't mind me. It's impossible to hear a word, but go ahead."

"Darling, you aren't ill or anything?" inquired one of the other girls, anxiously pushing forward. They all crowded round the sofa, staring with hard bright surprised eyes at their dearest friend, Pamela Merston, whose father gave her such a marvellous allowance, and let her have this quite lovely little flat all to herself instead of living with him in that gloomy barracks of a house at Wimbledon.

Pamela glowered at them, picking at the cushions in front of her.

"Oh, go and dance," she said at last. "Who cares if I can't hear."

"Why don't you go where you can hear if you want to talk?" suggested the young man called Tony. He had a round childlike face and a little brown moustache worn very high on his lip.

"Yes, darling," echoed Babs. "Why not take Gordon into the bedroom if you want to talk?—We aren't particular," she added softly.

The party hooted with joy at this sally. The man on the sofa, who had watched the whole scene with relish, unwound his long legs and stood up, stretching out a hand to Pamela.

"An excellent scheme," he said evenly. "We can talk in peace, and the children can work off their high spirits as they damn well like."

Pamela sprang up in one jerky movement and faced them with flushed cheeks.

"If I hadn't asked you here," she said fiercely, "I'd throw you all out on your necks."

She walked swaying to the bedroom door and disappeared with her escort.

"Well," said a tall girl with a short upper lip that kept her mouth permanently open. "Would you believe that? She must be ill or something."

"Something, I don't mind betting," whispered Tony to Babs, and moved off with her across the room. The others followed his example and began to dance. When he had gone once round the small space he returned to the subject of Pamela.

"This is the second time she's done it. Gone all jittery without the faintest warning and for no obvious reason, and then lost her temper. It's since she's taken up with this Longford fellow."

"Who is he?"

"Blessed if I know. Met him at Philip's myself. Thought he was rather wet, but I may be wrong."

"Well, if he's going to upset Pamela, he'll have to be eliminated."

Babs' small mouth set firmly. She couldn't do without Pamela, especially the pleasant lunches and cocktail parties, the smart black Jaguar car, and the suits and frocks that you could get from her second-hand, almost for nothing and as good as new. Babs had very little pocket money and had to live at home with fussy parents who were always objecting to her friends. Certainly she couldn't do without Pamela. She had been a fool to bait her; she must be careful to put that right sometime.

"Don't you think it would be tactful if we drifted off?"

The suggestion came from the tall girl. She waited till she had focussed the attention of the others and spoke again.

"I expect she's had bad news. I was just going to say, Robin is having some people in to-night and I know he wouldn't mind us gate-crashing. You've got a car here, haven't you, Tony?"

"Yes. Jolly bright idea!"

"Hubert's got a car, too. We'll easily fit into two cars."

"Right."

"Shall I tell her?" Babs moved officiously into the hall.

"Be discreet,—be discreet!" murmured Tony.

The tall girl pushed Babs on one side and knocked briskly at the bedroom door. Gordon Longford's voice said cheerfully, "Come in."

"That's presence of mind, if you like," remarked the irrepressible Tony.

Babs shouted, "Helen wants us to go round and see Robin. You don't mind, darling, do you?"

There was a moment's silence, and then Pamela's voice, somewhat muffled, replied, "Of course not."

The group outside the door grinned at one another and yelled back in chorus, "Thanks most awfully, Pam, for the lovely party."

They slung their coats over their arms, and dangling their hats in their hands trooped down the stairs into the mews outside where the two cars were parked.

Pamela Merston lifted her tear-stained face from the pillow.

"I shall go batty if you don't get it soon," she whimpered.

Gordon patted her shoulder. He was feeling bored, having comforted her steadily for nearly an hour.

"Don't worry, darling. Of course I will. Now what say to going out and getting some food? It's nearly nine."

"I don't want food."

"But I do. I work, my sweet. And I had a very light lunch."

The girl dragged herself off the bed and began to arrange the smooth black rolls of hair on her forehead. Her hands trembled violently. Gordon Longford got up and pulled the eiderdown straight where he had been sitting on it. Then, with a casual glance at Pamela, he strolled into the sitting-room and stood near the fire waiting.

As he shifted his weight from one foot to the other the telephone bell rang. He crossed the room quickly and took up the receiver.

"Who? Oh, you, Max!… Good… Good—Excellent!… Well, thanks for ringing me."

He put back the receiver gently and went to the door of the bedroom.

"Coming?" he asked.

Pamela, in hat and coat, her face restored to its conventional mask, nodded and picked up her handbag.

"You needn't look as if the end of the world had come," said Gordon, holding her as she passed him to kiss the back of her neck. "I promised you, and I shall redeem my promise,—let me see, to-day's Thursday—well, say Tuesday at the latest."

Pamela caught her breath; she clutched his arm and shook him.

"Really? You aren't saying that just to keep me quiet?"

"No. I mean it."

"Oh, darling!" She clung to him for a minute. "You don't know the relief! Let's not go out. I'll order some supper to come up."

"It'll be quicker to go out," answered Longford, who was genuinely hungry. "Besides, I must get home in good time."

"No, no," cried the girl, clinging to him again. "If we go out you must come back with me; I can't be alone. It gets worse and worse at night, rationing myself—you don't know. Sometimes I think I'll—" She broke off, shuddering and hiding her face against his coat. He said nothing; he was thinking, and his thoughts were not of her. Presently she raised her head and stood away from him. He crossed the room to a mirror and began to straighten his tie.

"You will come back here to-night," she insisted. "Say you will, darling. You must say you will."

Gordon Longford looked in the glass at his own long, narrow face. He approved of his fair hair and unusual amber-coloured eyes. He smiled faintly and spoke to his reflection. "All right. I'll come back to-night," he said.

2

THE MAIN ROAD GOING EAST FROM ROTHERHITHE
Tunnel is like any other of the South London throughfares.
It is broad, dreary and dirty, with tram lines down the centre
and on either side dingy houses in long rows broken at intervals by clumps of mean, untidy-looking shops.

On weekdays, and particularly on Saturdays, many of the
side-streets are transformed into markets, with stalls that
almost meet in the middle of the narrow road. Here provisions of every kind are supplemented by such luxuries as
jellied eels and tiny saucers of whelks and cockles, while a
rich harvest is gleaned by less honest traders who exhibit a
miscellany of old iron, enamel ware, and worn-out clothing,
which they manage with verbal skill to foist on to simple-
minded customers. On Saturday business increases as the
day moves on, so that by the evening there is a continuous
surging stream forcing its way into these side-streets, to lose
itself among the brightly-lit stalls, where the inviting Sunday
beef glows red and juicy under the arc-lights of the butcher's
stall, and the fruit and vegetables bewilder the eye in their

variety of colour and choice. Mothers with laden prams, the parcels in a mountain near the handle and the baby in a restricted space under the hood, push their way out of the maelstrom and pause as they reach the main road pavement and comparative freedom to yell encouragement to the string of children who struggle in their wake. It is possible to walk here, but not fast, as the pavement is still crowded. The young men, swaggering along to the cinema with their girls, have to step off the pavement to get round the family groups with their loads of provisions. The sweetshops, the tobacconists, the hairdressers, and the public houses all have their crowds of customers flowing in and out, enjoying their brief weekly leisure, preparing for Sunday outings, spending the weekly wage. The road itself is a menace to the careless motorist and a nightmare to the anxious one.

But by Sunday morning the noise has gone, and the packed crowds, and the yelling and pushing, the laughter and sudden anger. The side-streets are empty except for the piles of rubbish left by the stalls and swept into heaps against the curb. The main road is empty too. A few dirty papers blow backwards and forwards across it, a few people in Sunday clothes walk slowly along the pavement; a few trams clank past bearing visitors to distant families, uncomfortable in stiff collars and unyielding best shoes. The blocks of houses and shops, equally closed and silent, look drearier than ever. A stranger, travelling along this main road, and comparing it perhaps with other South London main roads and with main roads in Kentish Town and Dalston and Whitechapel, would reflect gloomily on the huge area of once beautiful country so defaced, and with so little resulting benefit to its occupiers. He would think of the rows of little streets stretching on either side of this road, joining and crossing one another until they opened into yet another thoroughfare, and another, and another. And he would put the hideous thought out of his mind as he travelled on, not knowing that for several miles he had been moving beside the bank of the river Thames.

For in some places along this road going east from Rotherhithe the streets on the left-hand side end at the water's edge in wharfs, in yards, in scrap-heaps, in narrow jetties, in small bays with promenades flanked by old dwellings, in little streets where the crumbling houses on the Thames' side stand out into the mud on wooden piles. Beyond them the river stretches and a different world begins.

The grime and squalor and ugliness are still there in the uncouth machinery leaning out over the wharfs, in the heavy work-worn barges, and even in the dark greasy substance of the river itself. But they are changed by the sea air blowing up from the estuary, and are cloaked and hidden by the blue-grey haze that hangs over the banks most of the year round. They are forgotten at the sight of broad swinging water, and sea-gulls turning and dipping to its surface, and the red sails of a barge working upstream from Rochester. The old men, leaning on the river wall, smoking their pipes, hear the shrill yelp of the tugs' sirens, and the deep boom of the steamers churning slowly down to the sea. The endless clanking of the trams two streets away is muffled, forgotten. It has no place in this wider freer world of gulls and lapping waves.

On the Sunday following the arrival in dock of the *San Angelo* with her cargo, the river lay tranquil and sparkling under a bright sun. There was no wind, so that, though the year was well-advanced, and the sun by midday had not climbed very far into the sky, the little beach under the river wall at the end of Lower Thames Street was pleasantly warm. More old men than usual leaned on it smoking their pipes and exchanging the gossip of the week. The children, swarming on the slippery oil-covered stones of the shingle, had for the most part discarded their shoes and stockings and were paddling in the spent waves, apparently careless of the winter chill of the water.

Harry Reed straightened his back and drew his hand across his hot forehead. His coat already lay over the rails of Jim Sawyer's boathouse verandah, and his pullover now followed it. He rolled up his shirt-sleeves and stood still for a few minutes, watching the sun on the water near the landing stage. Jim Sawyer broke in on his musing with a harsh cackle of laughter.

"Why don't yer tike yer shirt off and mike a job of it? Blimey, it's 'ot enough for Bank 'Oliday!"

Harry looked round at him and grinned. Jim Sawyer was spread on a deck-chair in the shade, reading *The News of the World*. He was six foot tall and weighed fifteen stone, but for all that he was surprisingly agile and sure-footed on the rickety contraption that served him for a landing-stage and in the tumble-down sheds that housed the four-oared boats of the Rowing Clubs. In his day he had been much sought after by rival clubs, for his weight and strength and unsurpassed knowledge of the river made him an invaluable oar to any crew that was fortunate enough to secure his services. However, with one or two intervals, he kept to his nearest neighbour, the "Fisherman," and as a member of that house's Rowing Club, had stroked their boat to victory on many notable occasions. He made his living on the river and by the river: no-one knew exactly how much he was worth, but many people speculated freely on the subject. Among these were the River Police, who had a few good reasons for wishing to know a little more, in a quiet way, about the sources of this particular income.

True, Jim Sawyer lodged and repaired the Rowing Clubs' boats and oars; in the summer he hired pleasure boats of a flat, up-river, and totally unsuitable type, in which the local inhabitants went for excitingly perilous trips. And at frequent intervals he journeyed to the vicinity of Commercial Docks and delivered to the Receiver of Wrecks sundry objects that he had gleaned from the Thames in the neighbourhood of his boathouse. But all this, though it was probably worth a sparing sort of comfort, did not spell affluence, and there had been times when Jim Sawyer had astonished his neighbours with a display of wealth quite disproportionate to his apparent means.

Take for instance the occasion when his wife, a sufferer from rheumatism, had missed her step on the stairs and fallen. There was every reason to think that her leg might be broken, but instead of sending for the ambulance and having her conveyed immediately to hospital, Jim had dispatched a message to his own doctor and at the same time had phoned for the attendance of the Portable X-ray Service. The doctor in the room above watched by the patient's side, and an admiring crowd below at the corner of Lower Thames Street and Wood Wharf stood round the Portable X-ray Service van, in the interior of which delightful unseen machinery buzzed and throbbed, while men darted in and out of the house, and the X-ray picture was taken through the bedroom window. When, in the "Fisherman" that night, Jim was asked how much the magic van had cost him he only waved his hand and ordered half-pints for everyone present.

That was all they ever got out of him on the subject, but it kept them wondering, and when, a few years later, Jim took a party of friends to the Derby in a private hire bus, and word went round that he had paid for the whole blooming concern himself, they were not surprised, but nodded their heads and said they knew as much. Meanwhile the River Police kept their eyes and ears open, and remained on terms of strict affability with Jim when they encountered him sculling his leisurely way about the river.

"Why don't you come outside?" said Harry, leaning his arms on the verandah rail. "It may be the last time you see the sun this side of Christmas."

"Don't care if it is. You don't see me mucking abaht on Sunday, sun or no sun; I likes me bit o' rest. It's all right for you, driving lorries all the week; mikes a change for you, don't it? But I sees the ruddy river week in week out. It don't 'old much fascination for me now, see?"

His shrewd little eyes twinkled at Harry and he lowered the paper to his lap.

"Got your boat ship-shape? I must say you save time draining 'er through that bung-'ole. Mind you don't forget it one day when you go off for a trip."

"I wouldn't get far without the bung," smiled Harry, "but I can swim all right."

"Don't say I didn't warn you," answered Jim Sawyer, and rustling his newspaper, plunged once more into the intricacies of the football news.

Harry went back to his boat and turned her over lovingly to rest on the other side of her keel. Because he had so little time from his work he had made a hole in her bottom through which he left her to drain during the week. In this way he avoided wasting time over baling her out when in his brief leisure he wanted to take her on the river.

He looked down at her with pride in his dark eyes. She

was clean and dry, her painter neatly rolled down in the bows. The thwart, newly varnished a week ago, shone in the sunshine. Harry put his sculls on board and pushed his craft carefully into the water, holding her in to the side of the landing-stage while he climbed on board. He sat for a few minutes bobbing up and down and still holding on while he looked about him. The river was quiet except for the gulls and few small dinghies like his own. Some had sails and floated silently backwards and forwards, boldly crossing the wide spaces of the river, which on weekdays were as crowded and dangerous as Piccadilly Circus to a bicycle, but now were as free as the Broads in winter. The beach, on the other hand, deserted when the children were in school, on Sundays was a play-ground where they screamed and tumbled with a zest made keener by the sharp air off the water. Hardly more than a hundred yards long, shut off at one end by Jim Sawyer's boathouse and at the other by a timber wharf, its surface a shingle that was black with mud and oil and strewn with every kind of filthy rubbish, it was a sorry pleasure ground indeed. But the children did not mind. They could paddle, they could wade in the shallows, dragging chunks of wood on strings, they could make ducks and drakes, they could pretend to splash water over their friends, they could souse their enemies. It was the only beach that many of them had ever known, and it was infinitely superior in entertainment value to trolleys in the streets outside their homes, or marbles in the gutter.

Harry grinned as he watched them. He had played on that beach himself, had made toy boats himself out of chunks of wood, and had begged trips on the river from a younger and slimmer Jim Sawyer. There seemed to be more kids than ever crowded on to the narrow space, and more old men leaning on the wall above, gossiping as they smoked.

A golden, unexpected head appeared among them and Harry caught his breath. It was that girl again, come after her kid brother, and was she a peach, oh boy!

He watched her as she pushed up to the wall to peer over and shout "Les!" in a shrill voice that carried across the water to where he sat, still holding the landing-stage and rocking gently with the rise and fall of the waves. Harry laughed to himself. She'd got plenty of life in her, and had it in for the boy, like last week. They must have dinner early at her home; perhaps she wanted to get out early. That would be it. She'd got a date, and they were having dinner early and the nipper wasn't back, so she'd had to come down for him. It hadn't half made her wild.

Harry looked about for the boy. He knew what he was like because he had watched a similar scene last week at about the same time. But he could not see him among the crowd on the beach, and as he shaded his eyes and tried again, he heard the girl's voice, filled this time with exasperation and a hint of anxiety.

"Les! Les! Come on home! You got no business messing down there. Come on! Dad'll take a strap to you when I tell him where you been."

The boy, whom Harry now identified, was up to his knees in the brown soupy water, gravely arranging ballast in a small dug-out log he had fitted up as a boat. He looked round and waved his hand. Then quite deliberately he waded further from the shore.

"Now he'll get it in the neck," thought Harry, and watched the boy trying vainly to roll up his trouser legs higher than they could go.

A solitary tug appeared in the distance moving rapidly down-stream on the out-going tide. Harry watched her easy swift advance, and envied the men on board. When he turned again to look at the beach, he saw that the girl had come down the steps and was standing on the comparatively dry shingle under the wall. She was bareheaded, and her light golden hair hung low on her neck with the ends rolled inwards; she had a little cluster of curls on her forehead. Her face was small and square with high cheek-bones and large round blue eyes. Her hands were pushed into the pockets of an old swagger coat, under which she wore a skirt and a woollen jumper that clung tightly to her figure, and even at that distance showed off its lovely shape.

"Do as I tell you, Leslie," she cried again, furiously angry. "Come here this minute! Oh, just you wait till I get my hands on you," she went on unwisely. Leslie put his tongue out at her.

"Yah!" he yelled back. "Come and fetch me, why don't you?"

Heedless of future retribution, he turned his back on her, and bent over his craft. Her reply was drowned in a long hoot from the tug as she altered course at the bend of the river.

Harry came to life suddenly and seized his sculls. Dreaming like that he'd be caught by the tug's wash if he wasn't quick and lose some of his fresh paint against the landing-stage! He swung the bows of his dinghy round across the stream and pulled frantically to get on some way. The first wave of the wash lifted him up, and as it did so he caught sight of the boy standing over his boat, with the water nearly up to his waist.

"Mind the wash!" he yelled wildly and sank into the trough behind the first wave.

"Mind the wash!" echoed the old men on the wall, waving their arms.

The boy looked up and tried to wade in-shore. But he was too late. The first wave plucked him off his feet, the second bowled him over, and the back wash pulled him out into the river, where he floundered choking, well out of his depth.

Harry took a grip on his sculls and began to pull furiously. The tide was running out and he knew that in a few seconds the boy would be swept down-stream to the timber wharf, off which four rows of barges lay moored. There would be little chance for him among their great hulks with the undertow dragging him down.

The girl too wasted no time. When she saw her brother stumble she screamed wildly. But the next minute she was out of her coat and her skirt, had kicked off her high-heeled slippers and was running down the beach. The old men, temporarily paralysed by the sight of her very shapely legs in the shortest of pink silk panties, recovered as she plunged into the water, and began to shout encouragement and to wave their arms for help. Commotion grew, the crowd increased, and eventually a policeman appeared above the wall, blew his whistle, and flinging his leg over the coping, dropped on to the shingle and dragged off his boots and tunic.

Harry, his eyes fixed on the boy, whose head appeared from time to time as he threshed the water, drove his boat across the stream in front of the barges. He began to wonder how he could possibly grab the boy without upsetting himself and making matters worse. But while he was feverishly manoeuvring for position, he saw the girl come up at a fast crawl, seize her brother, turn over, and look round gasping from her effort.

The crowd on shore cheered loudly, and the policeman paused in the act of dropping his tunic on the shingle. The girl could certainly swim, she had caught the boy and there was a boat at hand to pick them up. He thought he would probably be more useful on shore, and bolted for the nearest telephone box.

Harry drew level with the floating pair and shipped his sculls. The boy's head lay limply against his sister's shoulder; his face was blue and there was froth at his mouth and nose. The girl looked at Harry with terrified eyes, reaching out to clutch the side of the boat.

"I'll take 'im," said Harry quickly. He braced his feet on the thwart and took a firm hold of the boy's shoulders.

"Swim round to the other side and hold on," he ordered. "If I try to pull 'im out with the both of you this side, we'll all be in the water."

The girl let go and swam round as she was bid. When she had got both hands on the gunwale Harry heaved on his side and the boy was bundled into the bottom of the boat, where he lay in a limp heap, apparently lifeless.

"You better come in too," said Harry cheerfully, feeling very well pleased with himself.

But his triumph was short-lived. Warning shouts began again on the shore and, looking up, he saw that they had drifted rapidly down upon the barges, which were now only a few yards away. With a desperate effort he flung out his sculls, and pulled his boat round so that the girl should not be caught and pulled under. She saw the danger and, realizing that she had no chance of swimming clear, clung to the gunwale with all her strength. Harry made one more frantic attempt to pull away, but the great stern of a barge loomed above him, and as he struggled his scull struck its iron-clad side and splintered with a sickening crack. The boat spun about; he tried desperately to steady her and fend her off, but lost his balance and fell sideways. As his outstretched hand struck the side of the barge an agonizing pain shot up his arm, the girl screamed, the boat lurched once more with the force of his last strong pull and was still. She had wedged broadside on between two barges, and lay precariously aslant with the swift tide dragging at her and grinding her closer and closer into the narrow gap between them. Harry's injured wrist was imprisoned between the dinghy and the barge.

"Now what?" gasped the girl with a gallant attempt at levity. Her legs were being pulled under the boat by the force of the water, and her arms ached with the effort of holding on. But she knew that if she let go she would be drawn under the barges, and though she might have swum clear of one of them, a matter of eighty feet or so, they were here moored in lines of six. Besides, her young brother lay where he had been dumped and the colour of his face frightened her.

"Can't you do something?" she cried hoarsely. "Do something for Les! Don't you know artificial respiration? If you don't, I do. Give me a hand into the boat, can't you?"

Harry twisted round to look at her. Then without answering, he pushed with his free hand against the barge and tried to wrench out the arm that was caught. But he could not do it, and as the dinghy rocked and lurched and fell back on to his wrist he groaned aloud.

"What's up?" said the girl anxiously, seeing his face whiten. "Have you hurt yourself?"

As he continued silent, she pulled herself towards him along the side of the boat. She stared with large horrified eyes at his twisted, imprisoned arm.

"Coo!" she whispered. "Can't you get your hand loose?"

"No," replied Harry roughly, "I like it this way."

The girl bit her lip.

"I better swim off and get help," she said quietly.

Between pain and helplessness, he lost his temper and raged at her.

"Don't be a durned little fool! Fat lot o' good you'd do. 'Ow do you think you'd get clear of these bloody barges? You stay where you are and shut your face if you can't talk sensible."

They were so absorbed in their immediate need, the plight of the boy, and the terrors of their situation, that they failed to see the Police launch, summoned by wireless, bearing swiftly down on them. But the crowd on the beach saw her and raised a cheer as her clean lines sped through the water, raising a cloud of spray on either side.

"Now, then!" cried the cheerful voice of Sergeant Adams, "What's the trouble here?"

Harry answered bitterly, "The boy tried to drown 'isself and 'is sister 'ere followed 'is example."

"And what about you? Here, miss, catch hold!"

"Oh, I'm on a pleasure cruise."

Sergeant Adams, noting Harry's predicament, grinned approval.

"Don't you worry, son, we'll soon have you out of that."

A few brisk orders brought the stern of the launch end-on to the dinghy, her engine running quietly to hold her off the smaller boat. The girl, still clinging to the lifebuoy that had been thrown to her, was drawn rapidly on board. Then with great care and considerable skill, Sergeant Adams lowered himself into Harry's boat. The latter said quickly, "I'm all right. See to the boy. 'E's not dead, is 'e?"

Adams swiftly turned the limp figure over and, kneeling astride of it, began artificial respiration. In a few minutes the boy stirred and took a short gasping breath.

"He'll do fine," said the Sergeant presently. He crouched in the unsteady craft, hoisting Leslie in his arms. The constable acting as deck-hand in the launch leaned over and pulled the boy to safety.

"Give him a whiff of CO_2, Fred," called Adams. "He's all right, but he'd do with a whiff. And give us a boathook." He turned to Harry. "Sorry to keep you waiting, my lad."

"Don't mention it." Harry achieved a sickly grin. His arm felt numb and cold; it no longer hurt him. He was glad the kid wasn't dead.

The next minute he yelled aloud. Sergeant Adams had pushed the boat a few inches from the barge, and his released arm, carried outward by the current, hit the iron side of it with force. He caught at the useless limb with his sound hand and sank back shaking with pain. Sergeant Adams lost no time in transferring him to the launch, secured the dinghy on tow, and pulled away from the barges into the safety of the middle river.

The three victims of the adventure regarded one another sheepishly, keeping their eyes turned from their rescuers. Leslie was still coughing and spitting, but his colour had come back, and, though subdued, he took an evident interest in his surroundings and was beginning to appreciate his position as the central figure of the incident. The girl, who had with inward shrinking seen Harry Reed's distorted wrist and hand bound to a splint and supported in a sling, looked miserably from his face to her brother's and back again. He had not spoken to her since they were brought on board, so he must be angry with her, and quite natural, too. Leslie was a young limb, if ever there was one.

The launch drew in towards Jim Sawyer's landing-stage. Already the white shape of an L.C.C. ambulance could be seen behind the wall in Wood Wharf. A dense crowd surged about it. Sergeant Adams, having written down the last of the particulars of the accident, closed his notebook and prepared for action.

"Please, sir," said Leslie in a small hoarse voice, addressing himself to Adams, "I don't want to go in no ambulance. I want to go 'ome." He pushed his knuckles into his eyes and began to sob.

"Who said the ambulance was for you?" answered the Sergeant gruffly. "What you need is a good hiding."

"He won't have to go to hospital, will he?" asked June Harvey anxiously. "We live just at the corner of Upper Thames Street. I could carry him that far."

The crew of the launch looked at her thoughtfully. She had risen in her eagerness, and the heavy regulation boat-coat they had given her fell open, displaying the woollen jumper and the short panties clinging to her all the more tightly by reason of their wetness. Seeing the admiration in three pairs of eyes, she clutched the coat about her and sat down again.

"I suppose," said Sergeant Adams severely, "you've got a skirt and so on on shore."

Jim Sawyer was waiting for them on the landing-stage. He assisted at the disembarking and offered to carry Leslie up to the road. But Sergeant Adams, though polite, was distant, and continued himself to take charge of the proceedings. Jim beamed good-naturedly.

"Just as you like, Mr. Adams. But I've got Miss Harvey's

things back in the house, and I expect she'd like to put them on afore she goes much further."

The girl smiled at him gratefully.

"Very well." Adams made up his mind quickly. "Here, Fred, you take Miss Harvey up to Jim's place, and the boy too, and I'll see the young feller here on to the ambulance."

Harry went meekly. He was tired and his arm hurt worse than ever. Her name was June Harvey and she lived in Upper Thames Street. Her father was captain on one of the river tugs. That was all she'd told the cop and all he was likely to know. She hadn't said a word to him since it happened. Well, he didn't much care.

He followed Adams across Jim Sawyer's verandah and through the house to the front door. The Sergeant opened it and signalled to the ambulance, which began to back into position, while the crowd surged forward cheering. Harry tried to button up his coat; Jim had helped him into it, but it hung loosely over the injured arm and threatened to fall off. He struggled with it, but could not make the two sides meet. "Let me do it for you," said a faint voice at his elbow.

June Harvey slipped a small damp handkerchief through the buttonhole on one side and fastened it round the button on the other.

"I think that'll hold till you get there," she said anxiously. "I hope your arm's not too bad. I don't know how to thank you for what you've done for me and Les. I'm ever so grateful. I am really." Her voice broke huskily.

Harry looked down into large blue eyes full of pity and concern. He took hold of the loose shoulder of the police coat she still wore and shook it gently.

"That's all right," he said gruffly. "Don't you worry about

that. I'll be as right as rain when I get the bone fixed. And a nice little 'oliday into the bargain. Cheerio, kid. I'll be seeing you."

He ducked his head against the crowd and dived for the ambulance door. June stood by Jim Sawyer's side waving encouragement as Harry was driven away.

"Who is he?" she asked, as the white tail of the ambulance disappeared round the corner of Lower Thames Street.

Jim Sawyer drew her back into the house and closed the door.

"Well," he said, looking at her with his head on one side, "fancy you not knowing that!"

3

WHILE THE PEOPLE MOVED SLOWLY AWAY FROM THE bottom of Lower Thames Street, in Fripp Street, at the other end of Wood Wharf, old Mrs. Bowerman received a visit from the doctor.

Mrs. Bowerman was eighty-five, a powerful old woman with untidy, snow-white hair and several chins. She had lived in the Fripp Street house, the next but one to the corner of Wood Wharf, since her marriage, some sixty years before. And she had not only bought this dwelling but had also acquired the long lease of the next door house, number three. In this her eldest son and his family had lived until his death, when his widow, getting on for sixty, had left it to join her eldest married daughter, Mrs. Bowerman's tenth grandchild. After this bereavement many members of the family hinted to one another that the old lady didn't ought to go on living by herself with no-one handy. But, since her temper grew no sweeter with advancing years, and her liking for strong liquor increased as her bodily activity declined, no-one made any very definite plans for her disposal, though all were agreed that it was a crying shame to leave her where she was. The grandchildren in particular laid the blame on those unmarried Bowerman aunts and uncles who could very well have supported the old lady in decency and comfort, and the great-grandchildren, after listening to the endless discussions on the subject, had got her fixed in their young minds as a confused symbol of age, selfishness, inebriety and the wrath of God.

Meanwhile, old Mrs. Bowerman, dressed in an extremely dirty white frilled overall, and a greasy black straw hat with a drooping ostrich feather falling from its high crown, and wrapped in an even greasier fringed plaid shawl, tottered daily to the "Fisherman" in Wood Wharf, and returned carrying her foaming jug in one hand and a small loaf in the other. The Pope children and Mrs. Dunwoody's Violet at Number One scuttled out of her way as she passed them, and waited till her door was shut before they ventured once more on to the pavement.

But before the combined onslaught of age and severe winter weather, Mrs. Bowerman's indomitable spirit failed at last. The plaid shawl was not proof against the wind and rain of that biting November, and her lungs, so long her boast among asthmatical neighbours, succumbed to the heavy fogs that alternated with the gales and frosts. She contracted a severe bronchitis, confided in Mrs. Dunwoody next door, and went to bed with a bottle of rum at her side to sweat the fever out of her system. After three days Mrs. Dunwoody became alarmed at her continued prostration, and grew tired of ministering to one whom nothing pleased. Besides, she had a weak heart herself and stairs played her up shocking, so she sent Mr. Dunwoody for Dr. Ellis, and broke the news of her action to the patient when she heard the car at the door.

The doctor felt Mrs. Bowerman's pulse and took her temperature.

"You ought to be in hospital," he said in a tired voice.

The old lady heaved herself up on one fat elbow and looked at him with an indignant light in her shrewd little eyes.

"You ain't examined me lungs yet. 'Ow do you know I ought?"

She sank back and fumbled with the fastening of her nightdress. "Drat the thing! Why couldn't that girl 'ave stayed to give me a 'and? Always running off when she's wanted. That's Dunwoody all over. I don't go to no 'orspital not if you was to drag me there."

Grudgingly Dr. Ellis produced a stethoscope from inside his coat and prepared a small window-like opening in the nightdress over the front of the old lady's chest. He listened at the four corners of this opening and stood up. "Bronchitis," he said laconically.

Mrs. Bowerman squinted at the stethoscope with scorn. "I could of told you, without all that 'ere palaver," she said.

"I thought you wanted to be examined."

"I don't go to no 'orspital."

"How can you stay here, alone, with no proper nursing?"

"Mrs. Dunwoody, what was 'ere just now, she comes in and sees to me. I leaves the string in the door, see? I won't be bad long, will I, doctor?"

"I can't say. You are not as young as you were."

Mrs. Bowerman gave a fat chuckle of appreciation and pulled her purse out from under the pillow.

"Mrs. Dunwoody'll send for the medicine for me, doctor. I want something strong to cut the phlegm, see? 'Ow much do I owe you?"

"Half-a-crown. But you really ought to go into hospital. Look at your fire! It wants some more coal now. It'll be out before your neighbour comes up."

He took the half-crown and put it in his pocket; picked up his bag, hesitated, and put it down again.

"Where do you keep your coal?" he asked irritably.

"Downstairs. But don't you bother, doctor. Mrs. Dunwoody'll be back directly."

"And waste your wood relighting the blamed thing," muttered Dr. Ellis. He seized the shovel and made his way down the steep narrow staircase, holding on to the rope that lay close against the wall, and which was hard, black, and shiny, from years of use.

The ground floor of the house was empty alike of people and furniture. Mrs. Bowerman preferred now to live in one room, and since her bed was upstairs she had gathered her other necessities thither. The unwanted possessions downstairs had vanished one by one to supplement her old-age pension in paying her account at the "Fisherman." For over ten years now the front parlour and the back-kitchen had remained in their shroud of dirt and dust undisturbed except when Mrs. Bowerman filled her scuttle with coal from the wall cupboard under the sink, or drew water from the tap above it.

Following the old lady's directions Dr. Ellis groped his way along the dark little passage and into the back room. The door of the sink-cupboard was open, hanging by its single remaining hinge, and the coal was clearly visible in lumps inside, and in a generous sprinkling of black dust on the floor round about. The doctor kicked the door still further open and stooped to shovel up the coal. He was giving a last dig into the small heap when his shovel hit the back of the cupboard and to his great surprise it fell over with a resounding clatter and he found himself looking through the gap into the empty kitchen of the next house.

"What's up?" shouted Mrs. Bowerman from above.

"Nothing. At least, I'll tell you in a minute."

Dr. Ellis reached into the cupboard and pulled the dividing door into place, where it balanced precariously. He stood up brushing his hands together and gazing thoughtfully at the cupboard while he considered this curious phenomenon. Then he picked up the bucket and returned to the bedroom above.

"Trying to break up the 'appy 'ome?" inquired Mrs. Bowerman, after he had put some coal on the fire.

"Not at all. The back of the cupboard fell down into the next house. Why isn't there a proper wall there? It seems an odd arrangement to me."

The old lady chuckled.

"It was my son 'ad the 'ouse next door. 'E cut that 'ole through, so 'e could get at my coal if 'e ran short 'isself. The kids found it 'andy too, to come in and out, see."

"Has no-one lived there since?"

"Oh, there's been a good few since then, but they never knowed. I kept it fastened this side. Only the 'inge is weak now, and the other 'ouse being empty, I don't bother much."

Dr. Ellis crossed to the window and looked out.

"I thought all this street was coming down," he said.

"So it is when they gets me out and the Popes and Dunwoodys next door. But they got to find us somewhere to go, and I'm not moving till they makes me. I been 'ere sixty-two year, and I'm too old to make a fresh start."

Two tears of self-pity started to roll down Mrs. Bowerman's stout cheeks. Dr. Ellis picked up his bag again;

he must get on if he wanted any dinner; his housekeeper would be going out. Mrs. Bowerman tried to keep him a little longer.

"Aren't you in a 'urry to rush off?" she complained. "You better give me a sustificate, doctor, if you don't mind. I'll 'ave one for me club, and one to show the Council. They're boarding up the 'ouses this side to-morrow, right up to me. They wanted us out by the end of the week, to start pulling it down, but I won't be fit to leave then, will I?"

"I shouldn't think so. But you could always go into hospital."

"I won't go to no 'orspital, leastways not to the Institootion, and that's where you'd be sending me, I suppose."

"I'm afraid I couldn't get you a bed anywhere else. But it's a hospital now, not an institution, as you call it. You're not ill enough to go to the General, and they have to keep most of their beds for the cases sent in from their Outpatient departments."

Mrs. Bowerman did not bother to follow this explanation. She had got her certificate and that was all that mattered. Also the fire was burning up nicely. She lay back and closed her eyes.

Dr. Ellis promised to call again in two days' time and went away, shutting the bedroom door behind him. At the foot of the stairs he paused, looking back along the passage to the open door of the kitchen. He had not propped up the back of the peculiar cupboard very securely, but as the next-door house was empty it could not matter. He decided to leave it to the Popes or the Dunwoodys to remedy if they felt so inclined. He would have done it, but there was no time—there never was any time, and he was tired—always tired. He let himself out of the house and pulled the door close. The string, knotted to the latch inside, and hanging through a hole in the door, swung gently to and fro.

Gordon Longford stopped the black Jaguar car in front of the Harveys' house in Upper Thames Street. It was Pamela Merston's Jaguar, but she was spending this Sunday with her father at Wimbledon, and as the Rolls-Royce had been sent to fetch her, and Gordon's own Morris Ten was out of action, this was the obvious solution. He smiled to himself as he thought of what Pamela would say if she knew where he was taking her car. Then he forgot her as he knocked at the Harveys' door and prepared himself for the pleasant shock of seeing June's always surprisingly lovely face.

The door was opened by Mrs. Harvey. She was a thin woman with a not very agreeable disposition. Captain Harvey was away from home too much to suffer from it, but June and Leslie had endured much, and were at this time severally in rebellion against her unnecessary harshness.

Longford smiled with easy assurance. "Mrs. Harvey? Good afternoon. I've come for June. She promised me she'd come for a little run this afternoon."

Instead of inviting him in, Mrs. Harvey half-shut the door, and peering through the restricted opening she had made, said, "I don't know, I'm sure, if she'll be going out now. We 'ad an accident this morning. My boy was nearly drowned and June, too, by all accounts. She's in bed and to my mind she ought to stay there. But I'll tell 'er you called."

Longford thrust his hand against the door as it was closing upon him. He was not to be defeated so easily.

"But I say, Mrs. Harvey, June isn't hurt, is she? I mean, you might tell me a bit more. I'm a friend of hers."

What Mrs. Harvey would have answered is uncertain, though the sourness of her expression promised ill, but at this moment the window above the door was thrown up and June's head appeared.

"Too-de-loo!" she cried brightly.

Gordon looked up and retreated down the three steps on to the pavement. Mrs. Harvey, with an exclamation of fury and disgust, withdrew herself, forcibly slamming the door behind her.

"What's all this about an accident?" asked Gordon, throwing the maximum of anxiety and adoration into the look he cast upwards. June put her elbows over the sill and giggled.

"It wasn't me, it was Les. He fell in the river. Mum's made him stop in bed; he's ever so wild. She wanted me to, but I wasn't having any."

"Are you sure you're all right?"

"Of course I'm all right. What do you think? A little drop of water won't hurt me."

"Then are you coming?"

She leaned out and whispered.

"Has Mum gone in?"

"Yes."

"Then I will come. But I'm not ready. Do you mind waiting?"

"Not if you make it snappy."

June pulled in her head and Longford retreated to the car and climbed back into the driving-seat. He was accustomed to having his own way with women, and June was proving no exception to the rule. Of course, his position at "Lulu's" gave him some standing with her; she wasn't the sort of girl who would take up with any Tom, Dick, or Harry. Her mother looked the kind to have brought her up with some sense of values—the old hag. The memory of her thin, acid face was distasteful; he turned his thoughts back to June. It was extraordinary how much she appealed to him. Quite apart from her obvious attractions he found that she roused in him a feeling of unusual tenderness. She had kept him waiting nearly a quarter of an hour, and he was not feeling irritable, not in the least. It amazed him. He was prepared to believe that a grand passion had at last come into his life. How marvellous if it were so, and for her too, with all his experience of women, how fortunate.

He was so pleased with his thoughts, sitting idly in the car, looking up at the blue sky, that he did not notice the woman who was slowly making her way along the street on the opposite pavement. She was very untidily dressed in clothes that had once been smart; she wore no hat on her wild grey hair, and on her feet she had a pair of frayed plimsolls that had once been white. She walked uncertainly, often stopping and looking back with a vacant expression, as if she were not quite sure of her surroundings. Then she would turn and clutch the moth-eaten strip of fur more closely to her neck and move on with a dull despair in her eyes and on her lined drawn face.

As she turned on one of these occasions her eye fell on the car and Gordon Longford reclining comfortably in it. She started, and stared incredulous, afraid, then, as certainty grew upon her, in dreadful craving hope. He could help her if he would: she must make him help her.

She was careful, realizing the necessity for cunning if he were not to drive away at sight of her. She averted her eyes and walked a little distance up the road, then crossed and came back on the other pavement. She was sick with fear as she drew near the car. If he should start: if she should lose him now! She put both trembling hands over the half-open window and stooped to look in at him.

"Mr. Longford!"

Gordon Longford froze at the sound of her voice. He turned his head slowly and gazed at her. Though the change in her face was great, he knew who she was, and sat clenching his teeth together, cursing the evil chance that had led her to this encounter. He said coldly, "Well?"

Her voice shook.

"Oh, Mr. Longford, I couldn't believe my eyes when I saw you! I never would have thought to see you down this way. I'm stopping quite near here, Fripp Street, I don't suppose you know it. I've been—"

He interrupted her harshly.

"I don't think we have anything really to talk about, Mary."

"Don't say that, Mr. Longford! I'm getting desperate, really I am. I can't get work—how can I? You see what I've come to. Who'd give me a job in a shop in these clothes? Please, Mr. Longford, say a kind word to me. I've no-one to turn to. You knew that when you turned me out of my job, didn't you? No, I didn't mean that... Don't take any notice. I say spiteful things now without meaning it... I'm sorry I said that."

Gordon Longford looked at his watch. June would be out at any minute.

"What exactly do you want?" he asked impatiently. He had no wish to be discovered by June talking to this dreadful creature.

The woman's eyes brightened. She had approached him with no definite plan, only a wish to break her loneliness by speaking with someone she had known in happier times. But she now saw that fate had done more for her than that. For a few minutes her clouded mind worked freely.

"I see you're waiting for a friend," she said with a slow smile. "Near neighbours of mine: Fripp Street is quite close to here. It wouldn't take me much trouble to find out who lives in this house."

"If you need money, tell me, and I'll make some arrangement to send you some."

"I do need it," she answered, dropping her voice to a whisper. "I've spent what little I had put by. I've tried to get some dressmaking, but what is it, these days? Nobody wants sewing done. And what I earn goes—you know how. If you could help me there, now. It gets so difficult... and the price—prohibitive, as well you know. If you could help me, somewhere where it won't be too dear. That would be something like."

She put her head on one side and leered horribly at him through the car window. He frowned, racking his brains. It was blackmail, of course, but he would have to satisfy her—at present. Now who the devil?...

Suddenly his face cleared. He pulled out a pencil and a bit of paper and wrote rapidly.

"Here, take this," he said. The woman thrust the note inside her dress, and at the same moment June appeared on the steps, radiant in a bright blue coat with a bonnet to match on her fair curls.

"Go to that address," Longford finished quickly. "He'll fix you up. But for God's sake, scram!"

The woman glanced at June and moved away, well pleased with the results of her temerity.

"Who was that?" asked June in some surprise. She got

into the passenger seat, pulling the door shut, and as they drove past turned to look at the stranger's face.

"Oh, just a hard case," Gordon answered lightly as the Jaguar slipped away. "I gave her a half-crown and a blessing."

"Aren't you a snob?"

June's voice was mocking, but Gordon, glancing sideways at her, saw that her eyes praised him.

It was dusk when Gordon Longford and June left Richmond Park. It had been after three o'clock when they arrived, but June had insisted on a walk, to get the stiffness, she explained, out of her arms, and to prevent a chill. Longford was quite willing to leave the car and guide her across the brown and gold withered bracken and among the little copses of trees. He had a vague hope of improving the occasion, but June to-day lacked any subtlety of understanding. She strode along with easy grace, a delight to watch, and turned aside his attempts at seriousness in a way that jarred on his intelligence and further inflamed his senses. When the sun had disappeared in a crimson line over a heavy bank of dark grey cloud, June announced calmly that she was very hungry, and that they must go back at once to Richmond and have tea on the hill.

Now that the sun had gone, the cold November night rapidly undid the work of its warm rays and mist began to rise in the hollows. Longford led the way through gathering darkness to the abandoned car, and after a groping drive down the hill, drew up beside a tea-shop, which, with its wheelback chairs, chintzes, inglenooks, and warming-pans, was all that June desired in the way of quaint countrified luxury.

The tea was Devonshire and lavish. Longford ate a single scone and cream, while June polished off the rest of the plateful. She explained that she had not eaten her dinner because of the upset over Leslie.

"What exactly happened to him?" asked Gordon. He was not particularly interested, but he felt that the question was some time overdue.

June told him, making little of her own part in the affair, and mentioning Harry briefly. She was surprised to find that she did not want to talk to Gordon about Harry. This was odd, because to her father she had held forth in his praise until she was asked to stop. Longford roused himself to say, "You were lucky to get the river police so quickly."

"I should say we were. You wouldn't have seen me any more if they hadn't been there—and Mr. Reed, of course."

Gordon did not take this dreadful thought very seriously, and she was piqued by his indifference.

"It wouldn't matter to you, of course. I expect Madam could find hundreds of girls to replace me if I'd been drowned."

"Of course she couldn't. You are the apple of her eye."

"Go on!... You know her pretty well, though, don't you? How long have you been selling this 'Cynthia' stuff?"

"Years. 'Lulu' took it up before Miss Kemp was manageress."

"It's a bit of all right, isn't it? But terribly expensive, for what it is. Three guineas for a nightie. I think it's sinful what some people pay for underclothes."

"They can afford it, so why shouldn't they? And why shouldn't we give them the opportunity?"

"Half of them are such sights, and fat—would you believe it, I was showing one of those new peach satin cami-knickers one day last week and Lady Mingham came up to me and said, 'I think I should like these myself.'—Lady Mingham!—I ask you!"

"You mean the Dowager?"

"Do I not? Six yards round if she's an inch. The young one's all skin and bone, just the opposite."

"What did you do?"

"I said 'These are a model, Modom. But I'm sure Madam could get you a copy, Modom.'"

They both laughed. June speared a second cream-filled cake with her fork and ate it elegantly, cutting it up into small pieces. When she had finished she leaned back in her chair and licked the tips of her fingers. Gordon looked at his watch; he beckoned to the waitress for his bill.

"Just time to run down and look at the river," he said, "if you've quite finished guzzling those foul things."

"They're not foul. They're lovely. And it's not every day I get the chance of having them. I do think you're mean to speak like that in front of the girl. Anyone would think I was greedy."

"So you are—damned greedy. You'll get fat—like Lady Mingham."

"All right. When I do you can fire me."

He gave her a strange look, suspicious and guarded. "I wouldn't have any say in that. Miss Kemp is your boss. I only sell her the 'Cynthia' products."

"Does she own the shop then? I thought you said there was someone there before her, as manageress."

A shadow passed swiftly over his face.

"Yes, there was. Perhaps Madam Kemp bought it. How should I know?"

"Oh, all right. Keep your shirt on. Where's this river?"

They were silent as they drove down the widened main road and turned off along a narrow lane where the mist lay cold and heavy, pouring up to the headlights of the car as they moved forward with caution.

"It doesn't look as if we shall see much," said Longford sulkily.

June was nervous.

"I don't want another swim, thank you. We better turn back, Gordon. It's dangerous."

For answer he pulled the car on to the grass at the side of the road, switched off the lights, and took her in his arms.

"So that's it," thought June. "The dirty tike! Just like all the rest of them."

She was annoyed and disappointed. She had been out with Longford only twice before and on each of these occasions he had behaved like a perfect gentleman. She liked him, certainly, but not all that much.

Gordon Longford's mouth lingered on hers.

"Love me a little," he said softly, in the voice that seldom failed to get results.

But into June's mind had come suddenly a vision of Harry Reed's dark eyes shining in his pain-stricken face as he took leave of her, and she was hearing again his pleasant, familiar Cockney voice saying, "Cheerio, kid, I'll be seeing you." She knew that he would be as good as his word, and unexpectedly her heart sang for joy at the thought. She pushed Longford away.

"I'm tired," she said peevishly. "I don't want to be messed about. I want to go home."

Longford was deeply offended, and very angry, but still he was determined to subdue the common little slut. He made his way carefully back to the main road and drove slowly through Richmond to Hammersmith. The fog was thick on Barnes Common. It would not be difficult to pretend that he could not get down to South London till it lifted. If he could persuade her to wait at his flat till it cleared?...

At Hammersmith it was possible to see a few yards. June wound down the window on her side and peered out.

"It won't be so bad following the buses, will it?" she asked presently.

"I don't know. It's the lights in the shops that make it better here. It'll be awful down your way."

June did not appear to be listening, and they crawled on in silence. Then she said, "Would you mind if I got some cigarettes? I promised Dad this morning I'd get him a packet of Gold Flake, and then I forgot. I expect he's got some for himself by now, but I wouldn't like him to think I'd forgotten. Not but what they'd of been ruined in the water if I'd had them on me this morning."

Determined to indulge her in the hope of reward, Longford crept beside the curb until a tobacconist's shop appeared faintly through the fog.

"I won't be a jiffy," June assured him. "You don't have to come in with me."

He waited five minutes, then, as she had not returned, he got out and went up to the shop. There was no-one there. The young man behind the counter grinned politely.

"Cigarettes, sir?"

"Did a young lady come in just now to buy some Gold Flake?"

The grin broadened.

"There was a young lady come in, sir. She said if anyone inquired after her I was to say she'd decided the fog was too thick, and she was going home by train. She asked me the way to the station."

"Thanks. I'll have twenty Players."

Gordon Longford pocketed his unnecessary purchase, said good-night with an expressionless face, and retired to the Jaguar, raging in impotent fury.

4

THE FOG HELD AND THICKENED. LONDONERS WENT
to bed on that Sunday night coughing and spluttering in
spite of closed windows, and on Monday morning, Guy
Fawkes Day, awoke to find the same acrid yellow blanket enfolding them and blotting out the world. It was at
its thickest on the river and along the riverfront. In Fripp
Street and Wood Wharf it was not possible to see the width
of the pavement.

Number one, Fripp Street, had had a disturbed and trying night of it. To begin with, the fog-horns on the river had
boomed on a variety of notes from dusk onwards. Then Mrs.
Pope, a small, frail woman, who had suffered from asthma
all her life, began to feel the effects of the laden atmosphere,
and to cough as continuously as the sirens hooted. Her par-
oxysms disturbed her three children. They slept in a small
bed in the same room as herself and Mr. Pope. Winnie,
whose heart had been damaged by scarlet fever, and Ronnie,
the youngest, who had recently recovered from whooping
cough, both began to cough too. This made it impossible

for Ernie to sleep through their wrigglings and twistings, so he sat up at intervals and whimpered. The combined noise exasperated Mr. Pope, a chronic neurasthenic, and caused him to shout sundry curses at his family when it became too much for him.

In the room above, the Dunwoodys lay, indignantly awake, listening to the din. They promised themselves an ample revenge in the morning.

When it was light enough to see across the room, Mrs. Pope dragged herself from her bed, and wrapping a frayed coat round the bundle of rags that represented her night attire, searched for a few sticks in the grate and piled them on top of the burned-out cinders to make a fire. The feeble blaze held no warmth, but it was bright and cheerful. She crouched over it, coughing again as the chill air penetrated to her body.

Mr. Pope rolled over in bed, roused by the draught on his back from the empty place beside him.

"What the 'ell's the use o' that a day like this?" he demanded. "Best stop in bed in the warm. After the night we've 'ad. Lumme, I don't want annuver like that one."

"Get me the kettle filled, won't yer?" replied his wife, "The kids want their breakfast if you don't."

As she tried to rise she broke into fresh coughing and caught at the back of a chair to support her. Mr. Pope got up reluctantly. He pulled his trousers off the bed, where they had lain during the night to add weight to his covering, and dragged them on over the shirt that did duty both for day and night alike. He tied a greasy muffler round his neck, tucked it into the top of his shirt and shuffled out of the room. Mrs. Pope crawled back into bed where she sat with her arms round her knees and her bowed head upon them.

When Mr. Pope returned with the kettle and a shovelful of coals she looked up.

"You'll 'ave to get the doctor to me again," she gasped, "I've got a pain in my side something cruel. Shouldn't wonder if it's another touch o' that there pleurisy."

Winnie began to whimper. She had spent a considerable part of her short life in hospital and dreaded the word "doctor."

"Now then, you shut up," growled her father, giving her a box on the ear. "It's yer Ma's bad this time, so don't you start creating."

"Give 'er a bit of bread to keep 'er quiet," suggested Mrs. Pope.

Upstairs Mrs. Dunwoody dressed herself and her child, boiled a kettle and made tea. She poured out three cups, took up one of them, and then, seeing that her husband was sleeping soundly after the trials of the night, stepped out on to the tiny landing that divided the front room from the back. She stirred the tea in the cup, sipped a little from the spoon to see if it was correctly sweetened, and knocked at the back bedroom door. There was no answer. She knocked again and waited. Still no answer.

"Mrs. 'Olland!" No answer.

With an oath and a muttered comment that "some folk sleep like the dead," Mrs. Dunwoody deposited the cup of tea on the floor, screamed her lodger's name again through the keyhole, without result, and retreated to her own room, where she found her child exploring the sugar bowl with both hands. The culprit having been slapped, Mr. Dunwoody roused himself abruptly to inquire the cause of the "bloody shindy," and to receive a cup of tea by way of peace-offering.

"Did you take 'er in a cup?"

"I put one outside 'er door. She didn't condescend to answer."

"She may be asleep. After the night we've 'ad it wouldn't surprise me."

"That Mrs. Pope's bad again. I 'eard 'er telling 'im just now to go down to the Office."

"That means 'e'll get the doctor to 'er again."

The door across the landing opened noisily; they heard the cup rattle in the saucer as it was lifted and then the door was shut.

"'Ark to 'er 'and tremblin'. Been on the booze, you mark my words. And not a word to say for 'erself. I like that! Not so much as a word of thanks. I'm about fed up with waitin' on 'er, dirty lazy faggot! There's that Ronnie Pope 'ooping again. They've always got something, those kids. Always running down to the dispensary for Freeman. 'Ope 'e loses 'is way this morning. You can't see yer 'and in front of yer face outside."

The Dunwoodys stirred their tea and brooded on their wrongs.

Mr. Webb, the Relieving Officer, put his head round the corner of the door of Dr. Freeman's room at the Public Assistance Offices. The doctor had arrived and was taking off his hat and coat.

"Good morning, doctor. We wondered how you'd manage to get here in the fog. There's a string of people waiting to see you."

"Including Mrs. Pope, I suppose. No fog would be complete without her."

The Relieving Officer grinned.

"Worse than that, I'm afraid. Pope himself."

"Oh, my God! Then that means Dunwoody too, sooner or later."

"Pope's just got an order for his wife for you to visit her."

"Wretched woman! What can I do for her in a place like Fripp Street? I've a good mind to send her into hospital again. But they only keep her a fortnight; they never send her convalescent. It would serve Pope right to leave him in charge of the kids, but hardly fair on them. And he can't help his neurasthenia, poor blighter. It's genuine enough. What he wants is a nice quiet overdose of morphia."

"And Dunwoody with him." Mr. Webb spoke bitterly.

"Oh, Dunwoody. What he wants is a rope's end. Lousy little brute! Always taking cover behind his wife's weak heart. I bet he'll be up this morning to get an order for me to see her. If he does I'll fire her into hospital and leave him with the kid on his hands."

"I wish you would. Well, I only looked in to give you these certificates."

"Thanks."

Mr. Webb retired and the first patient came in.

Dr. Freeman worked rapidly. For the great majority of these cases, too poor to have a doctor of their own, there was little he could do. Nearly all of them were old destitute men and women, supplementing their meagre old age pension with a few free tickets for food and a handful of coals granted them by the Poor Law Administration. Their illnesses were in part due to their age and in part to their circumstances and misfortunes, both past and present. Dr. Freeman could encourage them with a bottle of medicine and help them with a pint of milk a day, but it was not in his power nor that of anyone else to effect a lasting cure of their complaints. There were others, too, not old, but equally hopeless, who attended the dispensary as regular visitors; those struck down in youth or middle age by tuberculosis, rheumatism, heart trouble and a number of more rare diseases. They had come to the end of their resources, their insurances, and their capacity for earning. The hospitals could do nothing more for them, but they still lived, in the worst possible surroundings, and the Public Assistance saw to it that they did not die too soon.

What more could Dr. Freeman and the Relieving Officers do? Their rules were clear, the amounts of the relief were distributed by a quite humane committee, and fixed in accordance with the money available. But that money was all that could be spared for what was, after all, but one of many public services.

Mr. Pope came in carrying a folded paper, the so-called "red order," authorizing the doctor to visit his wife. He had put on an old black overcoat that he had picked up cheap at the market. It was very much too wide for his thin shoulders, and accentuated the grey pallor of his haggard features. His cheeks were so thin that his forehead and nose stood out disproportionately large; he had several teeth missing. He shambled forward and held out the paper in a bony, trembling hand.

"Your wife bad again? Sit down."

"Yessir. I'd rather stand, doctor. The fog played 'er up last night something shocking."

"All right. I'll be round presently. Do you want her to go into hospital? You know I can't do much for her at home."

"If you think she oughter go, I'll try to manage, doctor. But Winnie gets that upset when 'er ma's away, and Ronnie's getting over the 'ooping-cough—"

"Do you want them all sent to hospital?"

"Not if you don't advise it, doctor, I don't."

Mr. Pope trembled so violently under the strain of speaking to the doctor and in the effort to arrange his wandering thoughts that he nearly fell down. He caught at the table with both hands and covered his confusion by coughing.

"You don't seem any too well yourself," said Dr. Freeman kindly.

"I know I ain't. But I mustn't grumble. I'm not near as bad as the wife. Will you be in this morning, doctor?"

"If I can. It depends on the fog. I shall be slow getting around, I'm afraid."

Mr. Pope retired humbly, to be followed, after one or two old ladies with bronchitis and bad legs, by Mr. Dunwoody.

Dr. Freeman settled his pince-nez more firmly on his nose. He disliked this little dark, round-faced man, with his shifty sloe-black eyes and his trembling lips and fingers. Deliberately, as Dunwoody handed him an order identical with that brought by Pope, he fumbled with the paper and let it drop to the floor. He watched with satisfaction the complete steadiness of Dunwoody's hands as he bent to pick it up. When the latter placed it upon the table he encountered the sardonic light in Dr. Freeman's eyes and trembled more violently than before.

"You want me to visit your wife?"

"Yes, please, doctor."

"I expect I shall have to send her into hospital."

"Oh, I don't think it's as bad as that, doctor. But I thought if you could excuse me attending the Centre, I could look after 'er at 'ome."

"If I send her to hospital you can continue to work at the

Centre. It's good for you. You might even get a job if you make yourself fit at the Centre."

Mr. Dunwoody's eyes glinted viciously, but his reply was humble and deprecating.

"If the wife went into 'orspital, I'd 'ave to stop 'ome to look after the kid, wouldn't I? She comes 'ome to dinner from school."

Checkmate, thought Dr. Freeman. He threw the "red order" into his open bag and rang his bell for the next patient. He was too angry in his defeat to dismiss Dunwoody civilly. The little man picked up his cap from the floor where it had rested between his feet and put it on with a defiant gesture. He wasn't going to be treated like mud and lie down under it, either.

"Will you be in this morning, doctor?"

"I don't know. Next, please."

As he was leaving the dispensary Dr. Freeman met Mr. Webb, also starting off on his rounds, but on a bicycle.

"I'm late, Webb. I get later every day. I shall give up this job and stick to my private patients and the panel."

"Oh, don't say that, doctor."

"It's those Popes and Dunwoodys. They're getting me down."

"You've said it." The Relieving Officer's voice was sepulchral.

"I thought Fripp Street was to be pulled down to build a block of flats?"

"So it is, when we've moved the Popes, etc., and old Mrs. Bowerman who lives next door."

"Mind you separate them, the Popes and Dunwoodys, I mean. They hate one another like poison, but if one of them comes up here, there's the other, next on the list. Put one of them in Tottenham and the other in Deptford."

"What a hope!"

Mr. Webb wheeled his bicycle out of the dispensary gate and disappeared into the fog. Dr. Freeman climbed into his car, consulted his visiting list, made the plan of his itinerary in his mind, and followed.

Captain Harvey was having a difficult and disagreeable day. His spell of duty began at eleven-thirty, when he joined the tug *Fatima* at Limehouse. She had two barges in tow, one to be dropped at Greenwich and the other to be delivered to the Angerstein Wharf. This done he was to drop down on the ebb to Tilbury and pick up four barges there, bringing two of them back to a factory on the river between Limehouse and Wapping and the other two to London Docks.

It was easier said than done. Though the fog had cleared a little by midday it was not possible from midstream to see either of the banks, and with all his profound knowledge of the river he found himself frequently at a loss for his position. However, in due course he arrived off Gravesend, turned the *Fatima* in the broad reach below it, and nosed his way back into the basin at Tilbury where he hove to between a couple of other tugs and looked about for his barges.

The confusion at all times when tugs are sorting out and collecting their charges is great, but on this day, augmented by the fog, it was greater than ever. Captain Harvey sent the mate, Tom Wild, clambering ashore over the close-laid tugs to see if he could find the barges, or alternatively, anyone who knew anything about them. After a long interval he appeared mistily on the quay-side, accompanied by a depressed-looking individual in a great coat and a yachting-cap worn back to front, who, he explained, had got two of the mucky barges tied up at the other end of the basin.

The *Fatima*, with a great deal of fussy ringing of bells and churning of the river, backed out of her position, sidled round the outer fringe of the turmoil, and pushed her way in backwards towards the quay-side, directed by the shouts of Tom Wild and the lighterman. The barges were attached to the stern of the *Fatima* side by side and lashed to one another fore and aft, and the mate came on board the tug.

"No sign of those other two, Tom?"

"Not a sight nor smell of them. Someone else must of took them by mistake."

"Drat this fog!" said Captain Harvey irritably. He resented muddles and interference with his work, and felt that the weather was primarily responsible.

"No good 'angin' round, is it?" inquired Tom.

"Oo said we were goin' to 'ang round, as you call it? We'll 'ave a job as it is getting back on time. This blasted fog won't get no lighter, believe me."

The *Fatima* was got under way and chugged off upstream helped by the now incoming tide. Captain Harvey was right. The fog thickened as the light faded; he began to use his siren at intervals. Near Greenhithe, however, it was not too thick for him to make out a tall, gaunt skeleton of piles standing out into the river. As he passed close to it a faint voice hailed him from nearby. The skipper slowed down to listen.

"Shouldn't wonder if them was your two barges," shouted up the lighterman who had joined them at Tilbury.

Captain Harvey leaned over the bridge and looked down at where he stood balanced on the bows of one of the barges.

"What's that?"

"Your two barges. That's Bob's voice: I'd know it any-wheres. 'E got 'itched to the wrong boat, I reckon."

Captain Harvey hailed the voice and a long conversation took place with the unseen. The outcome of it was that the *Fatima* performed a very delicate and skilful operation in the course of which the two abandoned barges were attached side by side behind the first pair. After this she resumed her course up river.

The second lighterman climbed calmly on board over the seething gap between the barges and the tug, and settled down on the deck near the engine-room ladder: the first lighterman followed. The engineer, standing on the second rung of his ladder, was looking on, with his face on a level with the deck. His work for the moment was in abeyance. He leaned his elbows on the top of the ladder and rubbed his hands on a piece of cotton waste.

"Fog gets in yer eyes, don't it?" he said cheerfully.

"Not 'arf." The lighterman in the yachting-cap spat vigor-ously, a good length that cleared the deck by at least two feet.

A grimy face appeared beside the engineer's. It was the stoker, Alf, a one-legged man of great height, with enormous shoulders and a pleasant vacant expression. He flicked the sweat off his forehead with the back of his hand and grinned at the second lighterman.

"Wotcher, Bob."

"'Ullo, Alf. 'Ow are you keeping?"

"O.K. Seen anythink o' Daise lately?"

"Nix. An' wot's more, I don't expect to, neither."

Alf was silent, gazing into the fog. The engineer glanced sideways at him and said cryptically, "They're all alike, to my mind."

The light faded rapidly as the *Fatima* churned upstream. The fog was patchy now, for the wind had risen and cleared those parts of the river where the banks were low and the water exposed. Here the boats could move freely, guided by one another's lights and the various familiar landmarks on shore. The intervening banks of fog, by contrast, seemed all the thicker and more menacing.

At about six-thirty Captain Harvey gave the wheel to Tom Wild and went down to his cabin, calling to Ted, the ship's boy, to make his tea. As he passed the engine-room he put his head inside to call out cheerfully, "Just past the Arsenal, Mac! We'll not be too late in at this rate. Fog's lifting. D'you 'ear the rockets? That's fireworks! There's been some beauties."

A deep voice shouted an unintelligible reply and the skipper swung himself down the ladder to his cabin. He took a spectacle case from one pocket, and a newspaper from another and, propping the latter against the milk jug and setting the former on his nose, disposed himself for a quiet half-hour of recuperation.

The tug drove steadily onwards dragging the four great barges in her foaming wake. She had passed Tate and Lyle's factory, where the wharfingers with their barrows, like the figures on an old clock, run in and out of the buildings up sloping corridors. She had taken the bend of the river at Blackwall and was making round the great loop by the Isle of Dogs. Tom Wild began to think it was time the old man took over again.

Quite suddenly the *Fatima* ran into a blank wall of fog. Not the difficult driving mists of the lower reaches, obscuring one minute and revealing the next, but a solid curtain of impenetrability, where even sound was muffled and came strangely across the unseen water. But sound there was, confused and alarming. This blanket, lying at the foot of the steep slopes of Charlton and Greenwich did not cover the higher ground, and so did not interfere with the Guy Fawkes celebrations there. So to the hootings of fog-horns and the booming and shrieking of sirens was added the thin scream and sharp explosion of distant rockets, distracting and exasperating the helpless steersmen on the boats.

Tom Wild was completely lost. He slowed down the tug until she was nearly hove-to, and edged forward with something like panic in his breast. The world seemed to have gone mad, blaring and shouting and splashing in the darkness about him. The engineer, McAlister, stepped up his ladder, took one look and disappeared below. His skill would be needed before long by the looks of it.

Captain Harvey was conscious of the ship slowing before he noticed the increased noise outside. He sighed, folded up his paper, put away his spectacles, and reluctantly swung himself up the companion ladder on to the deck. He had only just arrived there when things began to happen very quickly.

A siren shrieked—so close that the two lightermen sprang to their feet and ran forward to the foot of the bridge. Tom Wild replied and the *Fatima* blared out her indignation and alarm. Voices began to shout; another unseen boat gave tongue on a lower note. Harvey seized the wheel yelling "Get forward, Tom! I can't even make out the ruddy bows!"

But even as he spoke a faint red light shone straight ahead. He put the wheel over hard at the same instant that Tom yelled to him of the danger. The tug lurched sickeningly, but she came round in a brave sweep, missing by inches a dark shape on which bells rang, men gibbered and sirens screamed.

The *Fatima* was safe. McAlister and Alf were clasped in one another's arms on the engine-room floor, the lighter-men were hanging like monkeys to the superstructure of the bridge, and Tom was clinging to the donkey-engine on the forward deck of the tug. But Captain Harvey, his feet planted well apart and his back braced, swung in unison with *Fatima* and thanked his lucky stars—but too soon.

In the exhilaration of the narrow escape he forgot for a moment his string of barges lumbering behind. They took the sudden corner as heavy barges should, in a grand, slow, outward-sweeping curve. They were still coming round as *Fatima* slid alongside the obstructing boat, and as she continued her circular movement they drove broadside on across the stranger's bows. A collision seemed inevitable, but the fog, which had brought disaster so close, had also produced the means of avoiding it. The lighterman, Bob, whose job it had been to lash the mislaid barges close-hauled to the first pair, had, in his anxiety to bring to an end his uncomfortable vigil, neglected to secure the ropes as firmly as was needed; moreover, they were old ropes whose condition no-one had seen fit to report. They had stood the direct pull of the tug without slipping, but this sudden twisting strain was too much for them. Consequently, as the barges swung round, the gap between the two pairs of them, usually a negligible one, was increased, and as by a miracle the bows of the obstructing tug drove into it. The near set of ropes was wrenched away, the far set parted under the combined strain of the tug's bows and the rear barges' continued curving pull; the stranger lurched forward, and the *Fatima* drew off, shorn of half her tail.

There was nothing immediately that could be done about it. The stranger and the derelicts alike had disappeared into the fog: it would be madness to search for them. Captain Harvey swore, and cursed the lighterman. That individual was subdued and trembling, not only on account of his narrow personal escape from being flung overboard, but more particularly because he had been severed violently from his charges, and it was going to be distinctly awkward explaining to his employers how and why he had become detached from them at a moment when his presence seemed especially desirable.

"You was flung clear by the force o' the impac'," suggested the other lighterman, who had prudently retired to his own territory, and sat on the tarpaulin cover of his barge, lighting a pipe.

Captain Harvey snorted.

"Oh yeah! Bounced 'im off 'is barge up over the bows of the other tug, and 'e landed in a sittin' position on our decks, uninjured and dry as a bone!"

McAlister's head appeared for a moment.

"You wouldn't like Tom to put you overboard on the end of a line, would you? You'd mike a better impression, see... all wet."

The lighterman repudiated this plan and retired aft, sulking.

There was nothing to be done but to deliver the remaining pair of barges in accordance with orders at London Docks, and report the mishap to the Lighterage Company. This done Captain Harvey went home. To find the lost barges was not part of his job: the river police would undertake it, or the whereabouts of the derelicts might be reported from on shore. It was to be hoped they didn't cause any mischief on the river meanwhile. But he did not consider himself to blame for the incident, and he hoped the company would take the same view. After all, he had saved the *Fatima*, and his owners would take more account of that than of a pair of bloody barges.

"What is your name?"

"Mrs. Holland. Mary Holland."

"And what's the trouble?"

The woman took a crumpled note from her bag and handed it to Dr. Ellis.

"He said I was to come to you, and give you that." There was a hard defiance in her dull eyes. "He owes it me. He lost me my job. I'd have gone to him before only I didn't know where to find him."

Dr. Ellis read the note with a sinking of the heart. Another of them! There would never be an end to it, and he was helpless, bound by his own need.

"I see," he said aloud. He looked straight into her eyes and asked slowly, "Do you wish me to attempt to cure you?"

Mrs. Holland pushed back the untidy hair that fell about her face. Her hand was thin; Dr. Ellis noticed that the bones were unduly prominent and that, although the skin did not look as if it had been subjected to much hard use, the knuckles were grimy and the nails broken and black with dirt. He repeated his question in a sterner voice.

"Do I look as if there was much chance of a cure?" said the woman gloomily.

"There is always a chance, if you do your share of the work."

"Look here!" cried Mrs. Holland, "He wouldn't have sent me to you if you weren't O.K. So what's all this talk of cures? Give me the stuff and I won't bother you no more."

"Till next time."

"I might be dead by then." She relapsed into her former sullen state.

Dr. Ellis shrugged his shoulders, got up wearily and disappeared through the door that led into his dispensary. Presently he came out with a small packet wrapped in newspaper. He watched the woman as she stuffed it eagerly into her bag.

"You use a hypodermic?"

"Used to. But it got broken. I can't afford another."

"I'll see if I have an old one I can give you."

"Oh, doctor, I'd be ever so grateful. Then it would last. I shouldn't have to trouble you again so soon."

She was all eagerness now to be gone, to be back in her room, to be at peace. The doctor led her through the dingy waiting-room. The street door still stood ajar.

"I'm the last, aren't I? I hope I haven't kept you, doctor. And thank you, ever so."

She peered out into the fog. It did not seem quite so thick as on her way here, an hour ago. A small voice piped out of the mist, "Penny for the Guy, ma!"

She fished a halfpenny out of her purse. She was ready to endow the world.

"Bit late in the day, aren't you, sonny?"

Without thanks the boy snatched the coin and was gone.

Jim Sawyer trod cautiously to the extreme edge of his landing-stage, and listened.

From where he stood the shore lights behind him were hidden by the fog; it was thick in his lungs as he breathed. He flashed on his electric torch, turning its beam from side to side into the dense white wall surrounding him. He switched it off and listened again intently.

There it was, the slapping of water against a heavy boat, but nearer this time—so near that he felt he ought to be able to reach out his hand and touch it, whatever it was.

"Hoy there!" he called, but not too loud. After all it was past midnight; no object in rousing folks on shore.

There was no answer, and as the sound of his voice died away, the silence grew deeper than ever. Then all at once a fresh sound came out of the darkness, a scraping, rasping sound close at hand. He flashed on his light once more, and at the same moment he felt the boards vibrate under his feet. Then he started back in alarm, for a dark shape came softly towards him through the mist, nosing blindly along the landing-stage.

"Cor-lumme!" he whispered, "If it ain't a mucky barge!"

The derelict bumped and scraped at the landing-stage. Jim Sawyer, with only a second's hesitation, clambered on board. After all, if anyone turned up, he'd explain that he was looking for the lighterman, to see if the poor chap had come to any harm.

The swift survey was soon completed. Two bloody barges, and the ropes between them had not parted! But they'd been knocking about some time. The tarpaulin cover on one of them was torn and there were a good few wooden cases with their tops cracked. They were jumbled up a lot too; it looked as if one or two might be missing; there wouldn't be much harm...

By the time the two barges had worked free of Jim's landing-stage, that enterprising boat-keeper had succeeded in prising off one end of a wooden case that stood on his living-room table. The result was disappointing, for the case contained nothing but tightly-packed sheets of raw rubber. Jim looked at them in some disgust. A waste of time and energy, that's what it was. He'd have to notify the police and a fat lot of thanks he'd get, even if he was believed when he told them this box had been thrown out on his jetty. Well, they could take it or leave it, the box was going to the Receiver of Wreck in the morning for what it would fetch. He took up the box-end he had removed, and careless of the fact that he had it inside uppermost, set it in position and, picking up a nail, gave it a hearty thump with his hammer. The wood split, Jim Sawyer pulled out the nail again, and swore lustily.

But not in anger. It was in sheer astonishment that he blasphemed, for through the crack in the rough wood he caught sight of something pink and softly gleaming. The nail in coming out had pierced it and had pulled up a torn fragment into the gap. Cautiously now, and with great skill and care, Jim increased the split in the box-end, ran another one parallel to it, and by degrees forced it apart. He found, beneath the thin layer of wood he had removed, a gauzy chiffon nightdress, edged with a piping of thick satin. It was this piping that had been torn in his first ignorant blow, and that had shone so entrancingly when the light fell upon it through the split he had made.

"Would you believe it!" murmured Jim, quite startled by his discovery. He emptied the rubber out of the case and inspected the latter with great care.

The second nightdress was concealed in the bottom of it: a thick layer of rough wood on the outside, then the nightdress, then a paper-thin layer of wood glued inside, so neatly and with such skill that only a very close scrutiny discovered it.

Jim Sawyer shook out his two prizes and fingered them with delight. But as he did so his face changed again. He examined his hands, the whole nightdress, the one with the minute tear in it, the box, the rubber and finally his own hands again, and a look of frightened admiration and awe came into his small eyes.

"So that's it!" he whispered, still staring at the rose-coloured froth in his hands. "So that's it!... And me thinking it was all a rumour!"

5

MR. HOLMAN'S OFFICE IN LANCASTER HOUSE WAS fully occupied. That is to say, Gordon Longford lay at ease in the swivel-chair with his feet on the little table at the other side of the electric fire, and Max Holman sat on the desk itself, swinging his short fat legs and feverishly biting his nails. "There seems to be a fate against this consignment," remarked Gordon lazily. Having been roused from sleep, luckily in his own bed, at seven that morning, he felt that at eleven-thirty he was entitled to relax.

"And against us, too." Holman's voice was sharp with anxiety. "Why did that fool of a boatman call the Police? Why didn't he tell Listons or the Lighterage Company or any damned soul except those nosy parkers in their perdition launches?"

He fell to again on his nails, his head sunk in a despondent manner between his shoulders.

"The worst of you, Max," replied Gordon Longford with an elaborate yawn, "is that you're so impulsive. As far as we know no harm has come to the stuff through being located by the River Police. I've been on to both Listons and the tug company. The consignment will be fetched from its present uncomfortable moorings off the Saw Mills this very afternoon. That's a day late, but you can collect the 'speciality' to-morrow morning, and as the rest of the *San Angelo* lot comes up to-day, you can do it all together. It might not look well to go hurrying down after it this evening. Besides, when they say afternoon, they may well mean midnight or to-morrow."

"What about the shop?"

"I am hoping for the best. I shall go along there this afternoon and deal with one or two matters personally."

"You can?"

"I can."

There was a pause, each man pursuing his own train of thought in silence. Gordon Longford put out the stub of his cigarette and closed his eyes. The room was very quiet. He opened them again at the noise Max Holman made getting down from the table.

"What a restless devil you are, Max," he complained. "I want to rest. They rang me up at seven this morning. I ask you, seven! And I didn't get to bed till three, waiting up for news. It gave me a turn, I don't mind telling you, when Listons rang me up. I had visions of our goods floating all over the river."

"It wouldn't have mattered if they had," answered Holman.

Longford looked at him admiringly.

"Good for you! No, I suppose not. I never thought of that. Nothing worse than a customs fine and the necessity of inventing a new method. I'd be sorry though; this one has been so admirable, and I have quite an affection for it. Besides the work suits Martha, and…"

"Ah!" Max Holman, in the act of sitting down again, drew himself erect and nodded his head mysteriously. "Now you've reminded me. Before you got here this morning I had a call from Ellis. Who do you think has been to see him?"

"That's an easy one. Mary Clarke,—or Holland, I think she calls herself these days. She ran into me on Sunday, so I gave her his address to keep her quiet. He's one of our best customers, isn't he?"

"Was. But he's scared since his books were investigated three months back. He managed to pull it off then, but he daren't issue another prescription at present, and he rather wants to avoid new cases. Of course there's always himself; I send him down supplies from time to time. But it sounds a bit of a waste to me throwing good stuff away on Mary Clarke. Especially now we're likely to be short."

Gordon Longford roused himself for the first time since he had arrived at the office that morning.

"You're right there," he said quietly, and stared at the frosted glass window till his amber eyes darkened and glazed with the intensity of his concentration.

"Get Ellis now," he said at last. "Tell him to lunch with us at one-thirty, usual place. If he's out, leave a message; he's sure to be in at one. I have the glimmerings of an idea. You see," he explained to the wondering Max, "I've promised someone for this afternoon and if I use my reserve I've nothing till you get back from Listons to-morrow. Besides, I don't want a scene at 'Lulu's.'"

"Then you mean Miss Merston, I take it. If you want my advice, you'll cut out that bird. She's going to be more trouble than she's worth, by a long chalk."

"Perhaps," said Longford coldly, "you'll let me manage my own affairs."

Max Holman spread out his hands and shrugged his shoulders. In silence the two men settled down to wait for one-thirty.

There was something rather excessively discreet about the windows of "Lulu," but that may have been demanded by its proximity on the one hand to a very select bric-a-brac shop, and on the other to a high-class photographer. In such company it was but fitting that "Lulu" should fill more than half of her grey-green window enclosure with pink blossoms and hang upon a solitary stand one slender softly-glowing hand-embroidered nightdress, or one frail creamy lace-trimmed slip.

The interior of "Lulu" was also grey-green, from the thick soft carpet to the hanging-curtains of the fittings-rooms and the covers of the square-cut armchairs that stood ready to receive the exhausted customer. The shelves, cupboards, and counter were of glass supported by chromium-plated steel. June Harvey and a short brown-haired girl called Dolly took it in turn to keep watch in the shop, while Martha Kemp, in long black satin, appeared from the nether regions for consultations and fittings as required.

The morning of November 6th dragged slowly by and the day crawled on into the afternoon. A pretty girl gave a substantial order for her trousseau, and a lady of uncertain age and meagre figure bought herself a very unsuitable pair of georgette cami-knickers. June, having worked at "Lulu" for several months, no longer experienced feelings of envy when she made up the parcels, but in spite of her training she felt a slight pang as she slipped the cami-knickers into the grey-green paper carrier, and reflected on the skin and bone they were doomed to clothe. It did seem a waste, but then the right people never had the money,—or hardly ever.

She had her back to the door, putting away stock on the shelves, when it was opened and Gordon Longford came in quietly. She did not hear him, but she saw him in the glass front of the shelf. She decided not to turn round but to watch him and see what he would do. She wondered if he had been very mad with her on Sunday; well, it served him right, anyway. What did he take her for?

Longford reached the counter before he realized what she was doing. He laughed softly.

"That is a game that two can play, my sweet."

June spun round, pink and breathless.

"That'll be enough from you, Mr. Longford."

He held up his hand, still smiling, but with a look in his curious yellow eyes that was more insulting than his words had been. Before June could collect her wits he had moved to the door of the inner sanctum.

"Madam is in, I presume?"

"Yes."

"I have got something very pretty in my bag. I want you to show it to Madam."

"Can't Dolly?"

"Not tall enough."

June hesitated. Though in the ordinary way she took the mannequin part of her job in her stride, after Sunday she had no wish to parade before Longford. He noted her diffidence with satisfaction, anticipating in a forced performance the more pleasure for himself. He went through into Madam's room and presently Dolly appeared with a message that June was wanted inside. She found Martha Kemp dangling a pair of satin pyjamas over one arm.

"Here, dear," she said, holding them out to June. "Run along and put them on. If they suit you they'll be just what I want for Miss Temple-King."

As June, in the mannequin's cubicle, pulled off her neat black dress, she reflected that it might well have been worse.

The pyjamas fitted admirably. Martha was pleased, anticipating a quick sale and a repeat order, and Longford, in order to impress June with his position as agent for "Cynthia" products made a great show of writing up his book.

"You can have them in peach, black, and that duck-egg blue," he explained. "But we are only doing six dozen altogether in that design. So you can ask the exclusive price, as usual."

At this point voices were heard in the shop and a moment later Dolly's head appeared through the curtain asking if Madam could come, please. June turned towards the cubicle; she was anxious to get back into her clothes. But in one swift movement Gordon Longford barred her way, and laying his hands on her shoulders looked down into her stormy face.

"Don't be angry with me, beautiful. How can I help adoring you when you are so lovely?"

Feeling her soft shoulders through the satin of the pyjamas he almost believed it to be true that he loved her. In any case, he wanted her, and had been too successful in the past to fear failure now.

"Why did you run away on Sunday? You aren't a schoolgirl. It was unkind; it was rude too. Surely you aren't afraid of me."

June shook herself impatiently.

"I'll trouble you to let me pass," she said angrily. "I happen to be working, if you aren't. And I think you're downright mean,—taking advantage..."

Her speech was checked by a low fierce exclamation from the doorway. Gordon's hands fell to his sides; he moved away from her.

"They'll need taking up a bit on the shoulders," he said carelessly. "But I'd leave them as they are till you fit the customer. All right, Miss Harvey."

June whisked into the cubicle, taking in as she did so a vision of Miss Pamela Merston's two furious dark eyes in a pale haggard face.

When she came out dressed again in her black frock, Longford had gone, but Miss Merston was sitting in the shop near the electric fire, looking at an illustrated paper. A murmur of voices in one of the fitting-rooms showed that Madam and Dolly were attending to another customer.

June retired in silence behind the counter. Pamela, after one long cool stare at her, returned to the pages of her magazine. June felt embarrassed. She had no weapon against this cold, disdainful hostility, certainly none that she could attempt to use here, where the customer was always right. She busied herself tidying the already perfectly ordered shelves, and was conscious, whenever she turned away from the counter, of Miss Merston's dark eyes boring into her back.

At last the fitting-room curtains rattled aside. A girl in a coat trimmed with fur and a round fur cap hurried out. "Darling, have I kept you ages? I'm dreadfully sorry."

"Babs, don't be a hypocrite. You've been having the time of your life. Nothing she loves more, is there, Miss Kemp, than trying on belts?"

Madam smiled indulgently: there was nothing she liked

more herself, provided the customer, as in this case, was persuaded to buy the most expensive she offered.

"My turn now?" Pamela Merston half rose.

"Yes, Modom. If you will step this way."

June wrapped the belt in tissue-paper and put it in a bag. Miss Collingwood wished to have her account? No, Miss Collingwood wished the account to be sent to her mother.

Pamela Merston was at her friend's elbow again, eager, a little breathless, a small parcel in her hand.

"Finished, Babs? Right, come on. I'll drop you at Hyde Park Corner if you don't mind, because I've got to get home quickly. Got someone coming. No, no-one you know. Oh, do get a move on, darling. I'm in a hurry!"

"Well, I'm not. Don't rush me, Pam!"

June watched them go out of the shop, pulling on their gloves, fussing with their bags and parcels, and still wrangling in peevish, ineffectual, self-centred rage.

The single street-lamp in Wood Wharf was appropriately placed outside the door of the "Fisherman," and lighted up the burly red-faced individual who, seated on a barrel, pipe in mouth and net over knee, announced from his sign-board that tavern's homely name. Light also streamed through the "Fisherman's" windows, once formed of small leaded panes, but now covered with large sheets of glass, the lower frosted half of which bore the inscription "Courage" on the right, and "Ales" on the left, of the central double doors. The rest of Wood Wharf faded into darkness on either side, with only an occasional dim light behind a lace curtain to suggest that it was inhabited. Opposite the "Fisherman" a line of hoardings stretched the whole length of the street, closing up the fronts of the houses that faced the river. For these dwellings were doomed to demolition, together with their equally squalid neighbours in Lower Thames Street and Fripp Street, and when pulled down and cleared away would expose a great square space on which a new perpendicular warren, with modern convenience and room for ten times as many inmates, would take their place.

The landlord of the "Fisherman" foresaw great future prosperity from the coming of the new flats, though their overshadowing would darken his front. Still, he commanded a fine view of the Thames from his back windows, so he mustn't grumble. And so long as the customers had the river to talk about, they would come to his house to do so.

"I never see the fog so thick as it wor larst night, not in all my born days, I 'aven't."

"Did you see in the paper they'd found them barges wot cut loose larst night?"

"I knowed it without lookin' at no papers. I was down by the wall when they fetched 'em orf."

"When was that?"

"This arternoon. They drifted in to the Saw Mill Wharf, see. It took a bit of doing gettin' 'em orf. Tide was low, and water runnin' fast. You've seen it, 'aven't you, makin' whirlpools over them suction pipes;—give me the 'orrors, them eddies."

Jim Sawyer, thoughtfully sipping his pint nearby, laughed shortly.

"They're nothing to be scared of. You can't come to no 'arm in the whirlpools as you call 'em without you go swimming in 'em. When I wor a nipper I used to take my boat over 'em a purpose, just to feel the pull."

"Maybe you did, Jim. You was always a audacious kid. But I'd sooner you nor me for all that."

Through the tobacco haze that filled the "Fisherman" a patch of white caught Jim Sawyer's eye. He saw that it was the sling on Harry Reed's left arm. The casualty was practising darts by himself; he left the board in response to Jim's beckoning hand.

"Mending?" the latter inquired genially.

"Fine, thanks." Harry waggled his fingers and laughed. He displayed his neatly plastered wrist. "Fracture," he explained. "Same kind you get starting a car, they said up at the 'orspital. To think I been winding up the 'ole lorry for three years and now I get a bloody fracture falling against a damned barge."

"I wouldn't let that worry you. I broke my leg once on the river."

"'Ow was that?"

Jim Sawyer paused impressively, to allow of time for an audience to collect.

"It was in one o' these 'ere Regattas. I was stroke for the 'Fisherman' club in them days; I rowed fourteen stone three pounds. Well, we won, see, by 'alf a length, near enough, and naturally there was a lot of excitement on the followin' launches, the bookies yellin' theirselves 'oarse, and everyone leanin' over the bows and shoutin'. When we shot over the line the launches were so close on our tracks they couldn't stop, see. We was all finished out, layin' over our oars, and the cox that excited 'e was wavin' 'is 'and to the crowds on the shore and not payin' attention. So when the launch ran us down we was all took by surprise. 'Er bows cut us clean in two 'alves. Most of the men was thrown in the water, but I caught 'old of a rope that was 'angin' off the launch and 'eld on like grim death. It 'ud 'ave been all right only me foot was caught under the cox's seat. I didn't let go the rope but the bone of me leg cracked like it 'ad been a dry stick. They 'eard it go from the deck o' the launch, so they 'auled me up pretty quick. You'd 'ave thought I 'ad two knees by the way it moved. Didn't 'alf give me a turn, seein' it."

"Sez you." Harry cocked a sceptical eyebrow at the big man, but the rest of the company, accustomed to Jim's tales, received this variant of a well-worn theme in respectful silence or stolid indifference. Jim winked gravely, entirely unabashed.

"I'll 'ave to be going," said Harry. "I'm on the panel. They aren't 'alf strict."

"I'm going that way meself," answered Jim.

Outside the boathouse they paused to take leave of one another. Jim unlocked his door. A thought seemed to strike him.

"Come in a minute," he said in a low voice. "I got something for you."

Harry followed him into the room off the verandah.

"There," said Jim, opening a small cardboard box and lifting the tissue paper within. "What d'you say to making a present of these to your best girl?"

"Cor!" murmured Harry in genuine astonishment. Pink silk nightdresses were the last thing he expected to see in Jim's home. "Wherever did you pick these up?"

"I didn't. They was give me in the market: part of a debt that was owed me. But they're no manner o' use to me. You can 'ave them, and welcome. Your girl'ld be pleased."

"I don't 'ave no truck with girls," said Harry roughly. "Always wanting what they can get out of you."

He thought of June Harvey and how she had called round late on Sunday night to ask his mother how he was. He'd gone up to her house yesterday to ask after Les. He might just slip up there again now before he went home. Perhaps she'd go to the pictures with him, only it would have to be a Saturday at present, the early performance. But he wouldn't let on to Jim. Jim knew he took no account of girls.

The big man shut up the box and tucked it inside Harry's sling.

"If you ain't got a girl to give 'em to, try someone at 'ome."

"Why don't you?"

Jim snorted derisively.

"What, my old woman…crippled with rheumatism the way she is? Believe me, she's never been out of flannel since the day I married 'er."

Mrs. Dunwoody piled the dinner plates into an untidy heap, scraped up the bits of fat that Violet, to show her independence, had pushed off on to the table, threw these into the fire, where they sizzled greasily, and wiped her hands on her dirty overall.

"Now then!" she admonished her daughter, who was searching in the small fire-side cupboard for a lump of sugar. "You come out o' that, you young limb! Always got yer fingers into wot don't concern yer! The bobbie'll be after you, you mark my words."

This speech being accompanied by a vigorous shaking, Violet burst into a loud wail, which rose to a shriek as her mother cuffed her over the head and pushed her towards the door.

"I'll give yer something to cry for! Go and find Winnie. She's been moping ever since 'er ma went away to 'orspital. Go and 'elp 'er mind Ronnie."

"'E's got the 'ooping-cough, Mum."

"Well, so 'ave you 'ad the 'ooping-cough. You don't get it again, see. Do as I tell you,—take yourself orf. I'm going to the pictures."

"Can't I go, Mum?"

"No, you can't, and that's all there is about it. You go down to Winnie,—sharp now!"

Violet retreated down the stairs backwards, feeling her way from step to step. She was an only child and hated to leave her mother's side in spite of that parent's frequent bad temper. But once the plunge had been taken, and she was actually downstairs with the Pope children she enjoyed herself more than in her mother's irritable and nagging company.

Mrs. Dunwoody, relieved of her major burden, poured herself out a cup of tea from the tea-pot standing on the hob, and after a few seconds' hesitation poured out a second cup for her lodger. This she carried across to Mrs. Holland's door, but as usual there was no answer to her repeated knock. She turned the handle very gently, and opening the door a few inches, put her head into the room.

It was empty. The ashes lay unswept in the grate, the bed-clothes had been roughly straightened. A ragged flimsy pink nightdress, partly stuffed under the pillow, trailed over the edge of the mattress and hung down towards the floor. On a grimy plate on the small table under the window a dried up piece of bread-and-butter lay curled, a trap for smuts and dust. Some fish-bones sticking out of a piece of newspaper suggested the lodger's latest meal.

Mrs. Dunwoody put the cup of tea down beside the bread-and-butter and retreated to her own room, to emerge a few minutes later in hat and coat. At the foot of the stairs she remembered that she had not made up the fire. She stood and thought about it, but as she recollected her weak heart and the care she had been warned to take of it she decided to trust to luck and Violet, screamed her instructions through the backdoor, and departed.

Violet was a conscientious child. In the middle of the afternoon she remembered her mother's words and dutifully went upstairs to obey them. The fire was in a bad way by this time, but it responded to treatment. Violet watched it for a few minutes to make sure that it had recovered, and then slid down the bannisters to rejoin her companions in the yard.

When Mrs. Dunwoody came back about seven, having done her shopping after she left the cinema, the little Popes and Violet were sitting round the fire in the downstairs front room. Mr. Pope and Mr. Dunwoody sat with them smoking pipes and talking about the football pools. Mrs. Dunwoody detached her family from the group and led the way upstairs. "Wot 'ave you been doin' of?" inquired Mr. Dunwoody sourly, poking the welded mass of coals in his own grate. "The place stinks o' disinfectant."

"It's only a drop o' Lysol," answered his wife. "It's a 'ealthy smell, if you ask me. I did the stairs down with it this morning, on account o' Ronnie's 'ooping-cough. You can't be too careful, even if Violet 'as 'ad it."

"It makes a mucky smell, anyways," said Mr. Dunwoody obstinately.

His wife hung her hat on the brass knob of the bedstead and shook back her hair.

"You're never satisfied," she muttered.

Mr. Dunwoody, having stated his views, was disinclined to argue. Instead he put the kettle on the fire and shook the tea-leaves out of the pot into a dilapidated enamel basin that stood on the floor beside the hearth.

"'Ere, you Violet," said her mother, "Go and get the other cup. It's in 'er room. I took 'er in a cup o' tea afore I went out. She wasn't there, but she ought to be back by now. Ask 'er for the cup."

A few seconds later Violet came back and stood in the doorway.

"She ain't there, Mum. 'Er room's all dark."

"Well, leave the door open as you go in. The cup's on the table. You can see it if you leave both doors open. Waste of a good cup of tea, I call it. It'll be stone cold by now. Be careful you don't spill it coming out."

Violet did as she was told. A narrow beam of light from her own home lay across the lodger's floor. It did not reach the table, nor the window beyond it, and on either side the room stretched in darkness. Violet pushed open the door more widely until it met the end of the bed and would go no further. She tiptoed reluctantly into the room, and searched the table with her hands. A plate was there with a bit of bread-and-butter on it, and nearby a saucer, but no cup. As she shuffled sideways between the table and the bed, her foot struck something that clattered. Mrs. Dunwoody heard the noise and came to her own door.

"Whatever are you doing?"

Violet's voice, muffled by stooping, came back hesitatingly.

"The cup's on the floor, Mum. It's been broke. It's…"

A wild scream made Mrs. Dunwoody's heart stand still, and the next instant her terrified child flung herself into her arms shrieking and sobbing and clinging to her in an extremity of fear. For as she had stooped to pick up the broken fragments of the cup Violet had suddenly become aware of the lodger's dark bulk piled upon the bed, and as her groping hands sought the floor they had clasped the outstretched fingers of Mrs. Holland,—fingers that were icy-cold and stiff as pieces of wood.

6

Mr. Dunwoody in his shirt-sleeves, and for once in his life moving rapidly, summoned the two constables on the beat. One of them went upstairs to Mrs. Holland's room while the other tackled the hysterical Popes and Dunwoodys, who were inclined to take fright in the face of death, like refugees before an invading army. This unreasonable tendency having been suppressed, the constable engaged their attention by writing down their names and addresses while he waited for the results of his colleague's investigations. The interval was not long. The first constable returned downstairs looking a little sickly, and went away to call Dr. Freeman, who was Police Doctor for the district.

When pennies for the meter had been found and inserted and the gas in Mrs. Holland's room was lit, the story of her terrible end became clear. A bottle of Lysol, not quite half full, stood on the table. On the floor near the bed, where it had fallen from her out-flung hand, lay a broken cup: the fragments smelt strongly of Lysol.

"Seems to have fallen straight back on to the bed as soon

as she took it," said Dr. Freeman, "to judge by her present position. The mouth is badly burned of course, but no vomiting. I imagine she died pretty quickly from shock. One will be able to tell better at the post-mortem. She has been dead a couple of hours."

"Suicide, I suppose, doctor?" The constable was eager to end the grisly business.

"No doubt of it, I should think. Do you know anything about her?"

"Not much. She hired this room from the people across the landing. She's been here six or seven weeks, they don't remember. She was out a lot, looking for work, she told them; had been a dressmaker in a big firm,—didn't tell them the name. Kept herself to herself,—never mentioned any relatives. But she wasn't behind with her rent,—four-and-six a week she was paying. They don't know where she was before she came here."

"Sounds hopeful. Couldn't get any work, I suppose, poor devil, and took this way out."

Dr. Freeman examined the stiffly extended fingers of the right hand.

"She's not been used to rough work, anyway, so the sewing story may be right. Hullo, what have we here?"

He had pushed up the sleeve as he spoke and now bent his head to look closely at the forearm.

"Found something, doctor?"

The constable had turned away to avoid the sightless staring eyes that seemed to follow his movements. He looked round again.

"Yes. Marks of a hypodermic all over the forearm. Was she left-handed? No, there are more on the left, old ones by the look of them. Ambidextrous, evidently."

He took out a pocket lens and a torch and went over the arms again.

"Mostly old scars, but one or two fresh places that have bled too,—probably an old needle used clumsily. Diabetic, I wonder? In which case there ought to be some insulin about."

He looked all over the wash-stand, but there was nothing on it except a few crystals of soda in a cracked saucer and an old washing-flannel. The jug standing in the ewer contained a twisted piece of newspaper, half a bootlace, and two rusty hair grips.

"It's rather odd," said Dr. Freeman in a puzzled voice.

"What is?"

"Well, if the woman was giving herself regular hypodermics, one would expect to find a syringe and a bottle of insulin. That is, if she had diabetes. She looks pretty thin;—possible she was going downhill in spite of treatment and got depressed."

"I'll see if the other people know anything."

The constable went off to question Mrs. Dunwoody, while Dr. Freeman continued to search the lodger's room for the presumed hypodermic. He did not find it, neither did he find any insulin. But he established with some certainty that Mrs. Holland had no letters, no photographs, no bills, no receipts, no money beyond one shilling and threepence loose in the pocket of her coat, which she was wearing, no hat, no gloves, no change of linen, in fact no clothes at all except those she had on and a ragged pink nightdress that trailed out from under the pillow on the bed.

The constable reported that Mrs. Dunwoody had never heard any mention of diabetes, and that the lodger had a liking for two spoonfuls of sugar in her tea. Also that she had on rare occasions invited Violet into her room and shared with her some rich confectionery from the baker's at the corner of the main road. Also that it was Mrs. Dunwoody's belief that Mrs. Holland lived on air, for a square meal she had never seen on her table, only bread-and-butter and fried fish and such-like rubbish. But to Mrs. Dunwoody's knowledge she had shown no signs of incipient mental trouble and had never threatened to take her life.

"Which doesn't sound like diabetes, does it?" said Dr. Freeman, frowning at the corpse, which so annoyingly withheld enlightenment.

"But you'd say the cause of death was Lysol-poisoning, self-inflicted, wouldn't you, doctor?" the patient constable insisted.

"Lysol,—of course. Yes, suicide..." Dr. Freeman spoke absent-mindedly, for his thoughts were not on the poison bottle, which was obvious and uninteresting, but on the scarred forearms with all their implications, and most of all on the queer fact of the missing hypodermic.

Divisional Detective-Sergeant Chandler was given the unpromising task of identifying the dead woman. Considerable interest attached to her on account of the hypodermic scars on her arms, though nothing could be done in this direction until the results of analysis showed what drug, if any, was present in the body.

The post-mortem, which was performed on the morning following her death, showed little that Dr. Freeman had not already surmised from his external observations. The interior of the mouth, throat, and gullet, were severely burned, as also the lining of the stomach. Lysol mixed with mucus was present in this organ, but no food. A small quantity of Lysol had passed into the duodenum, the mucous membrane of which was also burned. It was evident that death must have taken place almost at once from shock. For the rest Mrs. Holland appeared to be about forty-five years of age, and though exceedingly thin, with hair already quite grey, did not show any evidence of gross disease in the various organs. The stomach and other important parts were sealed in glass jars and despatched for analysis, the coroner was informed, and the inquest arranged provisionally for the following Saturday, November 10th.

Since neither the room nor the neighbours were able to suggest the whereabouts or even the existence of any relations of the deceased, a description of her was printed and hung upon the outside of the Friary Road Police Station. No immediate results were to be expected from it, and after assembling the meagre facts already known, Sergeant Chandler decided to make another visit to Fripp Street to see what repetition would do in the way of supplementing them. There were two main questions for which he required an answer; the first, why had Mrs. Holland killed herself, and the second, why had she used Lysol, a notoriously painful method?

Thinking these things over as he went along he decided that the probable answer to both questions was lack of money. The few coins in the woman's pocket were all that had been found either in her room or upon her person. If she had come to the end of her resources and had no-one to whom she could turn for help, no parent, no brother or sister, no friend, she might, as many others before her, have preferred to die rather than to seek help from the authorities. But why Lysol? It was cheap, certainly, but so was gas,—in sufficient quantity that was to say, to achieve her purpose. And how much more pleasant. The Lysol rankled in Sergeant Chandler's mind, for he was a kind-hearted man, fond of animals and children, and the thought of unnecessary suffering was painful to him. Especially when it seemed to be caused, as in this case, by sheer stupidity.

Mrs. Holland's room had been locked up the night before, and except for the absence of her dead body and the fragments of the cup, was exactly the same as it had been when the constable and Dr. Freeman had examined it. The Lysol bottle and the saucer still stood on the table, also the plate with the piece of bread-and-butter, now almost unrecognizable in its shrivelled sooty state. The sergeant had seen the broken cup at Friary Road Police Station. All the pieces smelt strongly of Lysol and one or two had tea-leaves sticking to them. Well, that wasn't surprising; by the general look of the room he didn't suppose there was much washing up done there, either of china or anything else. There was no vestige of water in the room, no pail, no basin, except the china one on the wash-stand, no jug but the rubbish-filled receptacle standing in that basin. A small piece of hard dry soap lay on the window-sill and a dirty rag that had evidently done duty as a towel hung from the top rail of the bed.

After a prolonged and careful search through the bed-clothes and mattress, the empty interior of the rickety chest of drawers, and the equally empty built-in cupboard beside the fireplace, Sergeant Chandler assembled the Lysol bottle and the saucer and wrapped them into a neat parcel. He then left the room, locking it up again behind him, and knocked on Mrs. Dunwoody's door.

He found her in, and alone. Violet, after the shock of

the evening before, had been rushed away to an aunt who lived a few streets off, and was to remain there until after the inquest.

"'Er nerves was all to pieces, an' no wonder," explained Mrs. Dunwoody. "Takin' 'old of a dead 'and like that. It was enough to send a grown-up person silly, let alone a kid."

More likely to, in fact, thought Sergeant Chandler, who knew the self-protective callousness of the young.

"She had no idea Mrs. Holland was in?"

"No. She was playin' out the back with them Pope children. Noisy brats, they are. She didn't 'ear nothink of her comin' in, but it must a been before I got back, or else I'd 'ave 'eard 'er, see."

"You knew she was out?"

"Well, 'er room was empty when I took 'er cup of tea in after dinner."

"I see. That accounts for the tea-leaves in the cup, I suppose."

"Well, seein' it was my cup, and fresh out of the cupboard, I should say they was. And speakin' 'o that there cup of mine, 'oo's goin' to get me a noo one, I should like to know? I can't be expected to go buyin' crocks for people to throw on the floor, takin' poison, can I?"

The sergeant did not attempt to advise Mrs. Dunwoody on the subject of replacing her property, but endeavoured, with considerable difficulty, to obtain from her the correct times of the events of yesterday. She knew that she had reached the cinema in time for the first performance of the main feature, arriving during the last event of the newsreel. This provided accurate data for future research, but was not immediately illuminating. The time at which Violet had gone upstairs to put coal on the fire could not be settled.

The child had no idea at all, Mrs. Dunwoody said, and had only been able to say that it was still quite light. Chandler decided to see Violet in person later on, but he held faint hopes of getting more from her than a confirmation of her mother's statement. At all events she had noticed that Mrs. Holland's door was shut, and she was sure she had heard no-one entering the house during the time she was playing in the yard. This was not very helpful, since Mrs. Holland had in fact returned at some time before Mrs. Dunwoody herself. Putting aside the question of times, the sergeant returned to his main theme.

"Have you any idea if Mrs. Holland had had the Lysol by her for some time, or if she brought it into the house for the express purpose of drinking it?"

"I don't know, I'm sure, what she wanted with a noo bottle. There'd of been enough in the old one to 'ave done 'er in, and more besides."

"What do you mean?"

"I mean the bottle she give me in the morning to do down the stairs. As I says to Mr. Dunwoody, I says, 'You can't be too careful,' I says, 'what with Ronnie Pope 'avin' the 'oopin' cough all these weeks. There's no knowing what germs 'll be 'angin' round the 'ouse,' I says. So she give me 'er bottle of Lysol, and I scrubbed the stairs down from top to bottom and the landin' too. I'd of give 'er back the bottle if she'd of asked for it, but no, she must needs go and get a noo one."

"Have you still got it?"

Mrs. Dunwoody glared at him as if she suspected that he doubted her word, but she made no reply and produced from under her table a bottle of Lysol about half-full, the neck sticky and covered with dust and the label stained by the drips that had run down over it.

"It was like this when she gave it to you?"

"It was nearly full before I used it. But it 'ad been opened previous, if that's what you mean."

"Quite so."

Sergeant Chandler wrapped up the second bottle of Lysol, and prepared to leave.

"When can I 'ave my room back?" inquired Mrs. Dunwoody from the door. "It's bad enough 'avin' a suicide in the 'ouse, but if I can't even 'ave the use of the room…"

"You'll be able to use it after the inquest," answered the sergeant shortly. "Perhaps earlier."

"Not but wot I'm sorry for 'er, mind," said Mrs. Dunwoody, softening a little in the face of disapproval. "She 'adn't a job, and she wasn't well. It was only Guy Fawkes Day she was up at the doctor's."

Chandler who had started to go down the stairs looked up quickly.

"She consulted a doctor on the 5th? Who was that?"

"She didn't say. It was foggy that day if you remember, and I saw 'er come out in 'er 'at and coat. 'Wherever are you off to?' I says. 'I'm goin' up to the doctor's,' she says. 'My stomach's out of order.' 'And no wonder,' I says, 'with the mucky sort of stuff you eats.' I told 'er straight. 'You're ruinin' your inside,' I says. 'Nothink but bread and a kipper now and then. Get yourself a nice chop,' I says. But she wouldn't take no notice."

"You don't know who she went to?" pursued Chandler patiently.

"I expect it 'ud be Ellis, up at the corner of Barton Street. 'E's the nearest, and 'e charges less nor wot the others does."

Sergeant Chandler felt as he left Fripp Street that his visit had not been wholly unproductive. Mrs. Dunwoody's sudden regard for hygiene might have suggested Lysol to one who was contemplating ending her life. Perhaps she did not ask for the bottle back because self-consciously she feared her guilty purpose would be suspected; perhaps she could not wait once she had decided upon her course, but was impelled by a fierce longing for its completion to go out and buy immediately the means to attain it.

So much for the possible reason why Lysol had been used. As for the motive for suicide, what more probable than that Dr. Ellis, if indeed he had attended her, would be able to supply it. An incurable disease, a cancer, or perhaps mental trouble, incipient insanity; it did not always show, in the early stages. Well, there was no point in speculating; the doctor would be able to tell him. He began to see his way clear to the inquest.

Dr. Ellis's housekeeper, Miss Pollen, explained with regrets that the doctor was out. Wednesday was his half-day and there was no evening surgery. The usual hours were nine to ten in the morning, six to eight at night,—except Wednesday. The doctor usually went out on his half-day; he was in fact out now, and not expected back till late. Could Miss Pollen take a message?

Sergeant Chandler suppressed his impatience at this news, for there was nothing he could do about it, since Miss Pollen was ignorant of the doctor's whereabouts. He said that he would call the next morning during surgery hours. Miss Pollen, a stoutish middle-aged woman with a rather wooden face, promised to write down this message, and said the doctor would attend to it when he came in, and she hoped it was nothing urgent. Sergeant Chandler assured her that no life would be endangered by the delay, and went off feeling baulked and disappointed.

He walked slowly down Barton Street away from the main road until his progress was stopped by the river wall in front of him. On his right the great gates of the saw-mill yard towered above him. On his left a cobbled piece of roadway, edged by a row of small houses similar to those he had just passed in Barton Street, stretched to the corner of Lower Thames Street and Wood Wharf.

He rested his elbows on the parapet of the wall and read methodically through his notes. It became obvious that whatever Mrs. Dunwoody thought about the state of her child's nerves, Violet would have to be asked a few questions about the events of the afternoon before. Not about her finding of the body; no need to worry her to go over that, poor kid. The other people in the house had plenty and to spare to tell him on that head. But if she could throw any light at all on the time Mrs. Holland had returned it might be possible to trace the latter's movements. The shops had been singularly unhelpful, particularly the chemists, where the sergeant had hoped to discover the sale of the new bottle of Lysol. One of them thought he remembered selling a bottle of Lysol to a slatternly woman answering to the official description, but that had been more than a month ago. This might have been the first bottle, but as Chandler at the time of asking had not known of its existence, he had not pursued the matter further. Besides, it was unlikely that in such a neighbourhood Mrs. Holland was the only slatternly woman to patronize a chemist.

Sergeant Chandler detached himself with some reluctance from the wall with its pleasing view of waves and ships, and returning to the main road along Lower Thames

Street, boarded a tram and was conveyed to Violet's temporary home.

The aunt was at first indignant, then resigned. She said darkly that she knew what the law was, and that it wasn't no good for poor people like herself to get on the wrong side of it, but she dreaded to think what her sister, Mrs. Dunwoody, would say when she heard what had befallen her only child,—poor mite,—after all she'd been through,—laying her hand on that nasty corpse.

Violet, on the other hand, whose nerves seemed to the sergeant to be of stouter calibre than either her mother or her aunt suspected, was perfectly willing to be questioned by the tall thin gentleman who made a fuss of her and called her "dear." She was a naturally talkative child, fond of hearing her own voice and with insufficient scope for it at home. But however hard she tried to be helpful she could only say that she and the Pope children had played hop-scotch in the yard all the afternoon except when she went upstairs to put coal on the fire.

"Wasn't there anyone in the house at all?"

"No."

"Where was your father?"

"'E goes to the Centre. Dr. Freeman 'as 'is knife into 'im, so 'e won't give 'im a sustificate to say 'e can stop at 'ome."

This agreed more or less with Mr. Dunwoody's and also with Dr. Freeman's versions of the former's hard lot, so the sergeant went on.

"What about Mr. Pope? He has a certificate to let him off going to the Centre while Mrs. Pope is in hospital. Why wasn't he at home looking after the children?"

"'E isn't never at 'ome. 'E works on a job."

"Oh! What does he do?"

"'E 'elps a man wot sells betting slips."

Violet raised her eyes at her aunt's sharp warning hiss. The sergeant grinned; this gratuitous information was no concern of his.

"All right. And no-one came to the door that afternoon? No-one knocked?"

"I don't remember no-one."

"You didn't see Mrs. Holland come back when you were going up to do the fire or coming down again?"

"No."

"Did you see anything at all while you were going up or coming down; on the landing, on the stairs, in the passage?"

"No." She thought it over slowly. "But I saw Charlie Mason outside the door."

"Outside the front door?"

"Yeah."

"So the front door was open, was it?"

"Yeah."

"Tell me about Charlie. What was he doing?"

"Writing 'is name in the dust on the back."

"What do you mean—back? Whose back?"

Violet went off into a shrill cackle of laughter, and was with difficulty recalled to a sense of the occasion.

"Not a person's back. You aren't 'alf soppy! Dr. Ellis's car's back. 'E never cleans it, see."

"Oh." Sergeant Chandler was interested. "What was the car doing outside your house?"

"It warn't outside 'our 'ouse. 'E was in next door, to Mrs. Bowerman. She's been bad a long time. Mum's been seeing to 'er."

"I see. The car was there when you came down. Was it there when you went up?"

"I dunno."

"Did you hear it go? Was it long after you went back into the yard?"

"I dunno. You always 'ears cars. I didn't take all that notice. You better ask Mrs. Bowerman if you want to know."

"Now then, Miss," said her aunt reprovingly, but Sergeant Chandler got up with a laugh.

"Leave her be," he said kindly. "She's got her head screwed on all right."

All the same he wished she had been able to tell him at what time Mrs. Holland had come back to Number One, Fripp Street.

On the following morning Sergeant Chandler made his way, at the early hour of nine o'clock, to the surgery at the corner of Barton Street. The front of Dr. Ellis's house was no different in structure from the shops beyond it, but the large shop window was painted a dingy brown colour half-way up, and in the middle of this expanse of brown the doctor's name and hours for consultation were clearly set out in gold letters of considerable size. The door when pushed open sounded a bell, just as those of the shops did, and the patient walked straight into the waiting-room. Here wooden benches stood against the side walls and under the window, while in the middle of the room a small cane table covered with a worn piece of flowered lino-cloth supported a few tattered periodicals of mature vintage and a stunted ill-kempt aspidistra in a green pot.

When Chandler entered by the shop-door he found the waiting-room empty, but after he had sat on one of the narrow uncomfortable benches for a few minutes a door at the back of the room opened and a labouring man in a cap and muffler came out. He left the surgery door open behind him, nodding gravely to Chandler as he passed. The sergeant hesitated, but his doubts were resolved by a bell which rang loudly and impatiently in the doctor's room. He stepped forward and went in.

Dr. Ellis was seated at a table placed obliquely near the window. He was shuffling some papers as Chandler entered, and spoke without looking up.

"Good morning. Shut the door, please, and sit down. Have I seen you before?"

Sergeant Chandler hastened to explain himself. The doctor listened, drooping wearily in his chair, his chin held in his left hand, his other hand grasping a pencil with which from time to time he made small aimless patterns of dots on his blotting-pad. When Chandler ceased speaking he flung down the pencil, leaped to his feet and crossed the room to a set of card-index boxes standing on another table against the wall. He returned with the card he had pulled out, and sat down again, jerking his chair in close to the table.

"I saw it in the paper yesterday, of course, but I did not connect up. I am pretty sure this is the woman. She answers to your description and she gave the name of Holland— Mary Holland. I saw her once only, and here at my surgery. She complained of indigestion. I examined her and found no signs of anything beyond dyspepsia, gave her some McLean's powder and told her to see me again."

Chandler looked puzzled.

"You didn't notice anything special about her arms when you examined her?"

"No. I don't think I saw her arms uncovered. I only

wanted to see the chest and abdomen and in this bitterly cold weather they take off as little as possible, naturally."

"I see. Then from what you found you decided she was a case of dyspepsia?"

"Yes. That was my first impression. Had her symptoms persisted in spite of treatment I should have suspected more serious gastric trouble and had her X-rayed and so on."

"Did you test her for diabetes?"

Dr. Ellis looked startled, but almost at once he recovered himself and said with energy, "No, I didn't. This is a large, poor-class practice, and if I started making complete routine examinations of every patient I see at the surgery I should never get through my day's work. I do what I consider necessary to establish the diagnosis, having regard to the symptoms, and in nine cases out of ten I remove the symptoms and cure the patient. The tenth one goes to hospital."

Looking at the flushed face before him Chandler wondered at this unnecessary vehemence. He was not quite sure what he thought of Dr. Ellis. The man seemed to be capable and quite on top of his job, but there was something about him, a forced energy, a slightly theatrical air, that rang false. He decided it was probably his own imagination, and rose to go.

"I'm sorry I can't be more helpful," said Dr. Ellis smoothly. "But as I say, I only saw the woman once and that was on Guy Fawkes Day."

"It's a pity," answered Chandler, turning his hat over in his hands. "We can't fix the time she came home, you see. It's a pity," he went on, "you didn't look in when you were next door at Mrs. Bowerman's. That would have been a help whether she was in or out."

There was no missing the doctor's anger and confusion now. His body went stiff and he glared at Sergeant Chandler without speaking. The sergeant looked him straight in the eyes. They were queer eyes, some of the queerest he'd ever seen, very light grey with large pupils, one of which looked bigger than the other. Again he felt that there was something about Dr. Ellis that he did not understand. To gain time he walked slowly round the surgery, looking at the desk, the walls, the boxes of patients' cards and notes, the cupboards, and the small glass-topped trolley on which the doctor kept his bowls and instruments. A syringe lay in a glass dish of methylated spirit with a cover over it, and two thermometers stood side by side in a jar that had once held potted meat, their ends protected by a layer of cotton-wool and half their length immersed in a solution of Lysol. Chandler, looking at the opaque pale brown liquid, was reminded of Mrs. Holland's death and sniffed disgustedly.

"I hate the smell," he said. "But I suppose you have to use a lot of it."

The doctor was strangely pale.

"That or other disinfectants," he said slowly. "It's cheaper than methylated and doesn't evaporate in the same way."

Again Chandler looked at the thermometers.

"I don't know how they bring themselves to do it," he said. "The smell would be enough to put me off. Well, I'm sorry you didn't go up to see Mrs. Holland. You might have stopped her."

Dr. Ellis led the way to the door of his room. "I don't suppose I should have gone up anyway," he said with a short laugh. "But as a matter of fact I didn't know Mrs. Holland lived next door to Mrs. Bowerman. I thought it was some people called Dunwoody."

"Mrs. Holland was Mrs. Dunwoody's lodger," answered Chandler. "Don't come out, doctor, I see you're busy."

He made his way across the now crowded waiting-room and into the street. Dr. Ellis had told one lie at all events—an obvious and a stupid one too. For Mrs. Holland's address had been written plain to see upon her record card. Sergeant Chandler shook his head, more in pity than in anger.

In the waiting-room the patients sat, humbly listening for a bell that seemed disinclined to ring. But Dr. Ellis had something more important to think about than a crowd of petty ailments. He was sitting frozen in his chair, looking over the sharp edge of a precipice into a chasm whose depths were veiled in cloud, and all the more terrible for their concealment.

At last he drew the telephone towards him and took off the receiver with fingers that shook.

On Friday, Sergeant Chandler, after a morning and afternoon spent on other work, sat down to review his findings in the case of Mrs. Holland. The inquest was fixed for the following day, Saturday, and such evidence as there was had been collected. No-one had come forward to claim kinship or even acquaintance with the dead woman; it could not even be proved that the name Mary Holland was her true one. Her past history therefore was unknown, and with it presumably the real motive for her suicide.

But the post-mortem findings were at once informative and mystifying. The woman had died of shock following Lysol poisoning; there was no doubt of this. But there was found in her body a grain and a half of heroin hydrochloride, and the presence of the hypodermic scars on the arms was thus explained. Very well, thought Sergeant Chandler, here we have a drug addict, no money left, no supplies of her drug, can't afford to get any, decided to quit, buys some Lysol, does quit. Very pretty, very plausible, but what about those recent hypodermic marks? The report gave a definite statement with regard to the scars. Most of them were old, months old, but a few of them, three to be exact, were quite fresh. They had bled, suggesting an old or blunt needle, and had been easily identified.

Now here lay the snag. If Mrs. Holland had found a new source of supply, deprivation of the drug was not the motive for her suicide. If lack of money or the depression consequent on her addiction was the cause, why had she not used an overdose of heroin to lead her away in peace and comfort rather than a crude and fiery antiseptic to burn her brutally out of life? It was against all common-sense and the more he thought of it the more Chandler was puzzled, until he remembered that no hypodermic and no heroin had been found in the room in Fripp Street. Had she then come to the end of her fresh supply, and lost her instrument into the bargain? If not, how had she acquired those recent pricks in her left forearm? Confound the woman, why had she not left the usual explanatory letter behind her?

It was at this stage that Sergeant Chandler thought of Dr. Ellis and the visit that Mrs. Holland had made to him on the day before her death. He immediately set about investigating the doctor's record, and before long was rewarded. Dr. Ellis had been hauled over the coals by the Panel Committee for excessive prescribing of hypnotic drugs and for discrepancies in his poison register. Subsequently the case had come before the General Medical Council. The charge against him had however not been proved to the Council's satisfaction and he had been let off with a warning against carelessness and lax principles in the conduct of his practice. Certain chemists informed the police, and a watch was kept. But, apparently, the warning had taken effect, for no further action had been needed and his name was still on the Register. Nevertheless the coincidence was striking. A doctor, known to have provided addicts with drugs, in contact with a woman known to be a drug-addict. Moreover the woman had used a hypodermic recently, after a considerable interval had elapsed since her former injections. Of course she could have taken the heroin by the mouth meanwhile. It was cheaper than buying needles, and even a syringe had to be replaced from time to time. But then why had she suddenly gone back to injections, and why had the syringe vanished?

Sergeant Chandler began to take a sinister view of the doctor's conduct. Suppose he had been used to supply Mrs. Holland in the days before his exposure? What more natural than that she should consult him again when she was down on her luck? It might even have been blackmail on her part, the threat to spread a rumour about him and ruin his practice, such as it was, forcing him to give her what she wanted in order to keep her mouth shut. And in this case the doctor could not contemplate bringing her to justice, for the secret she threatened to expose was no mere scandal, but a crime itself punishable by law. He had escaped once by the skin of his teeth; with definite evidence against him he could not hope to evade conviction.

Suppose Dr. Ellis had gone up to see Mrs. Holland after his visit to Mrs. Bowerman at the house next door. Perhaps he had found the woman dead. What more natural than that he should remove the hypodermic syringe and the supply of heroin? The doctor had been distinctly uneasy when reminded of his visit to Mrs. Bowerman. It would account in a reasonable manner for the disappearance of the hypo-dermic outfit; it was very unlikely that Mrs. Holland, after only three fresh injections, had lost or damaged it. She would guard it as the apple of her eye; whatever else in her room she neglected she would not be careless of this. But it had gone.

And Dr. Ellis had told one important lie. He had pre-tended he did not know where Mrs. Holland lived. In Sergeant Chandler's eyes this confirmed his suspicions. The doctor had something to hide about Mrs. Holland. What was it? Had he given her the heroin? Had he been threat-ened by her? Had he tried to see her to argue her out of her intention? Had he even—?

The sergeant pulled himself up. No, Dr. Ellis could not have handed Mrs. Holland a cup of Lysol asking her to drink it down quickly and never mind the taste. Nor could he have forced it down her throat without a struggle, and there had been no sign of a struggle. Nor could Mrs. Holland have been made to take it while she lay unconscious under the influ-ence of the drug. But suppose she was just coming round and the doctor had arrived to find her in a drowsy state and had then handed her the fatal dose? She might conceivably have taken it. But that supposed that the Lysol bottle was all ready to hand, the second Lysol bottle that Mrs. Holland had bought on purpose for her suicide. You couldn't have it all ways, suicide, assisted suicide, and murder. Besides, the only finger-prints found on the Lysol bottle were those of Mrs. Holland herself. If the doctor had poured out the dose his prints would be on the bottle, unless he wore gloves. It was cold weather; he might well be wearing gloves. At any rate he would probably have rubber gloves with him in his bag.

On the other hand Violet, while not knowing the time, had seen the doctor's car while it was still light, but the post-mortem examination showed that Mrs. Holland had probably died after five o'clock, when it was quite dark. So it was unlikely that Dr. Ellis had seen Mrs. Holland at all that Tuesday afternoon—unless he came back again later, without his car.

Having let his thoughts gallop thus madly away with him, Sergeant Chandler took a firm grip of the reins and brought them back to a steady walk. This was going too fast altogether. The next thing would be to see Dr. Ellis again, put the wind up him by exposing his very silly lie, and see what further information he could get about Mrs. Holland and her heroin addiction. Then he could see old Mrs. Bowerman and check the times of the doctor's arrival and departure. If he had come straight up after his car stopped and had driven away at once when he left her, and if he had a satisfactory alibi for five o'clock, then these new suspicions fell flat. And in any case they got nowhere at all until it was discovered at what time Mrs. Holland returned to her room. And that, it seemed, was a thing of which nobody in Fripp Street or the neighbourhood had the very slightest idea. All the Pope children and Violet could say was that they had gone on playing after it was dark and had had tea given them by Mr. Pope sometime between five and six.

Sergeant Chandler looked at his watch. He would just have nice time to pop down to Barton Street, see Ellis, pop up to Fripp Street and question Mrs. Bowerman, and return to Friary Road Police Station to make a full report of his investigations to date.

7

LESLIE HARVEY WANDERED DISCONSOLATELY UP AND down the narrow beach near Jim Sawyer's landing-stage, from time to time picking up a stone and throwing it with languid air but accurate aim at the various pieces of rubbish that floated on the water. He was very bored. A cold in the head, drearily extinguishing the glamour of his Sunday morning adventure, had earned him a week's holiday from school. He should have been pleased at this, but he was not. In the first place he would have enjoyed telling his story with embellishments to his friends; in the second, having now realized the full advantage of being able to swim, he had wanted to make immediate arrangements for going to the baths and learning to do so. Instead of which his mother, expecting hourly the onset of pneumonia, had kept him in bed for two days, and then, irritated by his failure to live up to her anticipations, had allowed him to get up and go out, being only too glad to be rid of his incessant chatter and destructive, experimenting fingers.

So Leslie was at a loose end. To-morrow would be

Saturday when he could expect companionship. But to-day, Friday, his friends were at school, and he had nowhere particular to go. Presently, as on the three previous mornings, he found himself drawn by dramatic memory to the beach and the river where he had narrowly escaped from drowning.

The tide was low, so low that the water had retreated from the landmost end of Jim Sawyer's jetty, and the slimy, weed-encrusted piles stood clear of the water. Leslie approached them and idly began to pull the weed away. Presently he found several great nails sticking out horizontally from the piles, and unable to resist such obvious hand and footholds, pulled himself cautiously up and looked over on to the landing-stage.

There was no-one there. With a swift glance at the wall to guard against interruption from that quarter, Leslie pulled himself up a little further and rolled softly over on top. He crouched low, and then, as no warning shouts were raised, and no-one appeared to have noticed his behaviour, he wormed his way along the edge of the landing-stage towards the boathouse. In its shelter he would feel safe, and moreover, would find many fascinating objects to examine and play with.

Much to his own astonishment his purpose was achieved. He slipped unnoticed into the shed and wandered about, looking at the boats and oars of the rowing clubs, the loose rudders and thwarts piled against the walls, the small sculling boats in various stages of repair and ruin, the tools and benches and sacking, the piles of soft sawdust on the floor, the ropes and tackle, mast and sails of a dinghy which lay denuded of her centre-board, and, greatest thrill of all, Harry Reed's boat on which Jim Sawyer had been recently at

work with a restorative coat of paint. As Leslie gazed at her
he was filled anew with admiration of her owner and pride
that he had been the recipient of that hero's later attentions.
For Harry Reed had come up every night since the accident
to ask after his health, and to receive in turn the sympathy and solicitude of his sister June and, when at home,
his father as well. His mother, of course, never let on to be
pleased whoever came, but that didn't make any difference.
It would have been more sensible of Harry to have come
in the mornings when June was at work, because then she
wouldn't have taken up so much of the conversation. But in
spite of hints, more or less open, it had always been the evening after June came home, and each evening the visit had
lasted longer than on the night before.

Leslie looked longingly at Harry's boat and made up
his mind more firmly than ever that he would first learn to
swim and next to row and then, with the pennies he had
saved, amounting in all to three-and-sevenpence, approach
Jim Sawyer with a view to acquiring a craft of his own by
means of a sum down and deferred payments.

A hail from the river made him jump. He looked up to
see a police launch rocking gently a few yards off the landing. In the stern he recognized the cheerful brown face of
Sergeant Adams.

"None the worse for your ducking, eh?" the sergeant
called to him. "And can't keep off the river. I wonder Jim
lets you come down in his shed after the way you behaved
Sunday."

Leslie decided that, however unpleasant, his future safety
was best guaranteed by present candour. He approached
the edge of the landing-stage and put on a very pleading
expression.

"'E doesn't know I'm 'ere," he said in a faint high voice. "I slipped up over the piles. Don't tell 'im I'm 'ere, sir. I'll go back the way I come, straight, I will."

Sergeant Adams drew in a little closer to the stage. "You're a sight too fond of getting in places where you aren't meant to be," he said sternly. "If you're there without Sawyer's permission, you're trespassing, and you know what that means, or you ought to."

"Don't tell on me," begged Leslie, getting very red in the face as the tears rose in his eyes. "I wasn't doing no 'arm, only looking at Harry Reed's boat and that."

"I've heard that before," said Sergeant Adams. "Go on. Hop it!"

"Yessir." Leslie retreated slowly round the shed and stood, out of sight of the river, considering his next move. To go back along the landing-stage was risky, but in the end would have to be faced. To stay there was also risky and might, if the River Police noticed him again, rouse them to definite action. He began reluctantly to move back towards the shore.

"Cut round the corner of the jetty," ordered Sergeant Adams. "That boy's up to some mischief."

The driver of the launch was in process of obeying this order when a fresh exclamation from Adams made him look back. The sergeant was pointing at a battered wooden object that floated just under the corner of the landing-stage, caught by it and by a tangle of old rope that hung down over the edge. The launch pulled in closer and after a few abortive efforts, a square wooden box, rather the worse for its long immersion, was heaved on board. Sergeant Adams examined it briefly.

"One of the boxes off the barges that got loose on Guy

Fawkes Day and ran up against the Saw Mill Wharf here. There were several missing: we'd better take a look round, there might be more. Sawyer took one up to the Hole the day after it happened: probably pinched it off the barge, but we'll never know. Now then!" he thundered suddenly. "Get the hell out of that! I told you to move off ten minutes ago. Did you think I was just practising my speaking voice?"

Leslie Harvey's small face, scared but resolute, came round the side of the shed, followed by his skinny body. "I 'eard you shout," he said. "I thought you meant me, so I come back." He looked with glistening eyes at the wooden box that the police had salved. "Did it really come off them barges? I 'eard about them, but Mum made me stop in bed, so I never see them took off. Dad wasn't 'alf wild about it. 'E said…"

"Never you mind what your dad said. You've been listening, young nosy. You do what I told you or I'll take you in charge."

"Would you take me to the police station in your boat?"

Leslie came forward briskly. Arrest and imprisonment lost their terrors before the possibility of another glorious ride in the launch that had saved him and with the men who had brought him back to life. Sergeant Adams looked at the boy's eager eyes and relented inwardly. His voice, however, remained stern and chilled by authority.

"If you think you're going to get another trip in the launch, you're mistaken. Now, for the last time, hop it, or you'll be sorry you ever came here."

"If I find another o' them boxes," said Leslie desperately, backing a few inches up the landing-stage, "would you give me a ride in the boat then, mister?"

"*If* you find another box," returned Sergeant Adams, "it's your duty to take it to the nearest police station."

"Yessir."

"Now scoot!"

Leslie scooted. As he scrambled down the piles on to the shore he waved his arm to the launch which was moving quietly away up the river. Sergeant Adams smiled to himself. Not a bad kid, and persistent, like his father. He thought that he had probably not seen the last of Leslie Harvey.

The salvaged box was examined at Wapping by Detective Norris of the River Police. It was found to contain rubber and to be part of the consignment of that commodity known to have been purchased by Messrs. Listons of Limehouse, manufacturers, through a certain Max Holman, importer, of Lancaster House, Prince Albert Street. Nothing unusual was discovered either in the box itself or in its contents. It was decided to keep a careful watch on Jim Sawyer's landing-stage and its immediate neighbourhood, and also to a modified extent upon the resourceful boat-keeper himself.

Detective-Sergeant Chandler was unexpectedly delayed at the station. He ought to have put off his visit to Dr. Ellis until the following day, but he was keen, and felt that he had a chance of getting some really useful information. So, considerably later than he intended, he arrived at last at the doctor's surgery in Barton Street. He found the waiting-room empty and the consulting-room, with its door wide open, deserted. For a few minutes he moved about feeling rather at a loss, until he noticed on the waiting-room wall a bell-push surmounted by a piece of cardboard on which was written "Please ring." Obediently he did so, and waited. Footsteps sounded presently in the doctor's room and the housekeeper, Miss Pollen, appeared in the doorway. She explained shortly that it was after hours, and demanded to know if the case were urgent. Then, recognizing Chandler as the man who had on a former occasion asked to see Dr. Ellis, she said briefly that she would tell the doctor he was there, and disappeared. In a very short time she was back. "Dr. Ellis is on the phone just now. He will see you in a few minutes if you will wait, please."

As she turned to go, Chandler stopped her.

"Too bad of me worrying him so late, isn't it?" he began in a conversational voice, "But you see I've been working all day myself. Dr. Ellis is a very busy man, isn't he?"

"Doctors mostly are." Miss Pollen's expression indicated that she preferred not to gossip about her employer.

"It must be an awful rush for him, with the surgeries morning and evening, and the visits to put in between those times. I suppose he never gets a minute to himself except at meal-times and evenings when he isn't called out."

Miss Pollen was a trifle softened by the stranger's solicitude, and anxious to create a true impression.

"Oh, I don't know. Just after Christmas he's usually out all day, but we're fairly quiet at present for the time of year. He's been finished with the visits by four every day this week. That means a good rest for him before the evening surgery. Not that he doesn't need it. Doctors work harder than most people in my opinion. He generally looks fagged out."

"Well, I'm glad to hear he isn't being overworked at present. Home at four every day this week, I think you said?"

"That's right. Sitting by the fire with the paper. All but Wednesday—that was day before yesterday—his day off. He always goes out then, unless he's got a special case on."

Miss Pollen recollected herself and turned to go. "If you'll just sit down I don't think he'll keep you long."

She closed the door of the consulting-room behind her, and Chandler heard her go out by the inner door, shutting it also.

So Dr. Ellis had got home at four every day that week except Wednesday. And according to the post-mortem findings, Mrs. Holland had died at about five or a little later; earlier than five being most unlikely. The doctor's alibi seemed to be as watertight as Sergeant Chandler had hoped to find it leaky. Provided, of course, that Miss Pollen's statement was true. However, there was still the heroin problem. Without touching much upon Mrs. Holland's death, the sergeant thought he might be able to rouse Dr. Ellis to some response on this subject. He was right, but the information he received carried him no further.

"I said nothing about her addiction the other day," explained the doctor with a grave face, "because I consider my patient's confidence as binding, even after death. As a matter of fact, the poor woman told me of it herself, and I strongly advised her to go into an institution where she could be adequately treated. It is not a type of case that I could possibly undertake in a district like this in the patient's own home, as I expect you realize."

"Did you give her any drug to carry on with?"

"Certainly not."

Dr. Ellis stared indignantly at Chandler, but before the latter's steady meaning gaze his eyes dropped.

"Without referring to matters that don't enter this case, at least at present," said the sergeant carefully, "I think you know very well why we are making special inquiries about it here. The woman was an addict and she has been to consult you."

"We have gone over this ground before," said Dr. Ellis

briskly, rather too briskly, the sergeant thought, "and I have nothing to add to what I said then."

Sergeant Chandler had several things to add and was about to begin upon them when there was a knock at the door. It was Miss Pollen with a note. A man had brought it and was there an answer, please? Dr. Ellis unfolded the dirty, crumpled paper and read the message scrawled upon it.

"Yes. Tell him I'll come round at once. Is it Dunwoody at the door?"

"No, sir. I don't know who it is."

"Right. Tell him I'll come at once."

Dr. Ellis turned back into the room and tossed the note on to his table.

"Urgent call, I'm afraid. An old patient of mine, old lady of the name of Bowerman. Poor old thing, she doesn't want to go into hospital, but I think she'll have to give in before long. Will you come back later to-night, or to-morrow, or will you come along and continue the inquisition en route?" The doctor spoke in his usual rapid manner, and did not seem to be at all disturbed by the prospect of further questions.

Now Chandler had intended to see Mrs. Bowerman. If the old woman was to be sent into hospital there might be a considerable delay before he could question her. On the other hand, if he went along now he might be able to get in a few words after the doctor had finished, provided she was well enough to answer him. He made up his mind.

"I'll go along with you," he said.

"Right. Just as you like. I'll bring the car round to the front here. My garage is beyond the side door in Barton Street."

When the doctor had gone, Chandler picked up the note. It was quite short and very deficient in grammar, simply stating Mrs. Bowerman took worse and would doctor come at once. It was written in pencil on a scrap of coarse ruled paper; the writing was shaky and uneven, a typical uneducated hand. Chandler put it back on the table and went out into the street. The doctor's car was moving slowly towards him along the curb. It drew level with him and halted; Dr. Ellis leaned over to push open the door.

As Chandler climbed in he glanced back down the street. The doctor's garage door was open, but the house doors all appeared to be shut. The street was deserted except for a group of noisy children playing round a street-lamp and at the far end a solitary man leaning on the river wall.

Nine o'clock was striking as Dr. Ellis turned his car out of Barton Street into the main road. In Upper Thames Street Harry Reed detached himself from the doorpost of the Harveys' house and shuffled his feet on the top step. "Late as usual," he complained. "You've no business to keep me up 'ere jawing."

June laughed and gave him a push.

"I like that. Me keep you jawing, indeed. You don't have to stay a minute longer than you want to. I won't keep you."

Harry pulled her hair with his free hand. She yelped shrilly and would have smacked his face, but she remembered his crippled condition, and instead ran down the steps into the road. Harry followed with one easy bound and caught her again, this time with an arm round her waist.

"On the level, kid, I got to get 'ome now. What say we go to a picture to-morrow? Only it'll 'ave to be the second house."

"I don't mind if I do."

"Okay."

He drew her a little closer to him; June lifted her face expectantly, but no kiss came. Harry was staring into the distance with a set look on his face.

"What's eating you?" June asked. "Remembered you'd got a date with the other girl?"

"I don't have another girl. Look. There's something I want to give you. It's in my pocket. Let go of me a minute."

"Go on! I'm not stopping you."

June drew away haughtily, disappointed at this turn in the conversation, fearful that he should guess how much he now attracted her. She found she was being offered a small flat parcel.

"What is it? A present—for me?"

"Yeah." Harry's voice was embarrassed.

"Oh, well. Thanks very much, I'm sure. I think I'd better be going in now. Good-night."

She vanished before Harry had time to turn round. He swore softly: that was cool, if you like. He fumbled in his pocket for a cigarette and stood puffing at it while he considered the unaccountable and perverse moods of women.

Upstairs in her bedroom, June Harvey unpacked the parcel and discovered two rose-pink chiffon nightdresses of very superior quality. She was so astonished she nearly dropped them on the floor. They were good ones—real good ones. Why, at "Lulu's" they'd fetch forty-nine-and-six every time. They must be phoney, of course. Harry couldn't buy nightdresses worth forty-nine-and-six. Fancy giving her nightdresses: the sauce, if you came to think of it! And he didn't seem that sort of boy at all—never got fresh, like that cad, Longford.

She held the soft folds against her cheek. He must like

her to give her these, wherever they came from. And she did like him. When he held her up against him as he had done just now her knees went so weak she was ready to drop. But he hadn't even kissed her yet.

She pushed up the lower half of her window and looked out. "Harry!"

The glowing end of his cigarette moved.

"Harry, they're lovely! Thanks ever so. I shan't half feel posh..." She was going to say "wearing them," but felt that it might be indelicate and let her voice trail away into silence.

Harry grinned up at her.

"That's all right. Well, I'll come up for you to-morrow afternoon."

"I'll be waiting. Ta-ta, Harry."

"So long, honey."

June blew a kiss to him and retreated. Harry strode off down the road feeling slightly above himself. He had brought off his presentation, and it had been a success. He felt altogether too elevated to go home yet. Damn the insurance regulations. He was late already, a few minutes more wouldn't make any difference one way or the other, and they could only dock his money. Well, let them. He needed a drink to settle him before he went indoors.

As he crossed Wood Wharf to go into the "Fisherman," a car passed him. He saw that the driver was Dr. Ellis and that there was another man sitting beside him. Harry did not see which way the car went because he was inside the "Fisherman" before it reached the end of Wood Wharf.

Mr. Dunwoody, having no care in life but his own welfare and convenience, was scarcely equipped by nature for observing the Laws of Property. It was not that he was ignorant of the law, far from it. His experiences in life had made many of the finer points of its administration clearer to him than to some of his more stable fellow citizens. He would sometimes marvel at their ignorance when he read of cases in the newspapers, wondering how they could have remained for so long outside its clutches. It never occurred to him that their fault might be the single lapse in a hitherto blameless life. For his own hand had been against society from the beginning: against the parents who had made him put back the apples he stole off the stalls in the market when he was tall enough to reach up to them; against the school-master who had tried to teach him a string of irrelevant facts; against the employer who had tried to make him learn a job; and finally against the Public Assistance Committee and the magistrates, the former for granting him so bare a subsistence, the latter for curtailing his efforts to increase it.

So at last he had been forced to learn caution and a kind of wisdom. Honest work he would always be able to avoid, now that medical science had decreed that, the economic situation apart, physical unfitness rather than original sin was the cause of chronic unemployment, and that the term "neurasthenia," like the term "influenza," could be used to describe any condition that was not perfectly understood. For the rest he took what he could get, keeping a sharp weather eye open for that Law, which had, he felt, always directed an especially malign and suspicious glance in his direction.

Consequently, on this same Friday night, Mr. Dunwoody, a small sack in his hand, very carefully unlatched the door of the house next his own, and slipped silently into Mrs. Bowerman's downstairs passage. With the coal he intended to purloin from her poor store he looked forward to a warm week-end. After all, the old geyser was in bed, and Mrs. Dunwoody, properly instructed, could make up the invalid's fire with a few bits of rubbish and slack, and she would never notice the difference.

He stood in the passage listening for any sound from above, but all was quiet. He began to creep forward towards the back room. And then he stopped, checked by a sound from without. A car was coming up Fripp Street from the main road, and it was slowing down as it approached. That might be in order to turn into Wood Wharf or it might be in order to stop, and if the latter, it was probably the doctor come to see Mrs. Bowerman again. No-one else would call in a car at such an hour on an inmate of Fripp Street.

Just to be on the safe side, Mr. Dunwoody stole into the empty front room, and, leaving the door ajar, stationed himself behind it. As he did so it seemed to him that a cold blast of air enveloped him, causing him to shudder. The next minute his suspicions proved correct. The car crossed the road and drew up. He heard people getting out, and then the latch clicked as the string was pulled and the front door opened. Two pairs of feet thumped over the doorstep, and Dr. Ellis's voice called up the stairs, "It's me, Mrs. Bowerman... Dr. Ellis." And in a whisper to his companion, "Shut the door. I'll go up first."

Mr. Dunwoody was interested. Why had the doctor got someone with him and who could it be? His speculations, however were cut short, for at this point Dr. Ellis tripped on the stairs making a terrific clatter, and old Mrs. Bowerman yelled from above, "Gawd 'elp us! Whatever are you doing of?"

"It's all right," answered Dr. Ellis unsteadily. And no wonder, thought Mr. Dunwoody, it must have shook him up proper. "I only slipped. I haven't hurt myself." And Mr. Dunwoody heard him continue his way upwards.

The listener, having by now lost all interest in Mrs. Bowerman's coal, was mainly concerned with getting away from her house, but this was obviously impossible. The doctor's companion, whoever he was, remained below. He could hear the small rustlings and occasional breath sounds that betrayed one who waited. The murmured conversation in the room above seemed to go on and on. Mr. Dunwoody controlled his impatience with difficulty; it was essential that that other one should not discover him.

Presently the doctor came down again. A rapid conversation took place in tones too low for Mr. Dunwoody to hear more than an occasional word. "Ill" he heard, and "coal," repeated more than once, and then the two men went slowly and heavily along the passage and into the back room. A noise of scraping began.

Very cautiously Mr. Dunwoody moved round the door and put out his hand. A faint light shone from the back room; apparently a pocket torch was in use. It was also evident that Mrs. Bowerman's coal-scuttle was being replenished, for the scraping and rattling continued. He was wondering if he dared make his escape when footsteps suddenly crossed the back room causing his hasty retreat. But no-one came past, and he discovered when he looked out a second time that the object of the movement had been to shut the door of the room. The faint light still glowed from underneath it. He decided that he must wait till they had gone, and as he disliked standing for any length of time, he now lowered himself to the floor and stretched out his legs in the dust.

But he did not have to wait very long. The two men came back along the passage and, as before, the doctor mounted and the other stayed below. This time Dr. Ellis did not spend more than a couple of minutes upstairs. Dunwoody picked himself up and listened. He heard the front door open, he heard the two men go out, and before the door closed he heard the stranger say in a normally loud speaking voice, "Go down past the river."

Then the engine of the doctor's car started with a roar and the gears ground savagely.

Creeping over to the window, Mr. Dunwoody looked out. Through the dirt-encrusted glass he saw dimly the car turning into Wood Wharf and heard it grow faint in the distance. Then he tiptoed from the room and from the house.

8

"Good morning, Mrs. Dunwoody. Heart bad again?"

Dr. Freeman sighed as he flipped over the patients' cards to find her record. Mrs. Dunwoody sank into the vacant chair.

"Well, I 'aven't rightly come about meself this time, doctor. It's Mrs. Bowerman: I got an order. She says she can't afford no more visits from Dr. Ellis; 'e come once too orfen last night. She won't 'ave 'im at any price, she says. So I says to 'er, 'Why don't you 'ave Dr. Freeman?' I says, ''E's ever such a kind doctor, and you won't 'ave to pay nothink,' I says (because she's only got 'er pension, doctor, and wot she gets from the Relief. She did ought to 'ave 'ad you before, but you know what these old people are, they 'ates charity. Not but wot 'er children gives 'er somethink now and then, but nothink regular, if you see wot I mean.) So I told 'er straight, 'You can't go on like this, Mrs. Bowerman,' I says, 'It ain't doin' yourself justice, nor me neither,' I says. 'You layin' there gettin' no better, it's money down the drain,' I says, 'and I don't care if Dr. Ellis 'imself was to 'ear me.'"

"Do you mean the old lady who lives next door to you?" asked Dr. Freeman, taking a brief look at the red order.

"That's 'er, doctor. She's that independent, you wouldn't believe. And irritable! It's my belief she'd ought to be in 'orspital, where she couldn't 'ave it all 'er own way. She's real bad this morning, too; you can see it in 'er face. I noticed the change in 'er directly, when I went up first thing to put 'er kettle on."

"Very well, I'll come round when I've finished here."

As Mrs. Dunwoody did not move, he asked, "Anything else?"

"Well, sir, it's about my 'eart. We got to move out o' Fripp Street. I expect you 'eard it's all to come down our side to build one o' them big blocks o' flats. If Mrs. Bowerman goes to 'orspital, they'll get 'er 'ouse most like, and then we'll 'ave to quit at short notice. Wot I wanted to ask you, doctor, could you give me a letter to say as I didn't ought to 'ave no stairs? If I could get somethink on the ground floor it'd be better for the 'eart, see."

"Do you think there is any chance of getting something on the ground floor? Have you asked Mr. Webb if he can help you?"

"Mr. Dunwoody thinks 'e might 'ave the chanst o' some rooms if I 'ad a letter from you."

Dr. Freeman, realizing that there was certainly no chance for him of finishing his patients unless he gave way to her persistence, wrote a brief note certifying that in his opinion Mrs. Dunwoody, who was suffering from mitral stenosis, would benefit from accommodation which did not involve the climbing of stairs. Having sealed the note in an envelope, he handed it to her, thankful to find that it was successful in dislodging her from her seat, and that on this occasion neither Mr. Dunwoody's neurasthenia nor Violet's nerves were to be brought to his notice. She gathered up her string bag from the floor by her chair and made her way out, promising to prepare Mrs. Bowerman for his coming and await him at the old lady's bedside.

This she did, and Dr. Freeman an hour later found her sitting in the sick woman's room, with her feet on the fender and a cup of strong tea in her hand. On his arrival she retreated to the door, and after announcing that he had only to call if he wanted anything, went down to the street door and began an animated conversation across the bonnet of the doctor's car with a neighbour from the other side who had come over to remove her two-year-old son from the front mudguard.

Mrs. Bowerman was worse, and she knew it. Dr. Ellis's visit the night before had upset her, she had had a disturbed and restless night, and this morning her breathing was troubling her so much that when she started coughing she felt she would suffocate. She squinted up at Dr. Freeman and panted "Bronchitis... Been bad all the week... Wouldn't of sent for you, but Ellis didn't do me no good... Think you can?... Or am I goin' out this time?"

Dr. Freeman did not attempt to argue, but made a rapid and thorough examination. Then he folded up his stethoscope and delivered his verdict.

"If you go into hospital at once, which I propose to arrange for you now, you ought to be nearly well in about three weeks' time. If you don't go, I shall refuse to attend you, and you must take the consequences."

Mrs. Bowerman was so startled by this unexpected frontal attack, following the previous inward weakening of her defences, that she was rendered speechless. Dr. Freeman followed up his advantage.

"You'll be much more comfortable in hospital. They'll prop you up so that you can breathe easily and give you good food—much better than Mrs. Dunwoody provides for you, I'm sure."

The ghost of a grin appeared at the corners of Mrs. Bowerman's purplish lips.

"You never spoke a truer word. I'd like you to see the muck she calls rice pudding. My Gawd, if I'd of brought up my kids on that they'd not 'ave lived to neglect their old mother."

A shadow passed over Mrs. Bowerman's face as she spoke and tears gathered in her eyes.

"I'll be glad to get out of 'ere, come to that," she said in a low voice between gasping breaths. "After last night I'll be glad to leave." She spoke more to herself than to the doctor.

"Why after last night, specially?"

Mrs. Bowerman's face went blank, but she looked at Dr. Freeman with sharp eyes.

"Never you mind. You send me into 'orspital. I like you. You talk straight, you don't make no bones about it. And you done me more good already than all Ellis's visits. 'E come Sunday, Toosday, and last night, 'alf-a-crown a time, and nothink to show for it. You send me into 'orspital."

"All right. I'm glad you're going to be sensible. You'll be back here before you can say knife."

"Not 'ere, I won't." Mrs. Bowerman closed her eyes. "They wanted the 'ouse a while back. Well, they can 'ave it for me. I'll never come back 'ere no more."

Dr. Freeman patted her hand and murmured encouragement and consolation. Mrs. Bowerman opened one small indomitable eye at him, and muttered something which sounded suspiciously like "Garn!" The doctor settled his glasses on his nose and went downstairs to instruct Mrs. Dunwoody in the procedure to be followed for obtaining an ambulance and in it removing the patient to hospital.

Early that Saturday morning, at Friary Road Police Station, there was some anxiety and not a little indignation. Sergeant Chandler had failed to report the night before, he had not turned up this morning, and his evidence in the case of Mrs. Holland was due to be presented at the inquest on that very day. Much of what he would say was already known, but his latest report had not been made, and a good deal depended upon it.

Later inquiries dispelled the indignation and deepened the anxiety, for it was found that Chandler had not been seen at his home at all on the previous night, his bed had not been slept in, and he had neither sent nor left any message either to his own people or to the Station. It looked very much as if he had met with an accident. The London hospitals were questioned, but no-one answering to his description had been admitted or treated either as an out-patient or in the wards.

The coroner sitting on the death of Mrs. Holland, and informed of this strange mishap, took formal evidence of identification from the Dunwoodys; deplored the non-production of any relatives of the deceased, and adjourned the inquest for a week. Friary Road Police Station, genuinely puzzled and alarmed, and pricked on to fresh effort by Chandler's brother and sister-in-law who were by the afternoon in a state of panic, appealed for aid to Scotland Yard. The Yard was at first sarcastic, then interested. Finally it condescended to help, and a certain Inspector Mitchell, who had joined the Force in his youth in search of adventure and had never thereafter realized that his aim had been accomplished, was sent down to Friary Road to investigate the circumstances of the sergeant's disappearance.

The brother and sister-in-law with whom Chandler had lodged were not at all helpful. He had gone away after breakfast and they had not seen him since. He was often late in coming home, so they went to bed without any curiosity as to his whereabouts or qualms for his safety. They were not greatly surprised even when they found that he had been absent all night. But it had been a terrible shock to them when the superintendent at Friary Road had rung them up to inquire if Sergeant Chandler were ill. They had been quite sure until then that his work had kept him out. That was all they had to say, except that Mrs. Chandler kept asserting tearfully that she knew he'd had an accident, and Mr. Chandler insisted that some toughs unknown had done him in.

Mitchell went back to Friary Road and took up the question of Chandler's recent activities. At first sight there seemed to be nothing about them calculated to produce either accidents or enmities, but his attention was caught, in the case of Mrs. Holland, both by the queer features of the case, and by the amount of time and trouble the missing sergeant had spent upon it.

Mrs. Holland's heroin addiction, for instance. Was she a known addict, either under this name or any other? Apparently, Chandler had taken no steps to investigate this point, but then the report of the post-mortem analysis had only come to hand the day before. The question must be taken up at once.

Then the two bottles of Lysol. Apart from the curious

fact that Mrs. Holland had bought a second bottle on the day that she had lent one nearly full to Mrs. Dunwoody, was it known where these bottles had come from? Presumably one of the local chemists, but not by any means necessarily. Chandler's report was vague on this point. And no-one seemed to know where Mrs. Holland had gone on the day of her death or what she had been doing. They didn't even know what time she came home. Her means of livelihood were equally obscure: she was not known either at the Labour Exchange or the Public Assistance Department.

Inspector Mitchell sighed. Was it really important to know all this about a wretched obscure suicide? True, Chandler had put in some serious work on it, and Chandler unaccountably had disappeared. The Inspector went on doggedly with the report; if he got nothing out of it about Mrs. Holland, he was determined to discover what had interested Chandler so much.

Pretty soon he found it—in the person and behaviour of Dr. Ellis of Barton Street. The stupid lie about Mrs. Holland's address, the doctor's description of her case, the doctor's own distinctly questionable past, in which drugs figured prominently, all these pointed to some definite link between them. As Chandler had done before him, Mitchell began to wonder if the doctor had taken any direct part in Mrs. Holland's death, and again, as the sergeant before him, he was inclined to abandon the idea as fanciful. But a thought came to him which had not occurred to Chandler. Suppose Mrs. Holland had appealed to the doctor for a supply of her drug, and he, rendered timid by his previous narrow escape, had refused her. Might she not have committed suicide in despair, and Dr. Ellis, anxious to avoid being involved in her affairs, had kept silent for this reason? Here was a reasonable explanation with no extravagance about it.

It was annoying that Chandler had not made his report the night before. Unfortunately, it was also sinister and significant. For though he had not said where he was going when he left Friary Road the previous evening, it was very probable that he had made a second visit to Dr. Ellis's surgery, and whether the results justified it or not, it must have given the doctor a clear indication of part at least of what lay in the detective's mind.

At the end of the day Inspector Mitchell, sitting in his own room at Scotland Yard, was convinced that the suspicions which he now felt sure had been shared by Chandler were justified.

He had seen Dr. Ellis. He had had an exhaustive interview with the doctor and had taken him carefully over the ground covered by Chandler on his first visit to the surgery. He noted that on this occasion Dr. Ellis did not pretend ignorance of Mrs. Holland's address, and seemed to be unconscious of his former slip. He must therefore have made it on the spur of the moment or under the stress of some strong emotion, and then have forgotten the lapse. This was interesting and revealing; it confirmed his first impression of the doctor's instability.

He learned at once that Chandler had indeed visited the surgery for a second time the night before. Dr. Ellis gave a clear account of his conversation with the sergeant, explaining his knowledge of Mrs. Holland's drug addiction and his reasons for concealing it at the first visit. He described the urgent call, the visit to Mrs. Bowerman, when Sergeant

Chandler had waited for him in the hall of the old woman's house, and the drive back through Wood Wharf. He had dropped the sergeant at the river end of Barton Street and put his car straight back in the garage.

It was this clear, unemotional account of the sergeant's visit that Inspector Mitchell, considering his notes at the end of the day, found so very disturbing. For he had said no word to Dr. Ellis of Chandler's disappearance, he had given no reason for his visit or his questions. He had merely shown the doctor his warrant card and had been accepted as a matter of course. Almost as if Dr. Ellis had been expecting him. For though the doctor had mentioned that he had answered all these questions before, his protest had been half-hearted and mechanical, and he had not asked why Scotland Yard and not Sergeant Chandler had now taken up the subject of Mrs. Holland's suicide. Also he had his story very pat; it looked as though he had been over it in his mind more than once. He gave gratuitously all the relevant times, including the dates and hours of his visits to old Mrs. Bowerman, and the times of his return home on the various days of that week.

"Handing me his alibis in a stamped addressed envelope," thought Inspector Mitchell. But the facts appeared to be true; they had been confirmed by the housekeeper, who was also helpful in producing from the ashbin a crumpled, dirty piece of paper which she said was the note the man had brought the night before.

Inspector Mitchell smoothed out this scrap of evidence on his table. It told him nothing except that the urgent call had been made. On the other hand, it should not be difficult to trace the writer. The Dunwoodys had denied sending the note, and since Miss Pollen, who knew them both, had not recognized the messenger, this appeared to be true. But the Dunwoodys were not the only neighbours who were in the habit of visiting Mrs. Bowerman, and a search, tedious though it might be, would surely reveal which of her friends had been interested in her welfare. Unfortunately the patient herself was not able to help him. The hospital stated that she was worse, having developed pneumonia since she had been admitted; that her condition was precarious, and that no visitors other than relations were allowed. As he came away from the ward he met one frightened elderly daughter, summoned hurriedly to the bedside, and trying with present tears to make up for past neglect, who sobbed to him that Mother did not know her, but was raving about her eldest son, long dead and gone, and his little children, now all grown up and in homes of their own. So that line had petered out for the time being. Probably the old lady would go and die on them, and they never would get her evidence. The whole case, if, indeed, there was a case other than a simple suicide, seemed to be brought up short in every direction.

While Inspector Mitchell, with his usual painstaking quiet thoroughness, was going through all his notes again from the beginning, Detective-Sergeant Welsford arrived with a bunch of papers. He was a sandy-haired young man with a cynical outlook born of a cheerful disposition united to a low regard for mankind.

"This Chandler hasn't turned up yet," said Mitchell gloomily. "It looks bad for the poor chap."

"I know," answered Welsford. "You can't get abroad with the stuff like you used to. I suppose they're watching the airports as well as the boats?"

"Now what in hell are you talking about?" asked Mitchell.

"I was alluding to Chandler, Detective-Sergeant Chandler, Friary Road Station."

"Same here. I thought he was supposed to have disappeared, and as you've been looking into it, I thought you'd know by now what he'd taken and where he'd gone with it."

"You'd better look at this," said Mitchell severely. "If you can't do any better than talk scandal. For all I know he may be dead, then you'll be sorry for talking that way about him."

Welsford saw that his superior was in earnest and gave serious attention to the proffered notes.

"Well?" asked Inspector Mitchell after a suitable interval.

"It's not too good." Welsford ran his hand through his hair. "No trace of him after he left Dr. Ellis?"

"After his interview with Ellis, you mean. We know that it took place; the housekeeper spoke to him. But she didn't see him leave, because he never went through into the house at all—probably left, as he had come, by the surgery waiting-room door. We don't know if he really went with Ellis to see this old woman, Mrs. Bowerman. And we can't ask her at present; she's too ill. I went to her house, of course, to see if there were any signs of his having been there with the doctor, but the neighbours had been in clearing up the old lady's things and tramping everywhere. The house was in a filthy state; she's been living in one room for years. But at any rate, we do know Chandler had ideas about this case, and I agree with him that there are several things that want clearing up."

"About Dr. Ellis or about Mrs. Holland?"

"Both. We want to know why there was no hypodermic syringe in her room when she had been having recent injections and why there was no heroin when plenty was found in her body. We want to know whether she got her recent supplies from Dr. Ellis and, if so, where he gets his from. And there's another thing: I believe he takes the stuff himself. If you look at Chandler's description of him at the first interview, you see he was jumpy, tired-looking, and his eyes were funny, very light grey, pupils not equal, he says. Now when I saw him he was quite the reverse, calm and all that, answered questions without hesitating. I didn't get a very good look at his eyes, but to my mind the pupils were smaller than natural. Does that suggest anything to you?"

Sergeant Welsford nodded.

"Now if Ellis is an addict himself there might be several reasons for Mrs. Holland's death. She may have tried to get the stuff out of him and failed because he didn't want to part with any. But that wouldn't explain why her syringe had gone. Or she might have gone to him for her injections and not had a syringe of her own at all, and he might have got fed up with her coming and stopped her. In each case it might have led to her suicide. But Chandler had a strong suspicion, you can see it all through his notes, that Dr. Ellis had something to do with Mrs. Holland's death. If so, she must have been home before three, that is, before the doctor got to Mrs. Bowerman's and Violet Dunwoody went up to do the fire and saw his car at the door. Even so, I don't see how he got her to drink a whole lot of Lysol without any fuss, let alone a struggle. Now, looking at it from another angle, he wouldn't have wanted to get rid of her unless she was bothering him or threatening him, and either way making things dangerous for him. And if Chandler's come to any harm that confirms it because Ellis must have guessed he was suspicious."

"What if Chandler's all right, barring the hangover?"

"Then he'll turn up and tell us all about it," snapped Mitchell, who resented Welsford's flippancy.

"Marvellous."

The inspector looked up sharply, but there was respect in every line of his subordinate's face.

"I mean," continued the young man humbly, "he'll probably have a lot to say about the second interview, which isn't given in these notes."

"And I'd be more than glad to hear it," answered Mitchell gravely, "because I don't mind telling you, it's got me worried. I think Chandler found out something and Ellis knew he had. But I'm blessed if I know what it was."

"Surely he wouldn't do away with him for that. He'd know there was plenty more of us to follow it up and find out the same thing."

"That's true. Then it must have been some evidence Ellis overlooked in the first place but could destroy later."

"It might have been the missing syringe."

"No, Chandler would have got hold of it. It must have been something Ellis said or did."

"Perhaps Ellis only thought he'd given himself away and that's why Chandler hasn't put it down; he didn't really notice it."

Inspector Mitchell nodded approval.

"You're coming on. That was what I was thinking. But what the hell was it? And, anyway, what has Ellis done with him? The doctor was only away from home about half-an-hour altogether. His housekeeper knows when he went out and when he came back. And he certainly visited Mrs. Bowerman. Dr. Freeman, that's the police doctor at Friary Road, says the old lady told him so. Ellis says he dropped Chandler at the river end of Barton Street."

"He didn't say alive or dead, did he? He might have dropped him in the river itself while he was about it."

"You know, you aren't funny," said Mitchell thoughtfully, "though you may think you are."

Sergeant Welsford sighed.

"Any orders, sir?"

"You needn't take offence, Welsford. I was only telling you for your good. What would you do if you suspected this Ellis of getting supplies of drugs illegally?"

"Look for the rest of the gang, and try to trace his own record."

"Exactly. We're going to see if we've got his record. Mrs. Holland wasn't a known addict, did I tell you? And we're going to trace his telephone calls. I must say I'd like very much to get to know his friends."

Pamela Merston switched on the table lamp and the electric fire, flung her hat and bag on to a chair and sank down on the sofa.

"Turn the top light off, Gordon, it makes such a glare. Oh, thank God we don't have to go out anywhere to-night."

"You've been gadding about too much lately. You'd better have an early bedtime for a change. I can't stay long anyhow;—got to see a man on business."

"After eight on Saturday night? Who could possibly want to talk business at such a god-forsaken time?"

Longford disregarded her questions as he usually did, and taking out a small notebook, began turning over its pages in silence. Pamela watched him with an angry face. No-one treated her as this man did, not even troubling to be polite to her, indifferent to her beauty except when it suited him to make love to her, careless of her money, though he took it readily enough when he had need of it; above all, utterly impervious to any change of mood in her, so that her anger, her jealousy, her frequent unhappiness, her more rare tenderness, all passed him by, dashing themselves in vain against the hard encircling rock of his complete selfishness. If she had not depended upon him so much she would have sent him away long ago, she thought, raging inwardly, but he held her by what she needed from him, and by something strange and wild and exciting in his queer golden eyes when he took her in his arms to kiss her. Aloud she said, "If you don't want to be sociable you might chuck me over the evening paper. You've got one, haven't you?"

He took one from his pocket and with a preoccupied glance in her direction tossed it to her. Pamela arranged cushions behind her head, lit a cigarette and settled herself with her feet up. Her eyes travelled slowly over the pages: she was not at all interested in sport, and there seemed to be nothing but football news and hockey news and advertisements for winter sports clothing. But on one of the later pages a small paragraph caught her eye. It described very briefly an inquest on a certain Mary Holland, of 1 Fripp Street, South London, who had died by taking Lysol. The inquest had been adjourned.

"What is it now?" asked Longford, looking up at her startled exclamation.

"Half a mo. I've just seen something that reminded me…"

She got up and searched in the drawer of a small table that stood in a corner of the room.

"Here it is. Yes, it is Fripp Street."

Gordon Longford put his notebook away slowly and rose to his feet, apparently interested in her at last.

"Would you mind telling me what you are talking about?"

"Look…in the paper. There's been an inquest on a Mary

Holland, and it says the address was No. 1 Fripp Street. I meant to tell you, but I forgot. Someone called Mary Clarke, who said she was at 'Lulu' before Miss Kemp, well, she came here last Tuesday, I think it was—in the afternoon, anyway, just before four."

There could be no mistake about Gordon Longford's interest now. He was close to her, looking down into her eyes with a queer intensity that made her nervous.

"She really wanted your address, darling. But, of course, I didn't give it to her." He relaxed a little. "I told her she could write to you if she enclosed it in an envelope addressed to me, and that I would forward it on. Was she really at 'Lulu's'? Or was she a customer—like me?"

Ignoring her forced archness, Gordon said, "How did she come here? Why did she come to you?"

"She said Miss Kemp told her she might find you here."

His sudden fierce blasphemy frightened her. She moved away from him, but he followed her and took her by the arm. "Why didn't you tell me this before? I can't have people like Mary Clarke bothering you. Why didn't you tell me she'd been?"

"I forgot. And, anyway, I was going to tell you when she wrote. But Gordon...it's this!"

She pulled herself free and handed him the paper folded back at the paragraph about the inquest.

"You see the address is the same, and the first name. You don't think...?"

"Of course not. Why should Mary Clarke be Mary Holland?"

"I don't know. Only living in the same house it would be queer..."

"Whyever? Mary is a common enough name. And that's

a slum, Fripp Street. There are half-a-dozen families in each house."

"You know the street then?"

"No, I don't." His anger blazed up again. "But I know London, which is more than any of you pampered spoilt brats of successful business men will ever do."

"There is no need to be abusive," Pamela said coldly. "And I only wondered. I thought you would be interested."

"So what?"

"Nothing. Obviously." She sat down again and picked up the paper to read more of it. But before she could compose her thoughts and her ruffled feelings, Gordon Longford was on his knees beside her, pulling away the paper, uncurling her fingers and putting them to his cheek.

"I'm sorry, darling. I've been a bit worried lately. Forget about Mary Clarke and be nice to me. You don't know how I need it."

So she stopped thinking about the hungry-looking woman who had said she was Miss Kemp's predecessor, and she stifled the suspicion that his present tenderness was false and calculated, and she was nice to him. She could not help it when his mouth clung to hers, softening her heart. But after he had gone away, her thoughts went back to his queer anger, and she read the paragraph again. It was strange and rather disturbing. Mary Clarke of Fripp Street had been to see her on Tuesday and Mary Holland of Fripp Street had committed suicide on Tuesday. And no letter had arrived since then to be forwarded to Gordon Longford.

9

THE INTENSE COLD WHICH HAD ACCOMPANIED AND followed the Guy Fawkes Day fog gave place twelve days later to an unseasonable mildness and a fine drizzling rain. The streets, so recently a menace from the thin coat of ice covering them each morning, now betrayed the passer-by in a series of greasy mud-slides that were equally dangerous to the high heel and the rubber sole.

Leslie Harvey and his friends, however, were not to be confined indoors by a mere drizzle. The friends badgered their parents unmercifully until released, when they congregated outside Leslie's door with sacks over their heads in place of the mackintoshes they did not possess, and with a variety of uncouth weapons in their hands. They knew that Leslie's Ma took some circumventing, and most of them crouched under the railings to play marbles while they waited. At last the one who was keeping watch gave vent to a loud whoop. He had seen Leslie's face at the front window mouthing a message at him. The gang hustled one another a few yards down the street and there presently their leader joined them, covered like themselves with a piece of sacking. The whole troop moved away in the direction of the river.

Arrived on the beach the party split into three groups of three members each and gravely set to work. This was no mere game, but a serious effort organized by and on behalf of Leslie Harvey, whose recent aquatic exploit had raised him to a high place among the other members of his class at school. Leslie had explained to them the nature of the task suggested to him by Sergeant Adams. In fact he had let it be understood that the job was a definite commission from the River Police entailing unknown but supposedly great reward if it should be successful. In these circumstances his friends were only too willing to help him.

As the tide was coming in and a great part of the small beach already covered, their field of research was necessarily restricted. But they had an advantage in the weather, for it had cleared the wall of critical observers, and those who passed beside it had their heads down to the rain and were not inclined to loiter, but rather to hurry back to the shelter of their homes.

Leslie, as befitted a leader, chose what was in the present state of the tide the most interesting section of the shore, that which ran narrowly under the Saw Mill Wharf. In a short time it would be covered, but with a look-out stationed at the wider strip of shingle, and keeping close to the concrete wall itself, Leslie and one companion made their way carefully to the end, where the piles of the Saw Mill jetty began. The first row of barges lay off-shore about thirty yards, and into the little harbour formed by them and the jetty a thick scum of rubbish and weed and bubbles had been swept by the tide, and lay swinging up and down in a round noisome patch a few feet from the shore.

Leslie and his companion, with long iron bands, the derelict hoops of old barrels, found under the wall, thrashed the water patiently. After some time they were rewarded, less by their own puny efforts to create a current than by the impartial force of the tide. One of the iron hoops caught round a piece of log and a considerable portion of the mass broke off and began to move in-shore.

The triumphant whoops of the look-out attracted the other boys, who left their barren search round the base of Jim Sawyer's wall and ran back to join in the capture. Much straining and slipping took place in which everyone became thoroughly muddy, the protecting sacks fell off, and a good many feet splashed in and out of the river's edge. But great success attended their efforts. The core of the scum was solid, and when Leslie drew it up and pulled off the smaller rubbish clinging about it, he was awed and delighted to find that his prize included a wooden box, broken and battered indeed, hollow and empty, but in all outward respects similar to the one Sergeant Adams had hooked on board the launch off Jim Sawyer's landing-stage.

"Gee!" said Leslie in a voice of triumph. "The very thing I been lookin' for all along."

"Coo-er!" breathed his followers, and gazed at the leader with pride and admiration.

Chattering and splashing and jumping about with excitement the gang hauled their prize back to the safety of the wider beach near the steps where they crouched beside it waiting for further orders from their chief. Leslie Harvey hesitated. Now that it had come to the point he had to make a grave decision. Was it really worthwhile taking this all the

way to Wapping? Would Sergeant Adams really be pleased
if he did, or would he laugh at him for his pains? It was only
a broken old box after all.

A small child, there on sufferance because his older
brother had to look after him, began to pick at the broken
bottom of the box.

"'Ere, you!" said the look-out fiercely. "Take yer 'ands off
of that, will yer?"

The brother pulled his charge away, but immediately
took up his defence.

"'E warn't doin' no 'arm. Only pullin' orf that bit o' rag."

"Wot rag?"

Leslie bent over the box and examined it carefully.
"Gorblimey!" he said softly. "It's inside the lid. Look! Wot
d'you make o' that?"

The boys crowded round pushing one another out of the
way, leaning on one another's shoulders, shrill with interest
and excitement. Leslie's problem was solved.

"This 'ere's a police job," he said with importance. "I'm
goin' to take this 'ere to Sergeant Adams."

"Wot? All the way to Wapping?"

"Yeah."

"They won't let yer on a tram with it."

"I'm not goin' on a tram, soppy! I ain't got a copper for a
tram, anyways. Sid and Walter can 'elp me carry it, and the
rest of you can go 'ome, see. And don't you breathe a word
wot we found. Got that?"

The gang murmured assent and broke up, and Leslie
with his two companions set off together. They crossed
the Thames by the Rotherhithe Tunnel and made their
way from Shadwell to Wapping Wall. It was a long way for
three small boys to travel in the rain laden with an awkward

wooden box of considerable size, but they stuck doggedly to their purpose, not minding the distance nor the curses of those passers-by who were bumped and bruised by their angular treasure.

At Shadwell Basin they waited patiently, sitting upon their prize, while a boat moved slowly out of the dock and away into the river. When the roadway, which had been reared on end during this process, had returned to its normal position and the traffic had pulled across, they followed and plunged into the High Street, where the warehouses towered above them on each side, and all manner of carts and vans and lorries and trolleys and barrows were congregated, receiving and discharging goods in packages of every shape and size. Some went in and out through great doors opening on to the pavement, some, half-way up the buildings, were swung on derricks and cranes out of narrow doors opening on to space. The boys dodged and doubled, now on the footpath, now in the street, fearing both the moving vehicles below and the great swinging loads overhead, either of which, they felt, might at any moment crush the life out of them.

At last they stopped before a quiet red-brick building standing behind iron railings, whose tall blue lamp bore the name "Police." A door opening on the street in front looked close-shut and unpromising. But they discovered a passage at the side, with a distant view of the river beyond, and along this they ventured, Leslie leading the way.

The constable within said that Sergeant Adams was out on patrol and what did they want him for, anyhow. Leslie told his story and produced his box. The constable took their names and addresses and asking them to wait went away and returned after a while with a man in plain clothes who conducted them into an inner room. This man had a round face and very bright blue eyes. He addressed himself to Leslie.

"Now what's all this about a box? Is this supposed to be the box?"

Leslie told his story again and pushed forward the box to corroborate it.

"You say Sergeant Adams told you to bring anything you found here?"

"Not exactly, he didn't, sir. 'E said to take it to a Police Station."

"Why didn't you go to the nearest, then?"

"I thought I might see 'im, sir."

"Who? Adams? What did you want to see him for?"

"I thought 'e might give me a ride in 'is boat."

"So that's it." Norris laughed. "You've got a hope, I'm afraid. We don't carry passengers."

Leslie looked very crestfallen. His reward seemed to be fading into the unattainable, and he felt that in the eyes of his friends he had lost face. But the others, who had only imperfectly understood their leader's hopes, had kept their minds on facts not fancies. They nudged Leslie and pointed to the bottom of the box, where the mysterious rag was still protruding. Leslie seized the opportunity of prolonging the interview.

"There's something funny in the wood there," he said, and pulled the rag as he spoke.

The interest he aroused was gratifying. Detective Norris, with a sharp exclamation, bent over the box, and producing a small screw-driver from his pocket, levered up some of the splintered fragments. Then he paused.

"All right," he said kindly to the three boys, who were watching with round eyes and gaping mouths. "You can all go. But if you find anything else, take it in to the nearest Station, see?"

"Yessir," replied Leslie, and retreated with his companions into the outer room. The constable who had first attended to them was not there, and though they guessed that at any moment he would return, curiosity overcame them. They crept back to the still open door and applied their eyes to the crack. Leslie, manoeuvring for position, saw Norris pull out a length of gauzy pink material and shake it free. It was a nightdress, and as he looked, Leslie had a queer feeling that he had seen it before.

"Now then," said the deep voice of the constable behind him, "What do you kids think you're doing?"

They were round in an instant, backing warily towards the door. There was a buzz of voices in the passage outside and a tramping of feet. Leslie darted forward.

"I got another box," he cried, stopping Sergeant Adams on his way into a room across the passage with the rest of the patrols who had just come off duty. "It was up the Saw Mill Wharf. And it's got a nightdress shoved in under the wood at the bottom. The busy I give it to's lookin' at it in there."

He waved his hand behind him, at the same time that Norris, hearing his voice raised in shrill excitement, came out to see why he had not yet gone.

"'E said I couldn't 'ave no ride in your boat. I come all this way to get a ride in the boat, mister. Give us a ride, won't yer?"

"Not allowed to. You get your father to take you along in his boat."

"Mum won't let 'im. And I don't want to go in the old tug. I want to go in your boat, same as I did before."

"I see. Well, I'm sorry, son, but it can't be done. You'd better get along home now. It's a long way. Did you come on a tram?"

"No. We walked. We ain't got the fare."

Adams felt in his pocket.

"How much is it?"

"Frippence, sir. It's Saturday, there won't be no midday fares now."

Three pennies were handed to him. He looked at them dubiously and then at his companions.

"There's free on us, sir. It's frippence each."

Norris and Adams laughed so loudly that the other men came out to discover the cause of it. Leslie was embarrassed. "That's all you get," said Adams good-humouredly, "You can ride yourself and let the others walk, or you can all have a pennorth and walk the rest. Please yourselves."

And with that the three scavengers had to be content.

It was nearly one o'clock when Norris arrived at the rubber factory. Listons was housed in a square concrete building of recent make which had been erected on the site of an older structure after a very timely fire had gutted those inconvenient and crumbling premises. The insurance companies had felt momentary qualms but had no evidence, and Listons, with pious attention to the welfare of their workers, did themselves proud in the way of airy workshops and vast window space, while not forgetting to provide comfortable well-appointed offices for the senior staff.

It was in the finest of these that Norris found Mr. Bullock, the works manager, lingering over the end of the week's business, while his secretary, in the outer office, was putting the final touches to her make-up before leaving.

Mr. Bullock was surprised, but polite. He drew forward a chair for the visitor and offered him a cigarette which was refused. Norris explained that a box similar to the ones found earlier by a civilian and recently by the River Police had been brought to Wapping Station by some boys. There was no rubber in it, but in order to clear up the whole question of these missing boxes, he would like to have a statement with regard to the whole consignment, where it came from originally, whether direct or through an agent, how many boxes had been lost as a result of the accident to the barge, and whether there had been another consignment since then from the same source.

Mr. Bullock, who explained that he had a lunch appointment in the West End, was much put out by these questions. But he realized the futility of arguing and gave the information required, only remarking that he had given most of it before when the barges were located off the Saw Mill Wharf. Norris took down the details carefully, and asked, as confirmation, to see the invoices. Mr. Bullock ground his teeth and called for his secretary, but that young lady, anticipating some such move when she saw the visitor arrive, had prudently slipped away. It was after hours and her right, and she was not one to forego her rights in anybody's interest. So the manager had to find his own invoices, which he did in a thinly concealed fury. Norris, comparing Holman's with others produced during the search, was immediately struck by one singular fact. This was that the price charged by Mr. Max Holman for his rubber was very considerably less than that charged by the other firms who supplied Listons with raw material. Was this an inferior kind of rubber? he asked.

"Well, no," Mr. Bullock answered, looking a little uncomfortable, "Not exactly inferior."

"Then why do you pay less for it?"

Mr. Bullock hesitated: he had never much liked the arrangement himself, but his principals were always on to him to cut down expenses, and they had okayed the business.

"It's like this, you see," he began, "business is all round bad, as I expect you know, and we have to do the best we can. This fellow Holman wanted a workroom where he could do some experiments with rubber. He's working on some sort of process. So he put it to me if I could let him have accommodation here, and take his samples from the consignments he sends us, he would pay for it with a reduction in the price per box. He doesn't give any trouble. I don't know if his process will ever come to anything, don't even know what it is supposed to do, but he's no trouble. He doesn't come down every day, not above two or three times a week. That's all."

"I see." Norris was a little puzzled. "But why doesn't he pay you rent for his workshop, or whatever it is, and charge you the ordinary rates for the rubber? Wouldn't it make the books—er—clearer?" He meant more accurate, as Bullock was not slow to grasp.

"If you're suggesting there's any funny business in my books, you'd better be careful," he blustered. His temper, with the thought of Francie waiting in vain outside the Trocadero, boiled up in him and threatened to spill over. Norris took no notice.

"I wonder," he said quietly, "if I could see this workshop of Mr. Holman's."

"He keeps it locked up."

"Haven't you got a key?"

Mr. Bullock, after a little consideration, admitted grudgingly that he had.

"I haven't a search warrant, mind you," explained Norris. "So you don't have to show it me to-day. Only from information in my possession I can get one and it will be for the whole building. Just now I only want to see where this Holman works."

Mr. Bullock searched in one of the drawers of his desk and found a key. He then got up and led the way out of his room and along corridors to the main part of the factory. The men had all gone home and the large workrooms were deserted. On the ground floor, where the unopened boxes of rubber stood piled in a great room as big as a concert hall, there was a small office built of wood occupying the corner of it. Mr. Bullock halted outside and produced his key. "But you still don't know what Holman is trying to invent?" asked Norris innocently as they went in. Mr. Bullock glared at him, but said nothing.

A standing desk, with a top so high and sloping that it looked as if all papers placed on it would immediately cascade to the floor, was built in against one wall. At the other side of the room there was a carpenter's bench with a few tools on it, and beside it a table. This completed the furniture, except for an oil-stove of the Perfection type, very rusty, with its mica blackened by attempts to make it give out more heat than it could. The floor was littered with pieces of wood, sawdust, and nails. There was no rubber lying about, and no whole boxes.

"You say he takes samples of rubber?" began Norris, but Bullock interrupted him.

"I'll tell you just what he does, as far as I know it. He goes out on the floor there and picks out a few boxes, at random,

it seems. Then he brings them in here. He opens them himself and takes some of the rubber. The rest he puts back
outside after he's finished. I can't tell you what he does with
the rubber because I don't know. I think myself he takes it
home with him. As you see there is no real apparatus here.
You've got his City address and phone number; you'd better
see him about it. Now, have you done, because I'm half-an-
hour late already and it's keeping a lady waiting?"

"You needn't wait," answered Norris. "If you'll tell your
porter or watchman or whatever you have that I'm still here.
I'll put the key on your desk."

With this arrangement Mr. Bullock had to be content, but
he went away to placate Francie in a very disturbed frame
of mind. This perturbation lasted throughout the week-
end and plunged him into such depression that by Monday
morning he had decided on the drastic step of informing
Liston himself of what was going on.

Left alone Norris collected the larger fragments of wood
off the floor and examined them carefully. They were similar in appearance to those he had seen at Wapping Station.
The tops and bottoms, though he could not of course distinguish one from the other, were different from the sides
in that all of them had a thin layer of wood glued on one
side, evidently the inner side. This had been true of the box
found by Sergeant Adams which had not revealed any hidden object, and that brought by the boys, which had. It was
highly probable that Holman's activities in this so-called
workshop were connected with the presence of the chiffon
nightdresses in the box-lid. It was also obvious that there
must be a distinguishing mark either on the boxes or the lids
to guide his selection, for all did not contain contraband.
But for this he hunted in vain, both among the fragments in

Holman's room and among the untouched boxes outside. Not all belonged to the latter's consignment. Listons dealt with several importing firms, and these were easily distinguished from one another by their various labels or marks. But as far as Norris could determine the boxes supplied through Holman were all exactly alike, in shape, size, kind of wood, and markings. And yet, as he looked at them, Norris felt certain that in some at least lay hidden nightdresses of the same gauzy pattern as the torn rag at Wapping. He felt inclined to open all the boxes there and then and smash out their secret, but better counsel prevailed. If Holman were indeed engaged in a subtle and profitable smuggling trade, he must catch him red-handed. He must wait until the man himself was at the factory and then perhaps he would learn the secret of the selection. Also he must discover the ultimate destination of these smuggled goods. The tale would not be complete without that.

So he put back the key on Mr. Bullock's desk, and left Liston's to its week-end peace, determined that on Monday he would tackle Mr. Max Holman and his doings in real earnest.

"I don't like it, Max, and that's flat!"

"No more do I like it—that's why we got to slip Ellis a note telling him to lay off phoning me. I'm getting it from both sides now, and how long do you think it'll be before they join up?"

Martha pushed away her plate, the food on it half-finished. She was too much upset to eat. She leaned back against the red plush corner seat and looked at herself in the mirrors at her side. It was a scared face that she saw, framed in its girlish roll of yellow hair. It would have been white, but her make-up covered that.

"What exactly went wrong?"

"Everything's been going wrong this last few months. He's getting too clever for me, by half. First he takes up with a customer, a rotten little bitch with money, that—"

"Yeah! I know all about her. You don't have to tell me her life-history. I got it straight from the horse's mouth. She comes to me for supplies."

"Miss Merston does? Then he doesn't even have the sense to keep our system from her. The whole point of it was the customers never see him. Well then, he goes and falls for one of your girls and gets calling at her home. That was how he ran into Mary Clarke."

"Oh, she'd have found him out without young June Harvey. She came bothering me so often for his address or to give her some of you-know-what that I told her where Miss Merston lived, and said she'd better see if she could get at him that way."

Max Holman's eyes glinted angrily.

"You bloody little fool!" he whispered savagely, "I was coming to that. He's crazy mad at you. If it wasn't for me you'd be in queer street all right. You know the sort of man he is, or you ought to by now."

She shivered and pulled her fur coat round her. In spite of the gilt tables and the red plush chairs and the glittering chandeliers the hot showy restaurant seemed suddenly a chill place full of dark threatening shadows. She tried to toss her head, but the gesture lacked conviction. She felt for Holman's knee under the table.

"Can't we get out of it, Max, while the going's good? Go abroad or something. He scares me; it's that long face of his and the way his eyes are so close together and that queer yellow colour. You'll have to quit the office after to-day anyhow, won't you?"

"I don't know," Max Holman took her hand away from his knee, but squeezed it reassuringly as he did so. Damn it all, he was fond of the old girl, and she'd looked after him well, by God, she had. He'd have to see her through this.

"It depends," he went on. "There was this bloke, Norris; he's from the River Police. They picked up one of the lost boxes that had the nightdresses in, so they got one nightdress: the other end of the box was missing. He'd been down to Listons and found nothing. So he came on to me at the office, wanting to know what I do down there. I told him a lot of punk about experimenting with the rubber and a secret process, but he looked as if he knew it was all my eye. I said I didn't know anything about any nightdresses. It's lucky I've got out all the present lot. The next consignment will be in on the 30th. I'll have to let those go, and trust to luck the men don't break them out when they open the boxes. I've cabled for the new lot in the emergency code, so if we get through this break they can open every damned one and they'll find nothing."

"Won't they trace your cable?"

"I don't care if they do."

"And work out the code, or ask you for the key?"

"They won't learn anything." Holman felt safe here at all events, for the emergency code was merely a rearrangement of the wording in their usual code, and was only used when there was danger. It would need a very astute and persistent man to trace their cables and realize the significance of the two or three in which, though the sense was the same, the word order varied.

"What I don't like," he continued, "is that fool Ellis ringing me up. I'll bet they're watching his calls. The Scotland Yard dick has been down to see him about the missing you-know-who-I-mean. They know Mary Clarke doped, they suspect Ellis of having a hand in pushing her off, and now he's been trying to get me on the phone. I said it was a wrong number he was calling, but did the poor sap take my meaning? He rang again an hour later. I hung up on him and left the office. Now there's Norris on to me over the nightdresses. I had to give him my home address, so he'll be up pretty soon to see you. I told him you worked in the West End, and he left it at that. It's no good lying about that sort of thing, it'd give the game away, good and proper. And when he hears you work at a lingerie shop he'll be a bigger fool than I take him for if he doesn't think of nightdresses. What I don't like is that the Yard and Norris will connect any time now."

"They can't prove anything about that nightdress. It's been in the water. And the other two missing boxes have been found now, haven't they?"

"Quite right, honey. But one box was returned smashed up. It ought to have had the goods inside, but they weren't there. Perhaps they're in the river; let's hope so."

He called a waiter and ordered black coffee and liqueurs.

"Because you seem to me to be losing your nerve," he explained to Martha when the man had gone. She pouted, not ill-pleased with his attention, though she could not throw off her uneasiness. She said again, "Well, what do you want me to do?"

"Just slip a note to Ellis. There's a pub we generally meet at. I won't go in. I'll wait a few blocks off. You've never been to this place, and the dicks don't know you yet, so they're less likely to recognize you. Dress inconspicuous, if you can—you know, plain and no make-up—shove your hair up under your hat. Don't make out you know Ellis, he may be tailed. Bump into him and beg his pardon and drop the note in his pocket. Then come away before he tries to talk to you. If you can't manage it like that, and can't avoid him recognizing you obviously, just say a quiet word or two and pass the note over as before. It's to tell him we'll send anonymous information about Mrs. Holland unless he lays off, and that he's made such a god-awful mess of the whole business we're through with him."

"What if he tries playing the same game?"

"He daren't without pulling the noose up tight. It's round his neck already to my way of thinking."

Martha Kemp finished her coffee at a gulp.

"Let's go home, Max. I'd feel safer there."

"Don't worry, kid. You leave it to me. We'll quit all right while the going's good, but you leave it to Uncle Max to say the word."

She took courage from his brave words and dark smiling face. He was a great comfort to her, she thought, as she watched him, his short fat legs well planted, his bowler hat tipped up, carefully counting out his change. And anyway what was a poor girl to do, who was alone in the world, and had her living to make, and had been younger—well yes, certainly had been younger. Though Max didn't seem to mind that, bless him, and there was something in experience, say what you like.

She shook out a cloud of powder and applied a quite unnecessary layer of it to her face, where it lay in drifts along the sides of her nose and at the corners of her eyes. She touched up her mouth, curving the cupid's bow well above the natural contour of her upper lip. Then, seeing that Max was ready, she got up and minced after him to the lift, swinging her hips from side to side in what she believed to be the height of smart elegance.

10

IN THAT PART OF SOUTH-EAST LONDON IN WHICH
Fripp Street is situated early-closing day is on Thursday. On
that day the owners of movable stalls and barrows gather up
their goods at noon and go home, leaving a sabbath hush
behind them in the streets where on other days they shout
their wares from morning till night.

Mr. Sharp, who sold lemonade and other highly-coloured
drinks, oranges, biscuits, and several kinds of cheap boiled
sweets, packed up his belongings one Thursday morning
quite ten minutes before anyone else in the market, and had
turned his long heavily-laden barrow into the main road
before the first siren screamed the hour of twelve. He had a
removal engagement for the afternoon and there was much
to do in preparation for it.

Having reached his home, which had a convenient
though narrow backyard approached by an alley, he wheeled
in the barrow and pushed it into a wooden shed built against
the wall of the yard. The biscuit-tins were taken off and
stacked in a corner, as also the full bottles of mineral water.

The sweets and the large glass urn-like jar of lemonade, from which penny glasses of sickly refreshment could be run off by turning a tap, were for safety's sake carried into the house. Mr. Sharp then had his dinner, winding it up with a few minutes of relaxation with a pipe by the fire. At one o'clock he resumed his coat which he had discarded for home life, took out the empty barrow, a few turns of rope, and a few old sacks, locked up the shed, and departed on his mission.

He arrived outside Number One, Fripp Street, about twenty minutes later, having gathered in on the way a stalwart youth with long curly hair and a very small cap worn on the side of it. The three little Popes, whose noses had been pressed to their front window for some time, bounced up and down and squealed with excitement. Mrs. Pope went to the door and opened it, while Mr. Pope stood in the passage behind her and got in the way of those entering. He was feeling upset, and his face twitched even when he tried to stop it with his trembling hands. He smiled feebly at Mr. Sharp and the strong youth as they passed him stumbling over his feet, and murmured that "removals warn't much in 'is line."

Mrs. Pope had been home from hospital three days, and was not feeling very strong on her legs yet. But she managed to drive Winnie, Ernie, and Ronnie out of the front room and suggested that a start could be made there.

"Anywheres you like, ma," said Mr. Sharp obligingly. He hung his coat from a nail in the wall and attacked the brass bedstead. Mrs. Pope retired to the back room to make a large newspaper parcel of her pots and pans.

At first the work went forward swiftly. The bed, the chest of drawers with the clothes inside, the wash-stand, the two front-room chairs, were all laid on the barrow and lashed firmly in position. Mrs. Pope carried out a miscellaneous armful and tucked the pieces into any vacant spaces she could find. It was then that the hitch occurred.

A small cart came up the street, pulled by a depressed-looking donkey. The driver dangled his legs over one shaft, and on the other side sat Mr. Dunwoody.

"Move up a bit, carn't yer?" shouted the driver to Mr. Sharp. But the latter had the Popes' kitchen table on his head and was not feeling responsive.

"Wot the 'ell for?" he replied and turned his back on the new arrivals. Mrs. Pope, anxious to keep the peace, explained that the Dunwoodys were also leaving that day.

"They are, are they?" said Mr. Sharp, turning to stare fiercely at the donkey. "And wot's bloody well stoppin' 'em?"

The ensuing argument was lengthy and grew louder as it developed, so that neighbours from the other side of the street were drawn out to listen and appraise. Mrs. Dunwoody joined in from the upper window of Number One, and cutting off Mrs. Pope from the main battle, engaged her in single combat of particular virulence. All past disputes and differences rose up fresh and fierce from their suppression during the latter's absence in hospital, and Mrs. Pope, strengthened by her period of mental ease there, gave good account of herself in her turn.

Presently the onlookers began to tire of an entertainment that had become monotonous through repetition. Some said that "Popes 'ad started first, so they did ought to finish and get away," others advised strict equality and a turn and turn about method.

But in the end neither side prevailed. Leaving the principals to continue their argument in the street, Mr. Sharp suddenly grabbed his mate by the arm and dashed indoors. The donkey driver with a yell of rage followed, and the loading of the carts became a competition in which neither side had any very distinct advantage. For while Mr. Sharp's work was already more than half-done, his rival managed with skilful handling to block the exit from the Popes' back room with a part of the Dunwoodys' bedstead, and to keep the downstairs removers bottled up until the bulk of the furniture had been removed from the top floor. When finally released Mr. Sharp and the strong boy, after getting out the Popes' dresser, which had refused to go through the window in spite of great effort during the period of imprisonment, laid a trap of fire-irons at the bottom of the stairs. This, as a grand finale, was successful in overthrowing the enemy, whose vision was limited by the load he carried, and in breaking Mrs. Dunwoody's "present from Southend," one of her most cherished possessions.

The engagement slowly and painfully subsided from the exhaustion and breathlessness of the combatants, and the two families separated without saying good-bye. Mr. Sharp and his mate, with Mr. and Mrs. Pope assisting, and Ronnie perched on the front of the barrow, pushed off round the corner into Wood Wharf. The Dunwoodys, with Violet at one side of the donkey's head, started in the opposite direction to take up their temporary residence with Mrs. Dunwoody's sister. The neighbours exchanged a few jokes and decided that it was a scream, a caution, and a good riddance.

On the following Monday a lorry came with wooden planks and men, and the whole of the east side of Fripp Street was boarded up.

Inspector Mitchell felt that at long last he was beginning to make progress. Certainly, it was now a fortnight since he had begun to investigate the circumstances of Detective-Sergeant Chandler's strange disappearance, and that was a longish time for him to be at a complete loss, but now he felt he was on the right road and it was only a question of stepping on the gas. He thought it was a suitable moment to enlighten Detective-Sergeant Welsford.

"It's only a question of time now," he began confidently. "I admit we've been held up, but we won't be much longer. Like everything else if you stick to it you get the answer in the end."

"The only trouble is, to my mind," answered Welsford, "he may not be identifiable when we do get there."

"What do you mean—not identifiable? Who's going to do anything to Holman?"

"I wasn't thinking of him, whoever he is. I was thinking of Chandler. I hope they haven't cut him up."

"Oh." Inspector Mitchell was a little put out. Young Welsford was getting a bit too free with this wet-blanket habit of his. Still, it was true they had no faintest idea of the whereabouts of the missing man. In anger both with himself for his failure and with his subordinate for alluding to it, Mitchell went on.

"So you've not heard of Holman, haven't you? Perhaps you've forgotten we traced Ellis's telephone calls from the time I saw him first. You should train yourself to remember details, Welsford. It's details that count in this job. Do you call to mind now that Ellis got a number in the City, and the number said he'd got a wrong number? And he called it again later that day, and the number cut him off without answering? Well, after that he didn't ring that number again, and I must say I thought there was nothing in it and left it for a bit. But I got the name and address of the number.

It was Max Holman, importer, Lancaster House, Prince Albert Street. I haven't been there yet, partly because if they're as clever as they seem to be they'll be expecting me and if I lay off for a while they'll think perhaps I'm not on to them at all. But I've asked for any information that comes in or has come in already relating to this Holman, and now I've got it."

"Gee!" Welsford was genuinely excited. "What is it?"

"Holman supplies a rubber manufacturer with boxes of the raw stuff, sheets of it in wooden boxes. Some of the boxes got in the river. They come up direct to the factory by water, and one of these lost boxes got to the Thames Division at Wapping. They found a lady's nightdress hidden in the wood of the end."

Sergeant Welsford laughed heartily; Mitchell allowed himself a faint grin.

"It has its humorous side, I'll allow. But the point is this. Holman works, or pretends to work, at this factory, and opens some of the boxes, obviously to get at these nightdresses. The Wapping man, Norris, doesn't know how he chooses them. He went once when Holman wasn't there and again when he was, and got him to pick out a box and open it. Then he got Holman out of the workshop and had a look at the box-ends. Nothing doing. He still couldn't see any difference in the boxes himself. So we want to know how those boxes are marked and why the nightdresses are there."

"Isn't he just smuggling them?"

"Perhaps. But it's odd he should have been rung up by Ellis who maybe had something to do with the death of a heroin addict. It seems you don't get much ordinary smuggling these days, and nightdresses—I ask you? There wouldn't be enough in the whole consignment to make it worth the risk."

"No, I suppose not. But the nightdresses may be a blind to cover something else in the box; the drugs you mentioned, for instance."

"That's what I thought. Only if the nightdresses were located, the drugs would be too."

"They weren't in this case?"

"No, because the box had been in the river. Drugs would dissolve in the water."

"So you wouldn't find them in the nightdress either, supposing they were hidden in it?"

"Naturally, you wouldn't. Anyway this nightdress is a flimsy sort of affair, chiffon, they call it. Where would they put the stuff?"

"In the turn-up at the bottom—hem, isn't it?"

"Well, this hem is nearly as transparent as the rest of the garment—if you can call it that."

"I'd like," said Sergeant Welsford dreamily, "to see my girl in one of those. She'd look a treat."

"It's a good thing she isn't present to hear you," replied Mitchell sharply. "You keep your mind on the case."

"Yes, sir."

"You and me are going down to this rubber factory next Friday with Norris. Till then we'll leave Holman alone. Norris has got his home address. He has a flat in Eltham and a wife who works in the West End, but we'll go into his home-life later. He knows Norris has got a nightdress, but as I've kept out of it so far he won't know, though he may suspect, that we're working in with Norris now. I don't want to scare him before next Friday."

"Why?"

"Because that's when the next consignment comes in and that's when we're going to see if we can't catch him out over the boxes."

Inspector Mitchell began to write a few headings for future lines of research. Listons was the most promising by far, but the Ellis side of the question must not be neglected, and it had, after all, not been conclusively proved that the doctor had any real connection with Max Holman. As before, however, all inquiries at the Fripp Street end had come to nothing. Old Mrs. Bowerman was still extremely ill, and though the Inspector was allowed to see her for five minutes he did not gather much information from her, and what she did contribute was rambling and vague. But in spite of the difficulty of following her disjointed speech he found that two statements were unvaried in the course of many repetitions. She had not sent for Dr. Ellis the night before her removal to hospital, and she never wanted to see him again. Further inquiries had completely failed to discover who had brought the note to Dr. Ellis's house.

A second visit by Inspector Mitchell to Dr. Ellis's surgery and Dr. Ellis's housekeeper had not shaken the former's alibi for the afternoon of Mrs. Holland's death.

"If only we knew what Chandler found out that evening he disappeared," murmured Mitchell.

Welsford who, while his superior thought, had been amusing himself with drawing a picture of his best girl clad in chiffon, scribbled heavily over his composition and broke his pencil.

"That reminds me," he said, "You remember Miss Pollen in the surgery? When you asked her if anything had been changed she said Dr. Ellis had broken both his spare thermometers that used to stand in Lysol in a used potted meat jar, and he hadn't replaced them yet."

"Well, what about them?"

"The Lysol. I just wondered."

Inspector Mitchell snorted.

"All doctors have Lysol."

"Mine doesn't," answered Welsford. "He has Dettol. He says Lysol's out of date. It doesn't smell so bad as Lysol—Dettol, I mean—at least it smells different. And it goes a thick white with water, like milk. Not like Lysol, brownish."

"It's the alibi that bothers me," said Mitchell, coming back to the point. "If Chandler's been done in it's because Mrs. Holland was done in, and if she was done in, when was it done? You can't get away from that. If Dr. Ellis wasn't there, giving her the Lysol somehow, then she took it deliberately and it was suicide. And then where are we?"

"And where's Chandler then?"

The Inspector bent again to his notes and Welsford wandered over to the window where he began to hum softly to himself.

"What's that song?" asked Mitchell, "I seem to remember it."

"Too-ra-loo, roo-ra-loo, roo-ra-loo, ray," sang Welsford.

"Not that bit. The bit before."

Sergeant Welsford threw back his head and in a pleasant baritone delivered the penultimate verse of the old song.

"As Villikins was a-walking in his garden next day,
He saw his fair Dinah lying stretched on the clay,
A cup of cold poison was placed at her side,
And a billet-doux beside her to say how she died.
Singing, too-ra-loo, roo-ra-loo..."

"Shut up!" ordered Mitchell. "What did you say Dettol looked like?"

"Milk," answered Welsford in a hurt voice.

"And Lysol looks like tea. I've seen it at hospitals—tea with a lot of milk in it." Mitchell banged his fist on the table. "That's what Dr. Ellis's potted meat jar of thermometers looked like. Perhaps Chandler noticed it, perhaps he didn't. Ellis thought he'd seen it and he got rid of the jar with the thermometers before I went to the surgery. It would be a motive for getting rid of Chandler, too. That's what Mrs. Holland saw when she came in. It was what she expected to see—a cup of tea waiting for her, like Mrs. Dunwoody always gave her. And the stairs smelt of Lysol, the whole house stank of it, Dunwoody himself said, so she didn't notice the smell. It was nearly dark too; probably she was tired and thirsty and thought a cup of cold tea was better than no tea at all. You don't sip cold tea: if you're thirsty enough to drink it at all, you put it down quickly. Dr. Ellis didn't have to be there; he wanted to be rid of her and he took a chance. I expect the smell in the house gave him the idea and he had that new bottle of Lysol in his bag. God knows how I'll prove it. Even if it hadn't come off it would have scared her away from the district. She'd have known it wasn't accidental. But it did come off. A cup of cold tea—*a cup of cold poison!*"

"Singing too-ra-loo, roo-ra-loo, roo-ra-loo, ray," hummed Sergeant Welsford softly, but his eyes were bright and hard with anger.

Harry Reed's friend rested on his sculls and let the tide float him gently past the big cable ship at her moorings off-shore.

Next to Harry in the stern, hardly able to breathe with suppressed excitement, sat Leslie Harvey, who by dint of badgering his mother and enlisting his father's sympathy and support, had been allowed to take this Sunday morning trip. He held the rudder lines under his arms as Harry had shown him and felt very proud of the way he was coxing the boat, though his puny efforts unsupported by Harry's sound arm and the friend's watermanship would not have been enough alone to cope with the tide and the difficult navigation in those waters.

For over an hour they had moved lazily in and out of barge-roads and piers and round ships at anchor, seldom venturing into the rough water of midstream where the wind was blowing up the waves into white horses, but keeping to the comparative shelter of the little bays and artificial harbours made by the shipping near the bank. Leslie stared up at the cable ship as they floated past. She was lying high in the water with her great screw partly uncovered; there seemed to be no-one on board, though water was pouring out of the circulating discharge in her side.

"See the screw?" asked Harry as the friend turned the boat round and headed homewards.

"Coo!" answered Leslie. "Not 'alf! I wouldn't like to be near it when it's working."

"You certainly wouldn't. There wouldn't be much left of you if you got under that."

Leslie made a face of horror and felt that he was indeed getting his money's worth. There were a lot of dangers in this river; that was the fascination of it. Dangers and excitements, such as his encounter with the River Police and his visit to Wapping. He could not resist boasting of his exploits.

"If I tell you something, will you promise not to let on to Mum or Dad?"

Harry was amused, but he gave a solemn promise to preserve secrecy. The friend took the same oath. Leslie then told them of his recent adventures, not forgetting the final discovery of the nightdress and the interest taken in it by the police.

Harry became acutely uncomfortable. The boy's description of his find was only too vivid, and a picture of Jim Sawyer's great hand tucking a cardboard box inside his sling rose unbidden to his mind and stayed there. Harry knew about those lost barges: he had been warned by June never to mention them before her father. If what the boy said was true, Jim had been passing contraband to him, and he, like a sucker, had passed it on to June. He might have known Jim would be up to no good giving anything away. Come to think of it, it was queer he hadn't got rid of the nightdresses profitably while he was about it. It wasn't like Jim to lose a chance of turning a penny, honest or not. The more Harry considered it the less he liked it, but he was roused by Leslie prodding him with his elbow.

"Oh, look, Harry! See that lump of scum under the wall? It's just like wot I was telling you of. Couldn't we go up and look at it? Mr. Adams said if I was to see another o' them boxes…"

Harry's friend pulled towards the tangle of weed pointed out by Leslie. The wall under which it lay was some distance upstream from the beach and the Saw Mill Wharf, and the mud here was never wholly uncovered by the tide. The nose of the boat ran into the scum and through it while Leslie stared over the side, his sharp eyes on the look-out for another box.

"Now then," cried Harry as the boy leaned out and snatched at the water. "You mind wot you're about. I'm not going to life-save you a second time."

"It's a 'ankerchief," said Leslie unmoved, spreading his trophy on his knee. "An' it's got letters on it too."

"Initials," corrected Harry. "Chuck it back, Les. We don't want no dirty rags in this boat."

"No, I won't," Leslie protested. "Mr. Adams said if I found anythink in the river..."

He broke off and putting his finger in his mouth gave several ear-splitting whistles. Harry and his friend were taken by surprise; they had no time to stop him. The patrol in the police launch was also taken by surprise, but there was urgent need in the gestures of the small waving figure, and they drew nearer to investigate.

It was not, as Leslie had hoped, his friend Sergeant Adams but another officer, who was inclined at first to be annoyed and unwilling to hear Leslie's recital. However, when Harry had explained the boy's recent experiences and Leslie himself had pointed out the initials on the handkerchief he consented to take charge of it. He had heard at the station of the boy's encounter with Norris, and he had been instructed to keep his eyes particularly well open in this reach of the river, so he thought there would be no harm in delivering the present message.

At Wapping it was found that the initials on the handkerchief were those of Detective-Sergeant Chandler.

11

CONTRARY TO THE GENERAL EXPECTATION, MRS. Bowerman recovered. For ten days she suffered acute discomfort and by her rebellious and irritable behaviour saw to it that the nurses shared her troubles in ample measure. She frequently called upon the Lord to spare her this agony and to take her away, for she was quite ready to go. But apparently there was some diffidence in heaven over admitting so robust and truculent a spirit, and in the end she was sent back for a further period of chastening. In sleep her heavy face, now healthily pink once more, and surrounded by her snowy hair spread out on the pillow, presented an appearance of bland benevolence. Kindliness and wisdom and an ancient childish simplicity lay in its sleeping folds, so that visitors tiptoeing past her bed, and even the nurses who knew her only too well, would pause and say what a picture she looked. But sometimes, if they stayed too long or if a sudden noise disturbed the ward, her fierce little eyes would fly open, and the startled visitor would recoil before the angry contemptuous laughing stranger who took possession of the dear old face and twisted its lips to utter hoarse and terrible imprecations at their retreating forms.

When she was well enough to see visitors other than the cowed daughter and the subdued, uncomfortable grandchildren, she received a visit from the Pope family. They brought her a small present of grapes which she at once tucked away in her locker, and told her all their recent troubles, beginning with the unfortunate episode of the removal, and ending, as all their stories did, with the return of Mrs. Pope's asthma. They explained that they would have come before only they were settling in and getting used to a strange house. Mrs. Bowerman said she knew what it was, and Mrs. Pope didn't look up to much, she must have been overdoing it, what with the asthma and all.

"It's them stairs," said Mrs. Pope, leaning forward to pull Ernie away from the locker which he was trying to open. "We couldn't get the ground floor in the new place. A elderly couple 'as it, though they do say now as they're thinkin' o' leaving in a couple o' weeks' time. But it means goin' down for the water and coals and you know wot a drag that is with three children, and I mustn't send Winnie down for it on account of 'er 'eart; the doctor said not to run about too much."

Mrs. Pope smiled affectionately at her daughter, who was standing at the foot of the bed holding Ronnie's hand to keep him out of mischief, and patiently waiting to go home. "You certainly don't look up to much," said Mrs. Bowerman again. "But there's nothing like that asthma for pullin' you down. Don't 'e fetch the water up for you?" She glared at Mr. Pope as she spoke, making him tremble so much that his wife had to answer for him.

"'Is nerves 'ave been bad again. It was the moving done it.

'E's been down to the Dispensary and Dr. Freeman give 'im a tonic, but it don't never make much difference."

Mrs. Bowerman heaved herself up indignantly and plucked at her quilt to straighten it.

"If it 'adn't been for Freeman, I shouldn't be 'ere," she said. "If anyone could do 'im good, it'd be Freeman."

Mr. Pope looked apologetic, but continued silent and shaking. His wife hurriedly changed the conversation.

"It was a good thing you 'ad 'im in when you did," she began. "They say Dr. Ellis is getting queer in the 'ead. Mrs. Johnson, next door where we are in Wood Wharf Cottages, she called 'im in to 'er husband wot's on 'is panel, see, and 'e never come for two 'ole days. And when 'e did come 'e told 'er off for not fetchin' 'im sooner. 'E's been actin' strange at the surgery too. Don't remember you a second time, and flies off the 'andle for nothink at all. They do say 'e drinks."

"That wouldn't surprise me," said Mrs. Bowerman darkly.

She lay back again on her pillow with her eyes fixed on the wall at the other side of the ward. Mrs. Pope grew nervous. She felt it was time to go, but did not know how to do so without giving offence. At last she said timidly, "You'll be leavin' 'ere soon, I suppose?"

"I'm in no 'urry," answered Mrs. Bowerman. "I've got no roof over me 'ead now, so I might as well stop 'ere till they chucks me out."

"We weren't 'alf surprised at you givin' up your 'ouse so quick," said Mr. Pope, suddenly breaking his long silence. "An' it give 'em the excuse to get rid of us, too. It quite took us aback, 'avin' to leave in a 'urry, like we did."

Mrs. Bowerman drew a deep breath.

"I'd never go back there again, not if you was to drag me with wild 'orses. Never no more."

"But you always said…" Mrs. Pope was beginning, when Mrs. Bowerman sat up again, and beckoning both her former neighbours to draw closer, breathed in a harsh whisper, "It's 'aunted!"

"'Struth!" gasped Mr. Pope, falling back into his chair. His wife was less easily impressed.

"Your 'ouse? 'Ow d'you mean—'aunted? Wot by?"

"Next door, I mean. My boy lived there and 'e died there… Now it's 'aunted."

The lurid details which might have followed this disclosure were cut short by Ronnie, whose imagination was so wrought upon by the old lady's appearance and manner that he now broke down, and wailing loudly, demanded to be taken home. A nurse came running to discover the cause of the commotion and Mrs. Pope, flustered and ashamed, gathered her family together and hurried them away. The nurse saw them off at the ward door and went back to straighten the patient's pillows.

"What have you been doing to your visitors?" she inquired briskly. "Frightening them out of their lives with your ghost stories?"

The old woman's hallucinations were well-known, since they had survived the period of delirium and had persisted in spite of argument.

Mrs. Bowerman made a rumbling sound in her throat.

"That's right," she said hoarsely. "Blame the 'ole bloody shindy on me,—as usual!"

On the 30th of November Inspector Mitchell and Sergeant Welsford travelled down to Listons. The new consignment, unobtrusively watched from the moment of its arrival at

Tilbury, had been delivered at the scheduled time. Norris was already at the factory when the Yard men arrived and reported that Holman was in the building and had been at work for about half-an-hour. After making their presence known to Mr. Bullock, who was resigned, and had washed his hands of the affair both by informing his superiors and by terminating the firm's contract with Holman, the three men made their way to the workshop and tried the handle of the door. It was locked, but upon their knocking loudly at it, was opened by Holman himself. Norris, who had seen the importer at his office in Prince Albert Street, explained the status and requirements of Inspector Mitchell and retired into the background.

"You know what I've come about," the Inspector began. "There's something wrong with your stuff here. You've been told what we've found and it's my duty to go into it further."

"Anything to oblige," answered Holman with an insolent flash of his dark eyes. "Help yourselves—take your choice—carry on."

"We will," Mitchell said firmly. "I see you've got a box there unopened. Just open it for me, will you?"

"With pleasure."

Holman, closely watched by three pairs of eyes, took off the end of the wooden box at his feet, and lifted out the rubber. He made a good show of inspecting it and selected one sheet, which he laid on the carpenter's bench.

"I think Mr. Bullock explained to you that I am making experiments," he said. "I take samples that I think suitable for my purpose, and use them."

"Here?"

Max Holman smiled.

"No. Not here. It's hardly the place to conduct experiments

in. And you see I haven't got any apparatus here to do experiments with."

"Exactly," said Mitchell with meaning in his voice. "I had noticed that. And there isn't any apparatus in Eltham either, but I'll go into that later on. Now tell me, Mr. Holman, how do you select your boxes?"

"Oh, just at random. They're all the same as far as I'm concerned."

Sergeant Welsford picked up the box-end and taking it over to the carpenter's bench laid it down and split it from end to end. There was nothing there. The other end was similarly treated and proved equally unfruitful. Holman looked on with a well-assumed expression of surprise.

Inspector Mitchell concealed his disappointment. The man had anticipated this move; that was all. He did not propose to waste time in the workshop.

"I must ask you to show me the contents of your attaché case," he said.

"Certainly."

Max Holman opened his case: it was quite empty.

"I take the samples home in it," he explained. "So I bring it empty."

While Welsford stayed in the workshop, Norris and Mitchell went out among the boxes. Again they searched in vain for distinguishing signs: the boxes all appeared to be the same size, made of the same wood, of the same colour, marked in exactly the same way. They might of course arrange to open all these boxes, but would that advance the case? So far there was nothing to connect Holman directly with the nightdresses. The best thing would be to give him more rope and hope for results.

Having decided upon this course Mitchell returned to

the workshop, and collecting Sergeant Welsford together with the end of the box that had been opened in his presence, left the factory. Norris went back to Wapping at once with the trophy, while the two Yard men ate a hasty lunch before resuming work.

Their first move was to compare the fresh box-end with the one brought in by Leslie Harvey. Again they appeared to be identical.

"It's a beggar!" said Inspector Mitchell.

Sergeant Welsford dug out of his pocket a bundle containing a miscellany of objects.

"I picked these up like you told me to, off the workshop floor while I was waiting," he said.

Mitchell grunted approval.

"I was coming to that. Let's see what you've got."

The objects were spread out. They consisted of chips of wood, cigarette cartons, empty matchboxes, cigarette-ends, one cigar-end, struck matches, a few wood shavings, and some nails of different sizes.

"Half a minute," said Mitchell, "Hand us over that box we took to-day."

There were two nails sticking in the wood of it. Mitchell picked up a nail from the pile of rubbish and compared it with these. It was of the same type and length, but the head was distinctly smaller. The other nails were examined in like manner; two corresponded with those in the wood, the rest were of the first pattern.

"Now hand us that other box the boy found."

Welsford did so, and Inspector Mitchell sighed with relief to see a few nails sticking from its edges. They were of the smaller variety, identical with those found on the workshop floor. The two men looked at one another in triumph.

"Got him!" cried Mitchell, slapping the table so that the nails jumped and rattled. "And if I'm not much mistaken he's still down there thinking he scored off us fine this morning. We're going to give him the surprise of his life!"

But when Mitchell and Welsford burst into Holman's workshop the bird had flown. The floor was littered with boxes full of rubber and one of the firm's men was knocking the broken box-ends into place again. Mr. Holman generally did the job himself, he said, after he'd taken his samples. But to-day he was in a hurry.

"How many boxes has he opened?"

"Thirteen altogether, sir. He generally picks out about a dozen. They're all down on the floor in lines just as they come in off the barge. All 'e does is to pick out wot 'e wants, and I 'elp 'im carry 'em in 'ere."

"Were you helping him to-day to open these boxes?"

"Oh, no, 'e never 'as no-one to 'elp 'im open 'em. And, generally speaking, 'e knocks the ends on again 'imself, only to-day 'e was in a 'urry like."

"I'll bet he was," said Inspector Mitchell, taking a nail from his pocket and comparing it with those in the box before him. It was the same, the nail with the smaller head found also in Leslie Harvey's box and by Welsford in the corners of the workshop—the distinguishing nail that they had missed until too late.

"So now we know," said Welsford cheerfully, as they left the factory for the second time that day.

"A fat lot you know," answered Inspector Mitchell. "Thank God I had the gumption to have Holman tailed when he left here. We've got to get his attaché case from him before he unloads it on anyone. With any luck we'll find twenty-four chiffon nightdresses inside it."

"How d'you make that?"

"Twice twelve. One in each end of twelve boxes. Can't you do your twice-times? He's pulled off the whole consignment. There wasn't another small-nail box left in the lot. But we've got to hurry if we're going to get that case."

Inspector Mitchell was wrong. There was no difficulty at all in getting the attaché case. Max Holman was followed to the District Railway, on which he travelled to Charing Cross. At that station he locked himself, together with his luggage, into one of the inner sanctums of the Gentlemen's Public Convenience. Emerging very shortly afterwards still with the case in his hand, he took a train to Eltham and walked from that station direct to his own home. When accosted at the door of his flat he quite willingly opened the case.

It contained sample sheets of rubber and a few business letters—nothing more.

Harry Reed stood beside Captain Harvey on the bridge of the *Fatima* and admired the panorama. He had not, in his own small boat, ventured further down the river than Erith, and when, in gratitude for his taking Leslie out, Captain Harvey had suggested a return trip on the tug he had jumped at the idea. He liked the broadening reaches and the way the hills of Kent came down to meet the water near Greenhithe. He liked the distant view and the less-crowded banks. The Arsenal and the red-painted, red-flagged barges of explosive material near Woolwich were familiar to him, but the Smallpox Hospital provided more than a momentary excitement.

"See that covered slope running up from the pier?"

pointed out Captain Harvey. "You go up that on a stretcher, and you never come back, so the old story goes."

"Cor! Don't they never recover?" asked Harry in an awed voice.

"'Ardly ever. They say in the old days the bodies were run down the slope again and pushed into the river with weights tied to 'em to keep 'em down. They dursn't put 'em in the coffins they sent back to the relatives, for fear of spreading the disease, see."

"Cor!" said Harry again. He leaned out over the bridge and watched the Smallpox Hospital pier and its one white-coated attendant fade out of sight.

"Talking o' bodies," said Tom Wild, the mate, who had come up to take over the wheel, "'ave they found the body o' that copper they think must of got drowned?"

"Not as far as I've heard," answered Captain Harvey. "They've been dragging for 'im on and off the best part of a week. It was the nipper found 'is 'andkerchief when he was out with Harry here."

"They got 'is mackintosh," said Harry, "about the place where we picked up the 'andkerchief. That makes 'em think 'e can't be far off."

"You can never tell with the tides," said Tom gloomily. "Sometimes the bodies go up and down, up and down for months before they get in round the docks or up some back-water where they stick. Wot was 'e doing down on the river, anyway?"

"That's wot they'd like to know," said Captain Harvey. "Didn't you listen to the broadcast? It was in all the papers, too. Last seen in company with Dr. Ellis of Barton Street by the housekeeper when she took a note in to the surgery. Went in the doctor's car to Fripp Street, and Ellis dropped 'im at Wood Wharf Cottages at the bottom of Barton Street. No-one seen 'im since."

"'E was in the car with Ellis in Wood Wharf round about 'ar-past nine. I seen 'im," volunteered Harry.

Captain Harvey and the mate looked surprised.

"You ought to inform the police," Tom said when he had recovered from his astonishment. Harry shook his head.

"Not me."

"Why not?"

"They'd only ask me a lot o' bloody nosy questions about where I come from and what I was doing at the time. I'm still on the Insurance, see?"

"Wot did 'e want with Ellis, anyways? Freeman's the police doctor."

"Ask me another. Perhaps 'e wasn't there for 'is 'ealth."

Tom Wild took over the wheel and Captain Harvey led the way off the bridge. McAlister, as usual, when not actively at work, was standing on the engine-room ladder. He grinned at Harry.

"'Ow's the arm?"

"Doing fine." Harry waggled his wrist to and fro. It was weak and still receiving massage at the hospital, but it was out of plaster and he was using his sling less and less as the days went by.

"Enjoying yourself?"

"Fine, thanks. I wish I could bring my boat down here. Not so much traffic as there is off Jim's place."

"That's as may be. It's all right on a fine afternoon even when it gets dark early, like now, but in a fog!. . . Ask the skipper!"

Captain Harvey scowled and moved away without speaking. There was a hoarse chuckle as Alf, the one-legged stoker, appeared at McAlister's elbow.

"Don't talk to 'im of fogs! Ever since we lost them barges 'e's bin sore about fogs."

"I never got the rights o' that," said Harry. "Just what did happen?"

McAlister told him, with Alf putting in a word from time to time to fill out the story. At the end of it there was no doubt left in Harry's mind of the origin of the two nightdresses he had presented to June Harvey. They were contraband palmed off on him by Jim Sawyer for the latter's own safety and convenience. Well, it did not much matter. June was not likely to ask awkward questions, and no-one else would take any notice of them.

And then a thought struck Harry with unpleasing sharpness. Leslie, her own brother, living in the same house, and stupidly and unnecessarily attracted to the river police, had found a nightdress which must be of the same kind, and had gone officiously to their headquarters with it. How long would it be before he saw one of those belonging to June? Would the young limb recognize it, and into what course, if he did so, would his enthusiastic spirit then lead him?

Parting with his friends outside the "Fisherman" later on that same evening, Harry Reed found himself standing beside Jim Sawyer. He had not seen the boat-keeper for a week, and in view of his recent discoveries was not feeling very well disposed towards him.

"I'd like a word with you some time," he began as they walked towards Lower Thames Street together.

"Wot's wrong with the present?" asked Jim smiling.

Harry lowered his voice.

"You must of thought me pretty green to take those

nightdresses off of you without a murmur. You were right. I could kick myself now I know where they come from."

Jim passed his hand thoughtfully round his face before replying.

"I told you where I got 'em," he said at last. "Part of a debt wot was owed."

"Oh, yeah? Well, you can tell that one to the cat's grand-mother."

"I'm telling it to you," said Jim Sawyer severely. "Take it or leave it, that's my last word. And if you want my advice…" He stopped short and laid a ponderous hand on the front of Harry's coat, "If you want my advice—mind you, I'm only saying this for your good—I wouldn't go worritting around looking for trouble wot ain't coming to you if you don't look for it. Because if I'm right in thinking it's Miss 'Arvey wot's benefited by my little gift, then you don't 'ave to trouble your 'ead about it. I know wot I'm talking about, believe me."

"It's not so much myself, it's the idea of getting her into trouble," muttered Harry, who was not wholly reassured by Jim's voluble but vague pronouncements.

"If it ever comes to that," answered the boat-keeper with a noble gesture, "you can always blame it on me, can't yer?"

"I don't know as I can." Harry looked at the ground and scraped his feet. After all, Jim had been good to him over the boat: he didn't charge him anything for keeping her at his place. He wished he had said nothing about the night-dresses. He might have known it would be no good. He'd just have to trust to luck.

Jim Sawyer watched his young friend round the corner into Lower Thames Street before he turned with a shrug of his great shoulders to unlock his own front door. And though by this gesture he appeared to dismiss the affair from his mind, for quite five minutes more a slight frown remained on his forehead and a faint anxiety lurked in his shrewd small eyes.

12

"I DON'T THINK THIS ONE GIVES ENOUGH SUPPORT."

"No, modom. You are quite right. But if you will allow me—about half an inch here—like that…"

Miss Kemp, with a tape-measure hanging over her black satin shoulder, pinched up a small fold of the material at the front of the "foundation" garment she was trying on her customer. June Harvey advanced the pin-cushion and the required "lift" was secured.

"Now, modom, if you will turn sideways. There…isn't that a beautiful line?"

The customer, seeing her unruly abdomen temporarily under restraint, was inclined, against a more truly artistic judgment, to agree. It was better than anything she had experienced elsewhere for some time.

"Yes," she agreed, "It isn't bad. But the shoulder-straps need tightening now."

Again Miss Kemp held out her hand for pins and again June Harvey respectfully proffered them. The customer was gratified to see her shapeless bust assuming a fashionable outline. "Lulu" was evidently a good find.

"I want some nightdresses too," she said. "I wonder if you have got anything I should like. I don't want these indecent transparent things all lace and ribbon. I like a good thick crêpe-de-chine or washing satin, embroidered perhaps, but as plain as possible."

"I think I can show modom just what modom wants," replied Miss Kemp. She turned to June. "Is Dolly free?"

June looked out through the grey-green velvet curtain. Dolly was engulfed in a sea of yellow underwear which a smartly-dressed girl with a discontented face was stirring into confusion on the counter.

"She's serving, madam."

"Then you go." Miss Kemp took a bunch of small keys from her pocket and, selecting one of them, pushed the others on one side and handed it to her assistant.

"In my right-hand top drawer, Miss Harvey. The oyster set." She turned to the customer. "A special set I have designed for Lady Sylvia Pilchard. I could not give you exactly the same, modom, but I want you to see the material. You could order your own design."

As Miss Kemp had anticipated, the customer was both impressed by the clientele and flattered to find her own taste endorsed in such exalted spheres.

"And the suspenders," continued Miss Kemp, tackling her job with renewed vigour, "would modom like the back ones a little more to the side for convenience in doing them up?"

June Harvey went through the archway into Miss Kemp's room. The work-table contained a double set of drawers, three to each side, in which special orders and unfinished work were kept. Both the girls knew that these drawers were all kept locked. Madam had explained to them that otherwise there would be endless confusion, with things put in wrong places, sent to wrong customers, or wrongly made.

As June was walking quickly across the room with the keys in her hand, her eyes intent on the table, she failed to notice a small cardboard packing-box which lay in her path. She stumbled slightly, recovered herself with an effort, and dropped the bunch of keys to the floor. Fortunately it made no sound on the deep pile of the carpet, and June picked it up with a sigh of relief that her clumsiness had not betrayed her. But now she was in a quandary. The keys on the ring had all fallen together in their fall, and she had no means of telling which was the one she must use. Should she go back to madam and confess her mishap?—Before a customer! Certainly not. Madam had said the top right-hand drawer, or was it the left? Well, one or the other, and she knew the set she had been sent to find. Very, very good, very, very dull. Just like Lady Sylvia Pilchard herself, who always presented the same appearance whatever clothes she had on.

At first she could find no key that would open either of the top drawers. She thought it was a bit peculiar having all the locks different, but that again was probably one of madam's fads. Then she found herself opening the top left-hand drawer. Perhaps it was the left, though she still felt it really was the right. She looked in, and gave a little cry of surprise.

It was not the oyster set especially designed for Lady Sylvia Pilchard that lay within; it was not the tangerine pyjamas for Miss Huntingdon, nor the black cami-knickers for the Honourable Mrs. Bodde. It was a pink chiffon nightdress, the exact image of the one that lay under her own pillow at her own home in Upper Thames Street.

June half-lifted it from the drawer, and then, afraid of

being caught with it, hastily restored it to its original position and locked it up again. A frantic search revealed the right key for the other top drawer. June snatched out the oyster set and hurried back to the fitting-room.

The customer was dressed again and tidying her hair in front of the glass. She approved of Lady Sylvia's choice and ordered herself three nightdresses of similar design to the slip of the oyster set, choosing the same material in a pale green.

"I pity her hubby if she's got one," Dolly said as she wrote up the new order and copied out the measurements. "He'll think he's got into bed with a whole blooming aquarium."

June walked beside Harry Reed in silence. She was wondering how to broach the topic of the nightdresses without giving offence, and the problem was proving too much for her. Harry, after trying in vain to make her talk, decided that either she was tired or something had upset her at the shop. If he gave her time she would probably tell him. In the meantime he put an arm round her and guided her in the direction of the river wall. Away from the lights and noise of the High Street, and looking out over the dark water, she would tell him what was troubling her. It was of great importance to him that she should confide in him; of such importance that he was ready to show more forbearance than was usual to his energetic spirit. Because June was not like the girls he had so far known. For one thing she did not laugh so much, nor so loudly. She was always ready for a bit of fun, but never tiresomely insistent. She listened when he wanted to talk; she was not all the time angling for compliments. She was more beautiful than any girl he had ever met; he loved her more than any girl he had ever met. Hitherto he had been wary, keeping himself free from major entanglements, aloof in spirit even when at his best as a companion. But with June it was all different. He had only kissed her twice, lightly, swiftly, on saying good-night, friendly kisses that meant nothing. He was determined not to let himself go until he was sure of her. There must be no risk of being let down, because, unlike the others, she had power to hurt him deeply.

Their way took them down Fripp Street, which was looking more sordid and desolate than ever. For demolition had started on the houses on the east side, and above the hoardings a ragged fringe of wall showed, sticking up forlornly into the sky, bereft of the roof and chimneys it had supported. At the Wood Wharf end the work had gone further. Nothing could be seen of Numbers One and Two, and only the bare walls of the upper rooms of Number Three, dropping sheer behind the palisade, the ancient wallpaper peeling off in dirty strips, the fireplace suspended in mid-air with no floor below it.

As they came to the corner, a puff of wind off the river blew over the wall at the end of Fripp Street. It whirled round into Wood Wharf, came back from the houses there, rushed into the half-demolished buildings opposite and, swirling among the heaps of dust and rubbish, emerged as an obnoxious cloud of grit and filth. Harry and June stopped walking, ducking their heads to the assault. But June was not quick enough. She clapped her hand over her left eye.

"Got a speck in your eye?" asked Harry, concerned.

"Speck?—More like a brick, if you ask me."

"Well, come over to the light, and let's 'ave a look at it."

He drew her under the weak glare of the street-lamp at

the corner. June raised a face down which tears streamed freely. As the light fell on the injured eye she cried out with pain and shut it, dabbing at the lid with her handkerchief.

"Don't do that," said Harry, taking the handkerchief from her. "You'll only make it worse. Let's 'ave a look."

Gravely twisting up the corner of the handkerchief into a point, he raised her face and, pulling down the corner of her eye with one large finger, dabbed at it carefully. His hands smelled of motor-oil and his nails were not overclean—how could they be, working on a lorry all day—but they were gentle hands and comforting, and his aim was accurate. The offending grit was removed in one bold stroke and June looked up into Harry's face, her eyes still swimming and her lips trembling with gratitude and recent agitation.

Harry drew a deep breath. In her helplessness and her full willing response to his efficiency she was irresistible. He took her in his arms under the street-lamp and kissed her long and hard.

Later they stood close to the river wall at the end of Barton Street and watched the small lights twinkling up and down the banks. Near them the Saw Mill Wharf and the buildings behind it were in darkness. Only a faint hum from within showed that the dynamos were working.

In their new-found intimacy June at last opened the subject of the nightdresses.

"Don't mind me asking you, Harry, but where did you get those nighties you gave me?"

"Why d'you want to know?" Harry asked the question to gain time; he had not thought that she would be curious so long after the event.

"I can't exactly tell you. At least—well, I'd rather you'd say first."

"And I'd rather you'd say first." If there was going to be a mystery about the darned nightdresses it would be of her making, not his.

June hesitated. She did not want to explain her mistake at "Lulu," even to him. She had a feeling that Miss Kemp would be very angry indeed if she discovered what had happened, for that nightdress in the drawer was obviously not meant to be seen in the shop, not even by herself and Dolly. And here was Harry trying to get out of saying where he had bought the two he had given her. Had he something to hide as well? What was all this?

"I asked you a simple question. Why can't you answer it without all this fuss?" she cried, her voice sharpening in anger.

"That's right. Fly off the handle for nothing... Just like a woman!"

"Oh, Harry—you are mean! Really you are. I only asked you..."

"Yeah, I know you asked me. And I'm not telling you, see? It's no business o' yourn where I get you a present. Come on, kid. Snap out of it!"

But June pulled herself free and retreated along the wall, glaring at him with indignant eyes. Harry followed her, half amused by her temper, half anxious at its cause.

"I might have known you didn't care that for me," said June, snapping her fingers to demonstrate her meaning. "You don't know how to treat a girl right, you don't."

"Don't be so soft," said Harry, suddenly angry. "You ought to know better than to start creating over nothing."

"It isn't nothing. And you can't speak to me like that."

"Is that so?"

"No, you can't." June's voice rose to a shrill cry, and she

stamped her foot with rage. "I've a good mind to throw your old nightdresses back at you."

"Please yourself." Harry's face was stern, and his stillness frightened her. She had hoped to make him so angry that he would catch hold of her to shake her; then she would throw her arms round his neck and kiss him and pretend it had all been a joke on her part, and he would say he was sorry and tell her about the nightdresses. Damn the nightdresses! Why had she ever mentioned them at all? He might be angry, but she saw that he was not going to touch her; he was not going to make it up.

"I shan't then!" She burst into tears and sobbed. "I'd burn them sooner. Pretending to love me, and then won't do a simple thing like saying where you bought something. Why shouldn't I ask? What's the mystery in a thing like that? You didn't pinch them, did you? Or did you?—I'll never believe another word you say. I never want to see you again! I think you're downright mean. I hate you—get that?—I hate you!"

Harry's set face looked pale now in the lamplight. He swallowed once or twice and then very deliberately turned on his heel and walked away from her, past Wood Wharf Cottages and round the corner into Lower Thames Street, where his own home lay.

June dropped her head in her arms on the coping of the river wall and abandoned herself to her remorse and grief.

By the next morning she had recovered. Her proper pride asserted itself and with its return she felt convinced that Harry was solely responsible for the disastrous end to what had promised to be a very successful evening. This state of mind continued throughout the early part of the day, and coinciding with an appeal from Gordon Longford, who was visiting the shop on business, to give him her company on the following night, led her to accept an invitation which in happier moments she would certainly have refused. She had qualms about it on the way home, and wondered how to get in touch with Longford to put it off. But as the hours passed and no repentant Harry appeared to make his humble apologies and receive her tender forgiveness, her resolution hardened and she got out her evening frock, lace with a flower spray on the shoulder, and hung it up on the outside of her wardrobe to get out the creases. She would have to take it up to town to-morrow in a paper bag. It wouldn't go in her attaché case, and she could not take a larger case because her mother would raise Cain if she knew where she was going. She would say that she and Dolly were staying up to go to the Palladium. She would change at Charing Cross Station cloakroom after she left the shop, and get back into her everyday clothes before going home. She was determined to enjoy herself, to justify herself, to spite Harry, even if he never knew of it, and to stop the ache that would begin afresh whenever she thought of his quick dark eyes and wide smile.

And enjoy herself she did. Longford was determined to make the most of this unexpected opportunity. He took her to an expensive and fashionable restaurant where a dinner-dance gave him an opportunity to show her his skill. Dazzled by her surroundings, by the dresses, the people; warmed by exciting unfamiliar food and wine; surely she would lose her London-bred sharpness, her native caution, and yield to his subtle carefully-planned campaign? As he watched her sitting opposite to him in her not very distinguished frock with its spray of cheap flowers whose petals were bent and bruised from the close confinement they habitually suffered among her other clothes at home, he compared the lovely outline of her cheek and the fresh sparkle in her blue eyes with the jaded or artificial beauty about him, and took a cool satisfaction in his own taste. When he danced with her, gratified to find that in this too she did not fall far short of his own very high standard, he applied himself to perfecting their partnership and gaining her confidence.

June's spirits rose in spite of herself. She had to acknowledge that she was having the time of her life. She told herself that Harry was not worth worrying her head over, that the main thing for a girl was to have a good time while she was young, and that Gordon seemed to like giving her a good time—a marvellous time. So why not let him?

In this happy frame of mind she looked up into Longford's face as they danced and smiled so sweetly that he caught his breath and held her just a little closer, whispering, "You mustn't look at me like that if I am not allowed to love you."

"Look at you like what?"

"As you did just now. You are too lovely, June. You don't seem to realize what you do to me."

His cheek was very near hers as he spoke. She thought it might be only fair to let him kiss her once or twice later on. Aloud she said, "Poor Gordon, is it as bad as that?" and though she spoke mockingly, he saw that her eyes were kind, and that his victory was more than half won.

But he was too sanguine. As he followed June back to their table a shrill yelp of welcome made him turn. Pamela Merston, at a table nearby with Helen, Babs, Tony, and two other young men, was beckoning frantically to him.

Babs shouted, "Gordon, darling, what are you doing here?... We had no idea. We've only just come... How marvellous running into you. Come and join us."

"Who...?" Pamela was beginning, when she caught sight of June, standing irresolute a few tables away. Her face changed: anger and bitterness appeared for an instant, to be wiped off by a great effort of self-control, leaving only a cruel smile at the corners of her lips.

"Who's the new girl friend?" she asked, in a voice calculated to reach June. "Don't tell me you are entertaining the staff? How perfectly priceless of you, Gordon!"

He turned on his heel at that and took June by the elbow to guide her out of hearing. But she had seen and heard and understood. That hateful Miss Merston! It was just like her to turn up and spoil everything.

"I'm going home now," she told Gordon Longford in a fierce whisper. "You don't catch me staying on to be insulted by your friends. Nice friends, I must say! You'd better stop on with them. I'm going, I tell you."

They threaded their way with painful slowness between the tables.

"Who is it, darling?" asked Helen, turning her long face to stare at them.

"One of the girls in a lingerie shop we go to," put in Babs, anxious to back up her friend. "Gordon touts his firm's stuff there. I think this is carrying business enthusiasm a bit too far."

"Quite agree," said Tony solemnly. "Should never mix business with pleasure."

He winked at Babs and raised his glass towards Longford's retreating back.

"Here's how, old boy!" he called. "May your nerve never diminish."

A cackle of laughter greeted this sally. Longford set his teeth and June wilted, hurrying on between the idly staring ranks, who gazed and laughed and forgot what they were staring at. Not all Gordon's entreaties, his apologies for his friends' bad manners, his offers of further entertainment elsewhere, could prevail against her resolve to end the evening and go home. She ought not to have come to a place where she could be so slighted. She had never done it before, and she'd be seen in hell before she'd do it again.

Pamela Merston, with one uncomfortable young man at her side, sat and brooded while the others danced. Her jealousy grew, and her fury both with herself and with Longford. She drank steadily, and as her mind was slowly clouded, the swaying dancers and the swinging music, the monotonous chatter of voices and the metallic clatter of knives and forks, melted into a crazy whirling pattern over which the dark shadow of her revengeful purpose swelled and grew.

Dr. Ellis saw the last patient out into the street and locked the waiting-room door behind him. He turned off the light and went back into his consulting-room, locking that door also. The day's work was finished at last; a long day, not an unpleasant one, rather a dull one. Nothing to distinguish it from all the others, except that it was the last.

He sat down heavily in his chair and rested his tired head in his hands. At this time he need fear no interruption unless a patient should come to the side door in Barton Street. Miss Pollen was out on her Saturday evening stroll, which she always took during surgery hours since the patients admitted themselves to the waiting-room, and the doctor was sure to be in himself. From force of habit he got up and washed his hands at the tap in the dispensary, then came back to the table. No, he would not eat any supper: there was too much to be done. Miss Pollen would be back within the next hour, and by that time everything must be finished.

He unlocked a drawer in his desk and took out some foolscap paper. There was no need to go into great detail, but he must put down the facts,—the facts of his own misdeeds and the more terrible facts of the compulsion under which he had acted.

He looked back along the years to that time when his uneventful, honest, hard-working practice had suffered a sudden check through his own illness. Of all stupid unnecessary diseases shingles was the most cruel that could have assailed him. It dragged on for months with recurrences of excruciating pain, and though he went back to work in a few weeks' time, he could not get through the night without the heroin that had given him relief in the early stages. And so it had gone on. The shingles cleared up, the pain at last disappeared, but his craving for heroin remained, and in the security of his legitimate powers of prescribing he indulged his desire.

If he had only stopped at that. Why had the elderly man with chronic arthritis persuaded him, and the woman who had not been able to sleep since her daughter died? Why had he not pretended to help them and given them other drugs; or advised them to undergo a cure? He might have known that the word would go round, that ultimately his prescriptions would be noticed...

He turned back to his confession. It was bald enough, but plain and brief. The police did not want frills, they were not interested in his psychology. They would not understand the hell of the last few weeks, entirely cut off from those who had commanded him, forbidden to know even where the danger lay, until he had seen it for himself. The police would never understand his addiction; how he had fought against it every step of the way,—well, how he had fought against it at first. Tears of self-pity stood in his eyes. He would make them understand. He crumpled up the first page of the confession and started again. But he was soon dissatisfied, and a second sheet joined the first in the waste-paper basket.

Then panic seized him. Suppose Miss Pollen came back too soon? Suppose a patient called? Suppose even that the great discovery, so imminent now, had taken place and all public knowledge of it had been suppressed? Were the police already on the way? Would they come knocking on the door and find him there and his unfinished confession on the table? Not that!... He could face death, but not the months of waiting for his trial and execution, months of agony deprived of the heroin without which he could not now creep on from day to day.

He started again on a third sheet and scribbled in anxious feverish haste, not looking at what he wrote, striving only to make an end and be gone. At last it was done and he left it, a single close-written page, on his table, and took out his syringe and the tiny phial of emergency morphia tablets. It must not be heroin this time. He had become so tolerant to the drug that he dared not trust to its use. But morphia would serve; he would make sure with three times the usual lethal dose.

When it was done he put down the syringe slowly and sat back in his chair. Should he go to his bed or to the arm-chair in the sitting-room? He had no wish to sneak out of life, he would like to go with dignity. After all he had taken good degrees. If it had not been for that attack of shingles... Where would be the most dignified place to die?...

He had this urgent pitiful desire somehow to reverse the sordid decline of the last few years, to cancel it out by a final gesture. But in the end he stayed where he was, drifting about his past, sadly, resentfully, mistily, till his head sank forward on to his outstretched arms and he fell into the sleep from which he would never awake.

13

DR. FREEMAN LET HIS PINCE-NEZ DROP TO THE END OF their string, and rubbed his eyes reflectively.

"I always thought he drugged," he said at length.

Inspector Mitchell nodded.

"I was only discussing it with Welsford here the other day. Wasn't I, Welsford? We came to the conclusion there was some funny business going on. Was it heroin?"

"Can't say yet. Presumably, he used morphia sulphate to do himself in—the tube was on the table—empty. Don't know how many tablets he used—they were quarter grains—don't know how many he had left in the tube. I expect he took a pretty hefty dose to make sure of it. You haven't found any supplies of heroin at his house?"

"Not yet. We've got a special man on the job. Ellis may have destroyed his supplies. But I should very much like to know where he got them from."

"So should I, but I never shall, I suppose—even if you fellows find it out. Dog's life, this. All hard work and corpses. When anything really exciting turns up I never get a look in after the P.M. All the same I'd like to know why my late colleague chose this moment to depart."

Inspector Mitchell and Sergeant Welsford exchanged significant glances. Dr. Freeman leaped to his feet.

"I know when I'm not wanted," he said smiling. "And there are one or two of the living who need my attention." His face became grave as he added, "No more news of Chandler, I suppose?"

"I'm afraid not."

"And Mrs. Holland's inquest adjourned again for a month? Well, well. Good luck to you."

The door closed behind the Police Doctor.

"Nice chap that," said Inspector Mitchell. "And knows his job."

"You weren't exactly open-hearted about Chandler, were you?" replied the sergeant. "I thought they'd got hold of his hat now, and had hopes of getting out the body to-day."

"If Dr. Freeman read his evening paper he'd know as much as anybody else. I didn't tell him because I don't want him to go putting two and two together and making five."

"Because we only make it three, don't we?" answered Welsford. "But, arithmetic apart, do you think Ellis suicided because we found Chandler's hat yesterday?"

"I shouldn't wonder. You see I wasn't able to prove a thing about Mrs. Holland, though I was absolutely convinced he'd done it. I never should have proved anything. Take the syringe, for instance. It looked as if Mrs. Holland must have had one, but it had gone. Dr. Freeman was struck by that at the time her body was found and spoke about it to Chandler. Dr. Ellis had three syringes in his surgery, two old ones and one new one. Any of them might have belonged to Mrs. Holland, but how could we know it?"

"It says about the syringe in his confession, doesn't it?"

"Yes."

"Can I look at it?"

Inspector Mitchell handed over the crumpled sheets which he had retrieved from Dr. Ellis's waste-paper basket. Welsford smoothed them out and read through them. There was much that was irrelevant and obscure, but the story of Mrs. Holland's death was substantially what they had deduced.

The doctor's original intention, stated frankly, was to give Mrs. Holland an overdose of heroin while pretending to give her the usual dose. This course had been "suggested" to him. But unexpectedly finding her from home, his plans were upset and necessity as he saw it drove him to adopt a less certain method. He had Lysol with him, and the idea of the substitution coming to him as he smelled the antiseptic in the house and looked at the cold tea on her table, he lost no time in carrying it out. He drank the tea himself, leaving only just enough to impart the right cloudiness to the Lysol solution, and put the bottle on the table, some distance from the cup and saucer, where he hoped she would not notice it. He had to leave it to complete the picture of suicide. The syringe and a small quantity of heroin done up in a screw of paper he removed, the former because he had himself lent it to her, the latter for his own use.

"She must have noticed the Lysol bottle after all," said Welsford. "Because it was standing near the saucer, wasn't it?"

"That's right," answered Mitchell. "But don't forget she'd lent her bottle to Mrs. Dunwoody. I expect she thought it was that one come back. That was a bit of luck for Ellis."

"I don't expect he was used to that sort of thing," said Welsford kindly. "It doesn't seem to have been really his line—murder—by the way he acted all along. Look at this confession, now. First he writes it, and then he crumples it up and writes a long rigmarole about his drug-habit. Then he throws that away too, and leaves nothing."

"Ah!" said Inspector Mitchell. "That's just it." He took back the account of Mrs. Holland's death and pointed to the end. The confession filled one page of foolscap, but below the last line, right at the bottom of the page, there were some words, crossed out, at the beginning of a fresh line.

"You see," explained Mitchell, "those words 'It was H…' crossed out! Don't they suggest anything to you?" He did not wait for Welsford's answer, but went on, "Of course they do. That confession was not finished. There was going to be more of it, but he thought he'd do it differently, so he started again. Same thing with the second shot. That went wrong too. You think he gave it up after that?"

"I thought he might have," said Welsford dubiously. "Of course he ought to have said something about Chandler or his accomplices and…"

"Exactly." The Inspector was pleased. "Now you've hit the nail on the head. He did intend to write some more. That's why he put 'It was H' (for Holman, perhaps), and then decided to use a fresh sheet, and then chucked it away because he wasn't satisfied. But I don't mind betting he wrote it all up in the end."

"But there wasn't any other confession found."

"I think someone took it."

Inspector Mitchell leaned forward impressively, tapping the second confession with a large forefinger.

"All this about himself. He keeps saying it wasn't his fault. He was driven to it, he had to do it, he was threatened and so on and so on. The man who wrote that wasn't going to leave us to think he was solely responsible. And we know pretty well that he had been at one time in touch with Holman and that Holman shut him up as soon as he knew we were on to him. That's suspicious, if you like. Now I'll tell you what I think. You know Miss Pollen found the doctor dead when she came in; there was no-one else in the house. Well, the side-door was locked; she opened it with her key. But the garage was open and the inside door from the house into the garage was shut, but not locked. The two doors of the doctor's room were only closed to. The waiting-room door on to the street has a Yale lock. It was shut. It would have been quite possible for someone to go in through the garage, go into the doctor's room when he was dead or dying, take the completed confession and let himself out on to the street, pulling the door shut behind him."

"And as far as we know the most likely person to do that would be Holman."

"That's right. Finger-prints in the surgery won't be much help; too many patients been in. Besides if Holman was going to touch anything in the doctor's room after he found his body he'd wear gloves. But he can't have gone to the house knowing he'd find Ellis had committed suicide. He may have had an appointment and arranged to get in via the garage, and that was why the door there was unlocked. But in that case you would think Ellis would have hidden the confession. Anyway, Holman wouldn't be so careful in the garage. The finger-prints from the door there may be helpful. Then those small traces of oil in the kitchen passage and hall: they might, of course, be off the doctor's shoes, but they're more likely to have come off someone who didn't know his way about the garage and didn't want to use a light."

"That was Holman, you think?"

Inspector Mitchell frowned.

"I don't know how many of them there are, or how many of them we shall ever get on to. But we've got those night-dresses against Holman, and it's pretty funny that wife of his works in a lingerie shop. Says she owns the business, but she hasn't produced the lease of the shop yet. And here's another thing. You remember among Mrs. Holland's clothes an old pink nightdress, thin material? One of these drug nightdresses, obviously. Now did she get it from Ellis, via Holman? Or direct from our enterprising importer? She may have had a closer connection with the gang than we thought at first. Ellis gives no personal motive for getting rid of her: he implies that he was acting under orders. Then the doctor's housekeeper, Miss Pollen. She gave a description of the man who brought the note the night Chandler van-ished, and apart from the clothes it might quite well have been Holman. Size and build were right."

"We can't exclude Miss Pollen herself yet, can we?" sug-gested Welsford. "Though I should say she wouldn't be much of an asset to a criminal gang. Perpetual twilight in the top storey, to my mind."

"As I was saying," resumed the Inspector, ignoring this criticism of one who was, he felt, entirely trustworthy. "As I was saying, I intend to get to the bottom of that shop, and of Mrs. Holman, who calls herself Miss Kemp in business."

"I expect she is Miss Kemp too in private, if the truth was known," said Welsford, who resented being snubbed.

"Perhaps so. It's immaterial. But Holman's past is interest-ing. He started as clerk to a firm of importers—left them to set up on his own—went bankrupt, and then started again. I haven't got any information yet as to how he got the money to make a new start—and I'm waiting to hear. It might be interesting, I don't think it was Miss Kemp; she knew him then, but she wasn't in business and I doubt if she'd have that much saved."

Sergeant Welsford stretched his arms over his head. "What I'd like to know is how Holman got rid of those nightdresses out of his attaché case? They weren't hidden in his clothes; they'd simply vanished."

"He must have passed them on. Probably had an accomplice at the lavatories, and handed them under the partition between two compartments. Trouble was he didn't appear to recognize anyone either outside or inside, didn't speak to anyone either, and went on to his train alone."

"You mean he'd arranged beforehand they should meet outside and go into adjoining cubby-holes?"

"That's right."

"Then there must be someone in it besides Miss Kemp," said Sergeant Welsford firmly. "Because it couldn't of been her."

Inspector Mitchell looked shocked.

"Not in England, anyway," went on Welsford. "On the Continent, perhaps."

"What do you know about the Continent?" asked the Inspector with scorn.

"Only what I've been told," said Welsford humbly.

June Harvey was in a bad temper. Seen in retrospect, her evening with Gordon Longford appeared neither so glamorous in the early hours, nor so melodramatic in the latter part as it had seemed to her on her return home. She had not been able to think about it at all during the Saturday morning's work at "Lulu," but now, at home in her mother's kitchen, ironing her own week's wash, the whole party took on a sordid aspect, and even the innocent and unimpeachable food shared in the general condemnation. The root of the matter was Harry's continued absence. She had not seen him since the night of the quarrel and now it was another week-end, a precious week-end with five days' work between it and the next, and no plans made, nothing to do unless she went out to look for the friends she had neglected since she met Harry. And they would be so surprised, so sympathetic, so secretly triumphant. Damn them, she'd rather waste the time at home: it was bound to be a flop, whatever she did.

She spread her nightdress on the ironing cloth and clapped the iron on to it savagely. It *would* be *his* nightdress: everything conspired to remind her of him. The thin chiffon crumpled under her careless fingers and she pulled it straight impatiently. Just like him, it was! Not really good material after all. It had looked so posh and up-stage before she washed it, but look at it now! The colour had altered, the chiffon pulled when you ironed it so that goodness knows what shape it would be on, and the satin edging, that had looked so rich and rounded at first was nothing but a ribbon binding after all. Even when it was ironed flat and smooth it looked cheap.

She folded up the garment and hung it over the string suspended before the fire. Life was just one big disappointment; she might as well make up her mind to that.

"I say, June!" said Leslie's excited voice.

"Well, what is it?"

"Is that yours?"

"Is what mine?... Take your hands off! If you touch my things I won't half wallop you."

"Where did you get this nightdress, Junie? You might tell me. 'S important."

"I like that. Important! Who to? You? Just you mind your own business, young nosey. Go and play! There's no room for you in here. And leave that string alone, I tell you; you'll have it down if you aren't careful."

"It must 'ave cost ever such a lot. Wot did you give for it, June?"

"Well, of all the sauce! What's it got to do with you, I should like to know? As a matter of fact, I didn't buy it. It was a present—so there!"

"Coo! Funny sort of present. Who gave...?"

But June had had enough of Leslie's questioning. Moreover she did not want it known at home that she had accepted such a present from Harry Reed, the boy who had proved himself as heartless as he was fickle. She took Leslie by the shoulders and pushed him to the door.

"Take yourself off. I'm busy. Miss Kemp gave me that nightdress if you want to know. It's none of your business, but I don't care who knows it. Perhaps you don't know who Miss Kemp is?"

"Yes, I do. She's your boss at 'Lulu.'"

"Aren't you a clever little boy? Take care you don't have a brain-storm. And for God's sake, go, and let me get on with my ironing."

Leslie shook himself free, and made a face at her. "I'm not stopping you, am I?"

The door slammed behind him cutting short the skirmish, so Leslie retired to the bottom of the back-garden and began to throw stones at the fence. He had a weighty problem to decide. As a self-appointed member of the Thames Division of the Metropolitan Police it was his duty to report his new discovery to his superiors. But would this involve his sister in any trouble? Though he invariably bickered with June whenever he was with her, he had a secret admiration and deep affection for her, and always took her part against their mother. But his new enthusiasm, fed by the extraordinary luck of his discovery, could not be contained. He told himself comfortably that as the nightdress had been a present to June, it had nothing to do with her. And that being so, what a shock he would give them at Wapping! Even the plain-clothes bloke would sit up and take notice. Perhaps they'd give him a ride in the launch this time; he certainly deserved it.

June thought no more about her strange nightdresses and went to work on Monday entirely preoccupied by the problem of how to meet Harry Reed again without loss of dignity. A miserable week-end had taught her that life was no longer worth living away from him: she was ready to apologize for her share in their quarrel, but she wanted him to make the first move.

She was considerably mystified, therefore, when a round-faced man with very blue eyes walked into the shop and approaching the glass counter asked her in confidential tones if she was Miss Harvey and if she had a brother called Leslie who had fallen into the river and been rescued by the river police.

"It was Harry Reed rescued him, and me too," said June indignantly. "The police would never have been in time."

"Well, never mind that now," said Norris kindly. "This brother of yours has taken a fancy to one of our men, the one who was instrumental in saving him, and he's always dodging along to our place trying to get a ride in a launch, which he can't have, as he's been told."

"Why don't you see my mother about it?" said June, who could not understand why Leslie's exploits should involve a visit to "Lulu." "She's the one to stop him going."

Norris went on with his story.

"I don't suppose he's told your folk at home what he's been doing, and I won't go into that now. But from things we've heard there's something I must ask you."

As he spoke he drew a dirty pink rag from his pocket and began to spread it out. To her horror June saw that it was the remains of a nightdress similar to her own.

"Did Leslie give you that? That isn't mine. I put mine up to air last night, and..."

Norris stirred the rag with his finger.

"You have a nightdress like that one then, have you, miss?"

"Yes, I have... yes." She was about to say that she had two, but caution warned her to volunteer nothing at present. This was a policeman. If there was some trouble connected with these nightdresses, Harry's name must on no account be drawn into it.

"Can you tell me where you got it?"

That young limb, Leslie! She'd have a thing or two to say to him when she got home. In the meantime, best stick to the same story.

"I got it here," she said in a low voice, and her heart sank, for Miss Kemp stood in the doorway of the inner room holding back the curtain in her hand, and Miss Kemp's rigid face and wary eyes showed that she had both heard and seen. Norris, following June Harvey's frightened glance, turned also.

"Good morning, Mrs. Holman," he said pleasantly. "Perhaps I can have a word with you."

He picked up the rag as he spoke and dangled it from his finger.

"You'd better come in here, Dolly, if you've finished those shoulder-straps, you can go into the shop with Miss Harvey."

"I should like Miss Harvey to come with us," suggested Norris.

"Oh, very well."

Miss Kemp, keeping a firm hold on her temper and her shaken nerves, led the way into her sanctum and turned to face the detective. Briefly Norris explained the position. "Miss Harvey told her brother that you gave her the night-dress that is in her possession," he concluded. "I should just like to have your confirmation of that fact."

"I don't know what nightdress she's alluding to," said Miss Kemp sullenly, "I don't recollect giving her any nightdress."

Norris produced his decayed sample. Madam looked at it stonily and shook her head.

"I've never had anything like that in stock here," she said. She began to feel firmer ground under her feet.

"When do you say you were given this nightdress?" asked Norris, turning again to June.

"After the November sale," she lied glibly.

"But I tell you I never have that sort here or anything like it. You can go through the stock if you like."

"There aren't any in stock, I know," said June eagerly. "But there was one in the top left-hand drawer of this table only the other day. I saw it with my own eyes. I opened the drawer by mistake. You gave me the wrong key when you wanted that oyster set to show in the shop."

For a moment Miss Kemp appeared to be about to spring at her assistant and wring her neck. Then she controlled herself and stood silent, waiting.

"I'd like to see that drawer open," said Norris.

"Certainly." Miss Kemp unlocked the drawer and pulled it out. It was empty, as Norris had expected. The other drawers proved equally fruitless.

"There are a few trade samples kept in that drawer from time to time," explained Madam. "It is just possible I may have given them to the assistants after the sale. I really don't remember. Nor do I remember what they looked like."

"But you are quite sure you have nothing like this on the premises now?" asked Norris, folding up his specimen and putting it away in his pocket.

"Quite sure. Is there anything else I can do for you?"

"No, that's all."

Detective Norris had no more questions to ask because he now knew what he had come to discover.

June's discomfort and anxiety were not allayed, on reaching home, by the news that there had been a second visit to her home. The policeman who had called that morning for June's working address had been again in the afternoon and had insisted in seeing the washing on the line. Something about a nightdress June had been given at the shop.

"I suppose you did come by it honest?" asked her mother in her usual sour voice.

"What d'you take me for?"

"Then what's all the fuss about?"

"How the hell do I know?"

"Don't you dare speak to me like that! In front of Les, too!"

June snatched the offending garment off the line and took it to her own room. It was no good; she'd have to warn Harry, whatever he thought of her.

She stood outside his house in Lower Thames Street and sent in a message to him by his mother. Harry came out in his shirt-sleeves, his mouth full of bread and jam, a large sandwich in his hand. His eyes danced when he saw her and he mumbled cheerfully, "Wotcher, kid! Thought you was lost."

"Harry, the police have been down to our house, and along to 'Lulu'…asking about that nightdress. I thought—I thought you ought to know."

His face hardened suddenly.

"Quick work! When did you start laying information?"

"I didn't! You couldn't think… It was one I saw at 'Lulu,' a nightdress in a drawer there—just like mine. That was why I asked you where you'd got them."

"And I didn't say, so your suspicion was confirmed? That was it, was it?"

"No, it wasn't…it wasn't. Oh, how can you? I came down to warn you."

"That's right." Harry came close to her and his eyes blazed into hers. "You came to warn me because you thought I was mixed up in some funny business. Well, you can tell your friends the police there's nothing doin', see, nothin'."

June ran away up the road sobbing, her head held down, fumbling in her pocket for her handkerchief. Harry watched her go, and clenched his fists and cursed Jim Sawyer for getting him into this fix, and cursed himself. What if she had suspected him of something? Wasn't it natural that she should? Didn't it all look suspicious? Quite likely he was heading for trouble; he might have known better than to take presents from Jim. She had come to help him and he had driven her away with hard words. He had hurt her and she had hurt him as only those who love can hurt one another. Now she would never forgive him.

"I ought to be kicked," he muttered savagely to himself, and relieved his feelings by punishing the doorpost.

The work of demolition in Fripp Street went forward rapidly. Number One and Number Two were a heap of ruins; Number Three, shorn of its top storey, slanted up from that heap to the naked dividing wall of Number Four.

On the morning following June's unhappy visit to Harry Reed's home, two workmen, balanced one on either side of a peak formed by the chimney, were busy reducing this excrescence to the general level before razing the whole wall to the ground. With skilful well-aimed blows they first loosened, then cleared away, bricks and mortar, then stood and gathered strength for a fresh onslaught. During such an interval one of them looked down the short length of chimney remaining.

"Blimey, Bill, there's a nest down 'ere!"

"Nest—'ell! You don't get nesties a few feet over the kitchen range."

"I know wot I'm talking about. This 'ouse bin empty for years."

He plunged his hand into the chimney and giving a sharp tug, drew it forth triumphantly.

"There yer are! Wot did I say?"

Certainly he held a dark matted concave affair that might at some time have housed a sparrow family. Bill took it in his hand and looked at it with distaste.

"Rummy sort of nest. Made of 'air, ain't it?"

"Yeah. 'Orse-'air. Sparrows likes it for their nesties."

Bill in his turn peered into the chimney.

"There's a brick acrorst the 'ole. That's wot 'eld up the nest."

The other man spat on his hands and attacked the chimney. He was tired of the subject of birds. In a few minutes the next yard of brickwork bulged out and collapsed, while the two men retreated, shielding themselves from the falling bits. The dust cleared away, and as it did so Bill's hoarse cry made his mate turn back quickly.

"Christ A'mighty!" he moaned in terror.

Framed in the crumbling brickwork of the chimney, like a statue in its niche, a dead altered face looked mournfully out at them through dull unseeing eyes. A stained shirt covered the gaunt chest and skinny arms, whose hands were still walled up in the last unbroken piece of the chimney.

Bill stared from the face before him to the unsavoury mass of hair in his hand, and flung it from him with a yell that brought the workmen round about scrambling and tumbling to the spot, crowding round to see what had happened, breaking away to hide from what they saw.

The impact of their coming shook the frail structure of the ruin. While Bill and his mate stood, frozen with horror, the dead man swayed twice and toppled forward, and the bare scalped head of Detective-Sergeant Chandler bowed before them in the dust.

14

DURING THE NEXT TWO DAYS THE UNTIRING EFFORTS
of Inspector Mitchell and those under him produced a mass
of information, some of it irrelevant, but most of it very
much to the point.

The Popes and the Dunwoodys, having been the nearest
able-bodied persons to the presumed scene of the murder,
were questioned by the Inspector himself. The former had
nothing to say, but Mr. Dunwoody, realizing the seriousness
of his position, and the need for getting on the right side of
the law at the earliest possible moment, made a clean breast
of it, and described in detail his uncomfortable experience
in Mrs. Bowerman's house, only concealing the real motive
for his presence there. His wife, he affirmed, had sent him in
to see if the old lady was all right, and he had hidden himself
because he was afraid his motives might be misinterpreted.

"I'm not surprised at that," said the Inspector drily, but
he needed the man's co-operation and suppressed the rest
of what he felt inclined to say.

Dunwoody's story made plain the manner of Chandler's

death, which in its ingenuity and accurate timing must have been premeditated, and indeed carefully planned.

An accomplice, probably Holman, thought Mitchell, must have reached the house just before the car arrived and softly made his way in, hiding himself in the dark passage. The cold wind that Dunwoody remembered feeling as he withdrew into the front room was probably caused by this entry. The clatter made by Dr. Ellis tripping on the stairs was intentional, designed to cover the moment when the hidden murderer stepped forward and dealt Chandler the blow that had split his skull for the length of two inches in the left temporal bone. While the doctor saw Mrs. Bowerman above, and Dunwoody waited in the front room below, the murderer and his dead or dying victim had remained at the foot of the stairs. Dunwoody shuddered to think what would have happened to him if he had ventured at that moment to go forth, and remembered thankfully the strange small movements and breath sounds that had held him back. He described the journey to the back room, being positive that two pairs of feet had trodden the passage, the lengthy business of the filling of the coal-scuttle, the second ascent to Mrs. Bowerman and the final departure with the words "Go down past the river."

In the light of the recent discoveries made by the river police of parts of Chandler's clothing the purpose of this command was made obvious. The clothes were meant to be discovered, and to divert suspicion from the neighbourhood of Fripp Street. Since the buildings there were doomed, it was improbable that the murderer's intention was to leave the body in its immediate hiding place. It was more likely that Dr. Ellis was to take the opportunities presented by his visits to Mrs. Bowerman to dismember the victim and remove all recognizable parts. This plan had been frustrated by the old lady herself, first in her refusal to see Dr. Ellis, and her removal to hospital by Dr. Freeman, and secondly by her consent to the disposal of her house, which had led to the demolition of Fripp Street beginning considerably earlier than had been anticipated. These murderers, like many others, had over-reached themselves. Mrs. Bowerman's ghosts though clothed in flesh, had indeed taken possession of her dead son's house, and the noises that drove her in superstitious fear from her home were the fulfilling of their evil purpose, and had betrayed them in the end. No wonder Dr. Ellis had taken his life when he saw the place of concealment melting away day by day until only a chimney wall was left to cover his crime.

The manner of Chandler's death being discovered, the Inspector next turned his attention to the question of the accomplice. He had only two known associates of the doctor to suspect, Max Holman and his wife or mistress, Martha Kemp. The former had, as expected, produced an alibi for the night in question, but it was essentially unreliable, being merely that he had spent the whole evening at home in Martha's company, the lady herself being the only witness to the truth of his statement. Besides, shown a snapshot of Holman, Miss Pollen, the housekeeper, stuck to her conviction that he resembled the messenger who had brought the note. Moreover, she now remembered that when Chandler called on the fatal evening and she informed the doctor of his presence in the surgery waiting-room, the latter had at once gone to the phone, telling her to return to the waiting-room and say that he would be with the patient shortly. At that time she still thought Chandler had come for a medical consultation. As she left the doctor's sitting-room, where there was an extension of the telephone, he took up the receiver and gave a number. Without the assistance of a leading question she volunteered the information that the exchange she had heard called as she closed the door was "Eltham."

This was suggestive, but it was not convincing. Miss Pollen did not seem to be a woman given to flights of imagination: indeed ideas appeared to come to her singly, and to enter her mind after a sharp struggle with the resistance they found in their way. But she read the daily papers, so that it was not impossible for much of the fiction already overlying the case to have coloured her thoughts and warped her memory.

Time, however, justified the housekeeper thus. An appeal was broadcast for news of the doctor or the doctor's car on the night of Friday, November 9th. A few people described Dr. Ellis's visits to their homes during the afternoon, and one woman in Barton Street from her window opposite the doctor's house had seen him drive out of his garage at nine o'clock. Only one witness had seen the car later than that. Harry Reed, who had the whole evening fixed in his mind as the fatal time of the presentation of the mysterious nightdresses, and relenting his former determination to withhold his knowledge, described how he had waited for the doctor's car to pass before he crossed Wood Wharf to go into the "Fisherman."

Inspector Mitchell interviewed him in person on the third day after the discovery of Chandler's body and learned what he had hoped. There was another person in the car with the doctor after he had left Mrs. Bowerman's house. Obviously this could not have been Chandler; almost certainly it was the murderer himself. It was unfortunate that

Harry had been on the side nearer the driver, for though it enabled him to see clearly that Dr. Ellis himself was in the car, it made impossible any useful description of his passenger. The man was wearing a soft hat and a mackintosh but no further detail was available.

One thing, however, Inspector Mitchell learned which rather disconcerted him. He showed Harry a bunch of photographs including the one of Holman, in order to test whether the suspected man had been seen about in the vicinity of the doctor's house. Harry immediately pounced on this picture and declared that the subject of it was present in the "Fisherman" on the evening in question. He had noticed him because he was a new-comer, and rather different from the usual run of customers, though dressed like them, in workmen's clothes. Inquiries at the "Fisherman" elicited confirmation of this fact. The landlord himself recognized the photograph and stated that the man had come in about a quarter of an hour before Harry Reed. He noticed him because he was a new customer and he remembered him because he had not been in again. If this information was correct, and there seemed to be no reason for doubting it, then Holman was not, as Mitchell had supposed, in the car with Dr. Ellis. The third man, whose existence had already been inferred, was not only the murderer of Chandler, but was, perhaps, the leader of the whole gang. He it was who had ordered the doctor to "go down past the river." Had he planned the whole terrible deed, and the death of Mrs. Holland as well?

While Inspector Mitchell worked at and near the scene of the crime, other inquiries were going forward elsewhere. The next and last new consignment of rubber obtained by Listons through Max Holman was opened in the presence of the police. Not one single nightdress was found. It was noted that the cable despatched for this order was worded differently from other similar cables; it was decided that warning had been given, but how and to whom, could not be determined until information came in from the Dutch East Indies where the rubber firm was.

At the same time considerable attention was paid to "Lulu" in Mayfair. The question of the lease of the shop was solved, but not in a very satisfactory manner. The owner had let it on a long lease to a man who proposed to use it for the sale of domestic pets. This project having little success it had been sub-let to a woman of the name of Mounter. The pets fancier, who had later been successful in Eastbourne, had no recollection of Mrs. Mounter, having merely corresponded with her and seen her name on the sub-lease prepared for him by a solicitor. The solicitor had also dealt with the lady by correspondence, but the boarding-house to which letters had been sent could remember no-one of that name. Miss Kemp, on the other hand, persisted in her statement that the business was hers, that she had taken it from the last owner and that she had lost the lease. She agreed at a later interview that the name of the previous owner might have been Mounter.

All those people who had business dealings with "Lulu" were also sought out and questioned. Besides Miss Kemp herself there were two assistants in the shop, and a charwoman who came every morning between eight and nine. Three travellers for different firms that supplied goods were also constant visitors. Miss Kemp was her own secretary and one or other of the girls was sent out with the parcels that had to be delivered at nearby customers' houses. Other parcels were sent by post.

Of the travellers one engaged the attention of the police. His name was Gordon Longford and the firm for which he worked, "Cynthia Products, Ltd," was loud in his praise as a salesman. But what interested the Inspector was the fact that his last job had been that of clerk to a firm of rubber exporters in the Dutch East Indies. It was upon a reference from this firm, a good reference, stating his excellent business qualities and deploring his ill-health in the East, that "Cynthia" had engaged him. The man himself was perfectly willing to answer questions. He had no near relatives living, he said, but referred his questioners to some distant cousins in Dorset, who, rather surprised at a visit from their local force, nevertheless confirmed the fact that his parents were dead, and that he had spent some years in the East. Beyond that they knew nothing of him and had not seen him since he was a boy. Again the matter had to rest until the authorities in the Dutch East Indies were able to disclose what they had found.

"To think," groaned Inspector Mitchell, "that if I had only pushed the back of that coal cupboard, I might have found Chandler six weeks ago."

Sergeant Welsford made a sympathetic sound.

"If you had," he answered, "the whole gang would probably have melted away before we knew anything about any of them. As it is, we've got a good chance of cleaning up the whole pack."

"We'd have had a shorter job of it if Dr. Ellis's confession hadn't been pinched."

"But we wouldn't have got some valuable finger-prints on the garage door, which aren't Ellis's or Holman's or Kemp's."

"You're quite encouraging for a change," Mitchell was beginning, when the telephone on his table began to ring.

"All right," he said into the receiver. "Send her up... A Miss Pamela Merston," he explained to his subordinate.

Miss Merston's information was very much to the point. She explained her suspicion that Mrs. Holland and Mary Clarke were one and the same person, and with the knowledge that this woman had formerly been in command, if not the owner, of "Lulu," brought the case into an intelligible whole. Miss Merston, who gave her evidence quietly and simply, was able to recognize the post-mortem photograph of the dead woman, and to confirm the fact that she had preceded Martha Kemp at "Lulu." She had never heard her referred to as Mrs. Mounter. Asked for what purpose Mary Clarke had come to her flat on the afternoon of her death, Miss Merston became somewhat confused. She gave a rambling and incoherent explanation, in which a "friend who is a business connection of 'Lulu'" occurred several times. Inspector Mitchell insisted upon a more explicit answer, and the friend was stated to be called Gordon Longford, an agent for "Cynthia Products."

Mitchell and Welsford exchanged significant glances. This was indeed a step in the right direction. But from the moment she had made her revelation Miss Merston appeared to repent her loquacity, and the more the Inspector questioned her the less she would answer, until finally he decided that it was useless to continue the interview.

"Well, if that is all you can tell us, I won't keep you," he said, in the kind voice that had been the undoing of many witnesses. "If anything else should come to your mind in this connection perhaps you will let me know. I particularly want," he continued earnestly, "to establish quite definitely where Mr. Longford was on the night of—let me see—Friday November 9th."

"November 9th?" Pamela Merston was genuinely surprised. But as she remembered what she had read in the newspapers during the last few days, her face whitened.

"November 9th?" she faltered, and looked down at the floor. "Mr. Longford was at my flat that evening—that night, I mean."

"Do you mean he stayed at your flat—all night?"

"Yes," whispered Miss Merston, "I do mean that."

"She was lying, of course," said Mitchell, as he and Welsford made their way in the direction of "Lulu."

"Of course."

"Funny creatures, women. She came on purpose to do him down, and then tried to protect him. Why?"

"Jealousy, I expect. It takes 'em that way. *Cherchez la femme*—the other one, I mean."

They had not far to seek. Miss Kemp, forced to admit that Mary Clarke was her predecessor, acknowledged that she had taken the business over from her without a written agreement and without a lease of the premises, other than the original sub-lease to Mrs. Mounter, which was, Miss Kemp said, yet another name for Mary Clarke. She would not say how she had originally got in touch with the latter, only stating vaguely that she heard of her through friends.

Dolly and June were next interviewed. As neither of them had worked under the former proprietress neither of them was expected to recognize her features. Inspector Mitchell was considerably surprised therefore when June told him that she knew the face and would remember in a minute where she had seen it. He was overjoyed when she described her brief encounter with the woman who had accosted Gordon Longford on the Sunday afternoon when he had taken her to Richmond.

Longford again! And this time associated with June Harvey, the girl who had the suspected nightdress. It could not be just coincidence.

"And the next thing?" inquired Sergeant Welsford on the way back from "Lulu."

"June Harvey's the rival you were talking about. I'm not surprised. Miss Merston isn't a patch on her. Though what a nice girl like Miss Harvey can see in a fellow like Longford beats me."

"Perhaps she doesn't. A girl can go to Richmond on a Sunday afternoon and spend an evening dancing with a man without being committed to anything. I don't suppose she gets many chances of outings like that. She was most indignant when you asked her if Longford had given her that nightdress. Anyone would think you'd insulted her. And she sticks to it she got it from Miss Kemp."

"It's quite likely she did." Inspector Mitchell, while not allowing his feelings to influence his judgment, hoped, all the same, that this nice-looking kid was not mixed up with murder.

"After all," he went on, "Miss Harvey let Norris have that nightdress without a murmur. Not that it was any help, after being washed. Come to think of it, Miss Kemp is quite likely to have been trying to get rid of them. She wouldn't want to have any in the shop, knowing inquiries were being made. Of course, there was the one Harvey saw; probably waiting to be cleared to a customer. I'm convinced it's drugs at the bottom of the whole business. Maybe the Special Branch will have something to tell us by now."

Mrs. Harvey trod heavily along the passage to answer the front door.

"Oh, it's you, is it?"

Gordon Longford moved forward.

"Yes, it's me. Good evening, Mrs. Harvey. Is June at home?"

Mrs. Harvey pressed her thin lips together. She distrusted all men on principle, including her husband, and had no confidence in women, least of all her daughter. Whenever members of the opposite sex wished to see one another she was filled with foreboding; when the encounter took place in her own house she felt a personal affront.

"I don't know if she's in or out," she said ungraciously, "She wouldn't thank me if I did keep an eye on 'er. But I'll go and see. You'd better wait in 'ere."

She showed Longford into a dark and icy parlour sunk in a winter gloom that had covered the wall mirror over the mantelpiece with a frozen mist, and gave out an acrid breath of past fogs from the sooty lace folds of the window curtains. Here in a few minutes June came to him, a cardigan hanging round her shoulders, shivering at the change from the rich heat of the kitchen.

"Gordon, I never expected you to-day. Come out of this icebox."

"No, just a minute, June. Please, dear, listen a minute."

June looked at him curiously. His face was strained and had a worried look unlike his usual calm insolence of expression. She waited for him to go on.

"It's about that visit of the police to 'Lulu' to-day. I was in there this afternoon just after you left. Miss Kemp had not gone, and she was terribly upset by something you said to the flat...to the police. About a nightdress."

"Well, really!" June was angry. "I'm sick and tired of those old nightdresses! I never want to hear them spoken of again."

A strange light crept into Gordon's eyes. He laid a soothing hand on June's shoulder.

"Have a heart, darling! You can't blame me. It's this way. Miss Kemp is furious with you for saying she gave you the nightdress—or nightdresses—I don't know how many of them..."

"Two," said June defiantly.

"Well, then, she was all for firing you on the spot, but..."

"The old bitch!"

"Wait, dear, I haven't finished. She thinks you took it—them. Of course, I know you didn't, but I want you to tell me where you really got them, then I can make it right with her."

"What does it matter to you if she fires me?"

"Sweetheart, isn't that obvious?" His hand tightened on her shoulder. June shook herself free.

"It's no business of yours. I said I'd got them at 'Lulu,' and I won't say different to anyone."

"What's happened to the nightdress?"

"Which one? I gave the one to that policeman—the other's upstairs."

"Oh yes, you said you had two."

"Yeah." June was puzzled, but he seemed to want to help her. "Look here! Do you know anything about these nightdresses? What's all the fuss about? I'm sure I can't make any sense to it."

"If you'd let me have a look at the one you still have, I might be able to say. Is it a 'Cynthia' product?"

"It hasn't got the mark. I'll go and get it. I've not worn it yet."

She was gone from the room in a flash, and a very curious expression spread over Longford's narrow face. Leslie Harvey, crouched behind the sofa, saw it reflected dimly in the mirror and shivered. He had been watching for his friends at his usual station in the front room window when the stranger arrived. There had been no time to retreat; barely time to hide.

June came back in a very few minutes.

"This is it," she said.

Perhaps it was the way Longford looked at her nightdress, perhaps some sentimental thought of Harry's gift, or some anxiety for his safety should further evidence pass out of her hands. At any rate, say what he would, persuasion, entreaty, even the threat to her employment all failed to induce her to part with her property. Gordon might look at it, might handle it, but she was ready to go to all lengths rather than let him take it out of the house. In the end he gave way, and left her, June accompanying him to the front door to see him off.

When the room was empty Leslie crept forth from his hiding-place, snatched up the nightdress, which lay, where June had flung it as she went out after Longford, on the small table by the door, and darted through the kitchen into the yard. When the visitor's car had gone, he ran back swiftly through the house and away into the street.

"You've seen this man before?"

"Yessir. 'E comes to see our June."

"You know who he is?"

"Mr. Longford, sir. Something to do with the shop where she works. 'E's a wrong 'un!'"

"How do you know that?"

"'E tried to make June say she'd took them nightdresses. I 'eard 'im. Cunning devil!... Asking 'er where she got 'em. They was give to 'er. She said so. She wouldn't tell a untruth, not June."

"All right, son." Norris, sharing Mitchell's belief that Miss Kemp had palmed off the nightdresses on June Harvey to protect her own skin, was reassuring.

"They was a present," repeated Leslie. "But they ain't up to much, June says. They look all right like this, when they're new, but you should see them after they're washed. June showed the other one to Mum—all pulled out of shape, she said, and the satin binding all flat. Lost that rich look, she said."

Norris gazed at the nightdress as though he had never seen it before, then suddenly yelled "Scissors!"

A constable looked in.

"I said scissors, but never mind, a knife will do."

He opened the small blade of his penknife and stuck it into the soft rounded piping at the neck of the nightdress. From the hole he made, a trickle of white powder, the same white powder that had so amazed Jim Sawyer when it fell onto his hands from the tear in another nightdress six weeks before, dropped on to the table.

"Got it, by God!" cried Norris, and reached for the telephone.

In the ensuing bustle, the calls to the Yard, the orders and preparations, Leslie was forgotten. He stayed meekly where he was until Norris returned, ready to start.

"Please, sir, can I go 'ome now?"

"Bless us, I'd forgotten you were still here. You can come with me. I'm going down to your house now."

Leslie began to tremble with excitement.

"Are you goin'…are you goin'…in one o' them launches?"

"Now, you behave yourself. You oughtn't to be in this at all by rights. The less you say the better."

It was a proud exultant boy who sat, living his dream of bliss, in the small cabin of the police launch, as she sped down river to pick up the now smoking trail.

15

THERE WAS A SCUFFLE IN THE PASSAGE OUTSIDE DR. Freeman's room at the Public Assistance Dispensary. Voices were raised in protest or applause, and as the doctor stretched out his hand to the bell to repeat his summons for the next patient, the door flew open and Mrs. Bowerman, restored to the fringed shawl and the ostrich-plumed hat, tottered into the room, casting back over her shoulder a biting criticism of those who wanted to be the death of a poor old body, not long for this world.

"What's the matter, Mrs. Bowerman?" asked Dr. Freeman, as the noise outside was quelled.

"Turns indeed!" muttered the old woman throwing back her shawl. "At my time o' life—and me fit to drop. I'll give 'em turns! After all I bin through at death's door for weeks, they tries to keep me waiting, jawing about takin' turns! Never 'eard o' such a thing."

"It is usual," explained Dr. Freeman, "for the patients to come in here in the order in which they arrive at the

Dispensary. Still, as you've got in—out of your turn—you had better say what you want."

"I'll trouble you for another drop o' that cough mixture they give me up at the 'orspital. Wonderful good it was— cut the phlegm, lovely."

"Do you get much cough now?"

"Only since I got into my noo place. It's 'avin' the river so close."

"Where are you, then?"

"Wood Wharf Cottages, doctor. You see, Mrs. Dunwoody used to oblige me in Fripp Street, kindness itself, though no cook, I must say. But she done 'er best, and we can't do no more than that. She 'ad a back room downstairs she 'ad no use for, so I made arrangements to go there when I come out."

"Are you comfortable?"

"Mustn't grumble. Them Popes upstairs are a noisy lot, but it isn't 'er fault crippled with asthma, and you got to make allowances with children at Christmas time, I suppose. The river don't improve 'er cough, neither."

"You don't mean to say..." Dr. Freeman broke off, suppressing the outburst that rose to his lips. He changed the subject. "I suppose you're satisfied now about those ghosts of yours—that they never existed, I mean?"

"I reads the dailies," retorted Mrs. Bowerman with scorn, "To think 'e was a-murderin' o' that pore devil of a bobby right under my very nose, as you might say. Not content with makin' away with that Mrs. 'olland, next door..."

"Eh?" said Dr. Freeman sharply. "What's that?"

"Well, 'e went in next door the arternoon she died. Left me, not a 'alfporth better, mind you, and went out, me layin' there waitin' to 'ear the car go, layin' and waitin'. ''Lor love us!' I says to meself. 'Something's up with the works, or else 'is tyre's bursted.' Not a bit of it. Next thing, I 'eard 'im come out the door, next door, and start telling off the kids for climbing on 'is blooming car. The murderin' bastard! I'm lucky to be 'ere, meself. If it 'adn't a-bin for you, doctor…"

Dr. Freeman handed her the prescription and helped her to her feet. As she went away Webb, the Relieving Officer, put his head into the room. The doctor beckoned him in, and signalled to him to shut the door.

"I've just had a severe shock," Dr. Freeman began. "For five weeks I have rejoiced in the fact that the Popes and Dunwoodys had at last been evicted from Fripp Street. I imagined that they were scattered to the uttermost parts of London. Now Mrs. Bowerman tells me…"

"Don't go on," groaned the Relieving Officer. "It wasn't my fault. The Popes took the top floor when there was an elderly couple living below. They said they couldn't find anything else. The Dunwoodys went to her sister for a bit because they hadn't found anything at all. The elderly couple wouldn't stay on account of Mrs. Pope's cough—you know what it is."

"I do," agreed Dr. Freeman grimly.

"So their rooms were going to be vacant. Dunwoody came to me to ask for help, saying he couldn't get rooms on the ground floor and Mrs. Dunwoody couldn't live where there were stairs to climb. So what could I do? There they are together again, and worse than ever. I don't mind telling you, it's getting me down. They ought to have a Relieving Officer to themselves," concluded Webb gloomily.

"I agree." Dr. Freeman stabbed at the blotting-paper with his fountain pen. "But what's all this about stairs? Why can't Mrs. Dunwoody climb stairs?"

"You gave her a certificate, doctor," Webb was reproachful. "Dunwoody took it along with him when he applied for the rooms."

"God forgive me!" cried Dr. Freeman, aghast. "You're right, I did."

Inspector Mitchell's work was approaching its climax. Now that they had proved that the nightdresses carried drugs, the long-suspected motive, concealment of this traffic and the method of running it, was undoubtedly the true one. The various pieces in the jig-saw puzzle of the double murder of Mary Clarke or Holland and Detective-Sergeant Chandler were fitting into place, giving a coherent story which revolved about one central figure, Gordon Longford.

Information of a very suggestive kind had come in from the Dutch East Indies. Longford's career there had been neither so satisfactory nor so uneventful as the rubber firm's testimonial to "Cynthia Products" had suggested. He had from the first developed acquaintance and friendship with the less desirable elements in the business world there, in spite of the fact that his own firm was entirely respectable and respected. Later he had been involved in some trouble with an employee of another firm, which had led to the dismissal of the latter and to a severe reprimand for Longford. This man's successor was young and newly arrived from England. It was noticed that Longford went out of his way to make friends with him, but that the friendship after a time began to wane. The next thing that happened was that Longford on a short leave went up-country, with the young man, apparently reconciled, as his companion. A week later Longford returned to work, stating that his friend had stayed on to get some more shooting, his leave not being over.

Nothing more was ever seen or heard of him. After an interval in which anxiety developed into alarm an expedition was organized to search for him, but nothing was found on the further side of the camp where Longford had turned back alone. Those locals who had been of the latter's party said they had left the other man well and happy and promising to follow in a few days' time. Of the locals who remained with him there was likewise no trace for several months, but later some of them came back to their former homes.

It was about this time that an ugly rumour grew up that Longford had made away with his friend. It was remembered that they had quarrelled formerly and that the young man had hinted once or twice that Longford would soon see himself in Queer Street. As this rumour coincided with the growing desire of his Company to be rid of him on account of his general behaviour, though he was competent at his work, he was advised for his own sake to go back to England, and provided with a testimonial calculated to assist him on arrival. So, after an interval embarrassing to his former acquaintances and coolly enjoyed by himself in openly flouting convention in the most notorious local hotels and brothels, he left for home.

But the most interesting part of the report from Mitchell's point of view related to the dismissed employee of the rival firm. This man's fault proved to be an attempt to peddle heroin and cocaine, notably to certain local suspected addicts. It was not discovered who was responsible for providing this man with the goods for which he was to act as agent or middleman. But it was safe to conclude that his friendship with Longford had introduced the latter to the principals in the local branch of the trade, and that his present system had been worked out in the East before his return home. It was obvious that whoever was in charge, whether as originator or as agent, must be able to see the order cables from England, for it was clear that the trade had stopped from the time Max Holman's altered wording had reached the East Indies. The Special Branch had no suggestions to offer. The present system had been undetected during its period of use. The only thing to do now was to wait until a new route was invented, keeping in the meantime a close watch in England on the addicts, known to have been supplied from this source, and an equally close watch in the East on the rubber firm concerned.

So far it had been impossible to trace the method of substitution of the prepared boxes. The factory that made the boxes supplied several rubber firms in different parts of the country, including that from which Max Holman obtained his supplies. Since the police cables had arrived from England inspection had been carried out at every stage in the making and packing of the boxes, but the smugglers must have been warned, and would probably never use that route again. As usual the principals were, and would remain, undetected.

In any case Mitchell was not concerned with this aspect of the case. The Eastern drug-smugglers were criminals outside his province, but he had their henchmen, guilty of the worse crime of murder, at hand and already in the net, while he sought the last piece of evidence he needed before closing it up.

He had ample proof now of Longford's complicity. The man's finger-prints, given voluntarily with those of the other agents who represented their firms at "Lulu," had been found in several places in the Harveys' front parlour. They were also proved to be identical with those found on the inside door of Dr. Ellis's garage. It was probable therefore that it was Gordon Longford who had removed the completed confession from the doctor's desk on the night of his suicide. It was also likely to be he who had entered Mrs. Bowerman's house before Dr. Ellis and Chandler arrived, and who had dealt the fatal blow. Holman, luckily for him, was proved to have been in the "Fisherman" at the time. Mitchell had tested the time taken by a car to drive out into the main road from Barton Street, along to the end of Fripp Street and down it to Number One. A man walking or even running from the river end of Barton Street past Wood Wharf Cottages and along Wood Wharf itself would hardly be able to reach the house first. Therefore Holman, after delivering the message, must have waited at the river wall until he saw the doctor's car come out and Chandler get into it, and then must have signalled to Longford waiting at the Fripp Street end of Wood Wharf. This would give the murderer time to go quietly into Mrs. Bowerman's house as soon as he saw Dr. Ellis's car turn into Fripp Street.

There was only one objection to this theory, Longford's alibi given by Pamela Merston, and it was to break down this alibi that on the dark and dreary afternoon of December 29th, Inspector Mitchell and Sergeant Welsford went to interview her at her own flat.

They found her sunk in an armchair by the fire, her feet in a pair of dirty satin mules thrust out before her, doing nothing, brooding with heavy eyes on the flames. She did not rouse herself or try to be civil. Even to move her head in their direction seemed an effort too great for her to attempt.

"I have interviewed two friends of yours," began Mitchell,

"a Miss Barbara or Babs Collingwood, and a Miss Helen Tregard. They are both quite positive that you accompanied them to a party on the evening of Friday, November 9th."

"So what?" Pamela spread out the fingers of her right hand and began to study their nails.

"That does not agree with what you told me the other day when you came to Scotland Yard voluntarily to give information regarding Mary Clarke, alias Holland."

"Do you mean to say you haven't cleared all that business up yet?"

"Now Miss Merston, it's no good beating about the bush. You did accompany these two young ladies to a party, did you not?"

"Probably. I really don't remember. We often go out together."

She yawned slowly and deliberately.

"Then Mr. Longford was not here on that evening?"

"Yes, he was. After the party. I said before he was here that night."

Inspector Mitchell changed the direction of his questions. "When did you last see Mr. Longford?"

Miss Merston's hand clenched on the arm of the chair.

"Just over a fortnight ago."

"Where?"

In a few short bitter sentences she described her encounter at the restaurant with Longford and June. Mitchell looked curiously at her. She did not seem the sort to take any love affair seriously. But perhaps, even so, she could be jealous. What a fool Longford had been! His infatuation for June Harvey had wrecked his prosperous drug-trade, led him to instigate murder, to accomplish murder himself, and finally to secure his own betrayal by alienating his wealthy mistress. Carefully choosing his words the Inspector goaded her on.

"He has been a friend of Miss Harvey's, has he not, for some considerable time?"

She raised her eyebrows.

"How nicely you put it! Gordon Longford is not the sort of man with whom a woman has 'friendship.' But don't let me make improper suggestions about little June Harvey."

"He visits her home," answered Mitchell, heavy and deliberate. "He was down there only the other day." He did not describe the purpose of Longford's visit on that occasion but went on, "From what I can see he seems to be almost engaged to her. Of course I may be wrong, but I thought it was genuine. Now, perhaps you can tell me…"

Pamela Merston stiffened in her chair.

"No!" she cried. "I don't want to listen to any more. I don't want to hear anything about her, or him. I hate them both—I hate everybody!—I hate you, coming here forcing me to speak. You know perfectly well I lied to you! You know he wasn't here that night, that I only said it to shield him. All right—I've said it now…" her voice sank to an exhausted whisper. "Go and do your third-degree stuff somewhere else… Can't you see…I'm all in?"

Inspector Mitchell came nearer, and looked down at her with a grave face. Welsford licked his pencil and began to write.

"He has been giving you drugs, too? I am right, am I not?"

"Yes."

"You got them at the lingerie shop, 'Lulu,' concealed in the piping round the neck and sleeves of chiffon nightdresses?"

"Yes."

"The nightdresses were purchased by you originally from

Mary Clarke, alias Mrs. Mounter, and later from a woman called Martha Kemp, both acting under the instructions of Gordon Longford?"

"Yes."

"How much did you pay for each nightdress?"

"£75."

"How long did the supply in each nightdress last you?"

"About a month."

"Miss Merston," Inspector Mitchell put his hand on the arm that now hung limply over the chair. "Miss Merston, I do earnestly beg you to go at once to your father's home in Wimbledon, tell him everything, and let him put your affairs in the hands of his solicitor, while you yourself enter a nursing home for treatment. I cannot say what action may be taken against you when this case comes to Court; it is not my place to advise you, it is for a solicitor. But I can tell you one thing. Longford is a dangerous and desperate man, and if it comes to his knowledge that you have given information regarding him, there is no limit to what he may do."

She raised weary sullen eyes to his face.

"You get to hell out of this," she said.

On the evening of December 30th, at a cheap hotel in Newhaven, Max Holman and Martha Kemp were arrested on a double charge of selling and being in possession of dangerous drugs, notably heroin, and of being accessory to the murder of Detective-Sergeant Chandler.

Max Holman said nothing: Miss Kemp on the other hand decided to make a statement.

At about the time the Newhaven arrests were being made, Gordon Longford let himself quietly into Pamela Merston's flat. He found her lying on the sofa in the sitting-room, uneasily trying to read. She started when he came in, but welcomed him with a smile.

"Why, Gordon, you're quite a stranger. I thought you had given me up for good. How is your affair with the little shop-girl prospering?"

Longford paid no attention to her gibes, but took the book from her and sat down on the edge of the sofa. Under his steady brooding gaze she faltered and grew silent. He said, "What did you tell the busies? Come on, out with it. I won't ask you why you double-crossed me because I know. It was just your damned jealousy, wasn't it? You couldn't bear me to look at another girl. Even when you were amusing yourself with your own friends, you couldn't allow me the right to have an evening on my own, or to give anyone else a treat."

"You know perfectly well it was more than that! I saw you, in the shop that time, and the way you looked at her. You're tired of me. You thought I'd let you go if you neglected me enough. Well, you went a bit too far."

"I asked you," repeated Longford stonily. "What did you tell them? I'm in a hurry; I can't stay here arguing with you. I'll give you two minutes."

"Don't be so melodramatic," Pamela's lip curled scornfully. "I told them nothing about you, only about Mary Clarke and Mary Holland being the same person. Why shouldn't I tell them that? You never said I wasn't to? And I asked you about her. You could have warned me if it was important."

"You knew it was important, all right. You had it in for

me, and you went about it the best way possible, you dirty little Judas!"

He controlled his anger, leaning forward over her body, his hands on her shoulders.

"What a fool you are, Pam. Where will you get the stuff from now? I've gone out of business—too dangerous—besides, they know... Martha'll be leaving too—to-morrow. Did you tell your friends at the Yard that you were a dope-fiend? Or did you confine your remarks to me?"

"I tell you I didn't let them know a single thing about you. Except that I gave you an alibi for the night the detective was—killed."

She could not look at him now. His face seemed to have grown thinner since she had last seen him, longer and thinner. Now with its pallor and tautness it frightened her. His curious amber eyes concealed his thoughts: they gazed down at her with the coldly impersonal stare of an animal.

"You gave me an alibi—how generous of you! And how easy for the dicks to make their own deductions. You would have helped me more by silence." He paused and then asked slowly, "So you think I killed Chandler?"

"Didn't you?" The words were out before she could stop them, and she clapped her hand to her mouth and shrank away from him.

"What a state you're in, my sweet. Nerves again, my poor little darling."

The venom in his voice made her blood run cold. He leaned closer to her, pressing her back on the couch, and then, without altering the position of his body, shot out a hand and turned off the table lamp.

"No, Gordon, not now, I'm tired." Her voice was suddenly peevish, exasperated. "After the way you've been slanging me, you can't expect…" His hands moved softly from her shoulders and met about her throat. "Darling, put the light on again. I tell you I won't… Gordon, you're hurting my neck… Let me go… Don't Gordon, I meant it, I… What are you…doing?"

His voice in the darkness was dull and heavy. "I am killing you."

16

It was New Year's Eve. The day broke cold and dark, with a dull yellow sky that soon began to drop a steady rain on to the busy lighted streets. June Harvey travelled to her work packed with other business girls in crowded vehicles where the atmosphere was oppressive with the smell of damp mackintoshes and cheap face-powder. She splashed along the street towards "Lulu" sheltered closely under her umbrella, and nearly collided with Dolly, who was standing before the shop gazing blankly upward.

"For goodness sake, girl!" cried June, recoiling, "Whyever don't you go in? You'll be wet through."

"It's shut up. I can't get no answer," replied Dolly.

"Coo! You're right." June tested the door and found it locked. She looked about her helplessly. "This is a nice set-out, I must say. On a day like this, too. Lucky it's Monday, and she paid us up on Saturday. I don't know what we'd better do, I'm sure."

The assistant in the bric-a-brac shop next door looked out into the street.

"No-one's been able to get in this morning," he volunteered. "The charwoman came and couldn't get an answer, so she went away again. But I heard the police were there yesterday."

Dolly and June exchanged glances.

"You don't say! Well, there doesn't seem much point in staying. Thanks ever so much for telling us."

The two girls walked slowly away together. Dolly was indignant.

"I do call that the limit. No notice or nothing. I shall go straight down to the Labour Exchange. Are you coming?"

"No, I'm going home. I think I'll take the week off. I could do with a rest."

"It's all very well for you, living at home. Well, see you again some time!"

"Ta-ta."

"Ta-ta."

June went straight home, greatly troubled by the morning's revelation, and by her own conviction that the nightdresses were at the bottom of it. How would this affect Harry? If only she knew in what way he was mixed up in it. She did not believe that he could have done anything really wrong, but boys like him were reckless and headstrong; it might have been some foolishness…

Her mother was disagreeably surprised to see her back so early, particularly as her daughter would give no coherent reason for it. June went up to her bedroom and sat for a time thinking over the situation. Then she wrote a short note to Harry Reed, explaining what had happened and imploring him to come up and see her that evening. She thought she might be in danger. Please forgive her for her bad temper. She had never suspected him of anything, but it might be serious for both of them.

If he had ever cared for her at all this humble and piteous appeal should bring him to her side. She took the note down to his house and left it there for him.

With the rest of the day to get through till six o'clock might bring his answer and, she prayed, himself, June strolled homewards, making a detour into the High Street to buy sweets and a newspaper. On the front page of the latter, with photographs and lurid headlines, she found an account of the murder of Pamela Merston.

New Year's Eve had long been set aside in the Harvey family for Mrs. Harvey's annual visit with Leslie to the Lyceum Pantomime. Neither rain nor snow nor frost nor fog could put them off. If there was a tram running, they went.

The obstacles on the present occasion were more serious, but Mrs. Harvey was not in any way daunted by them. Reporters, anxious to interview June about her connection with Martha Kemp, who had been charged that day at the Police Court with sensational crimes, were brought up short on the threshold of her home. Mrs. Harvey had nothing to tell them, and she was speaking on behalf of her daughter when she said that June had nothing to tell them either. She was comfortably off, thank you, and did not approve of taking money from newspapers, article or no article. She had no photographs of her daughter, and had no intention of letting any be taken. She'd be obliged if they'd take themselves off. This, after some argument and no success, they were forced to do.

The police fared better, but received no encouragement to make themselves pleasant. A single visit, however, served to confirm and expand June's original story. She had received two nightdresses, not one, after the sale which had taken place early in November. She thought she had said two the first time; she was sure she had said two to Mr. Norris, and, anyway, he had got the second one, because Leslie had taken it to him. She had seen one nightdress in the drawer at "Lulu."

Sergeant Welsford was as lenient as his conscience would allow him to be. With Inspector Mitchell, he believed that Martha Kemp had got rid of the nightdresses to avoid their discovery in her possession. The time of the sale had coincided very closely with the beginning of the police investigation into Max Holman's activities. November was an unusual time to have a sale. He did not understand why June had withheld the second nightdress until Longford's visit. Perhaps she wanted to keep it, and was afraid the police would take it from her as they had the first. It was the sort of thing a girl would do if she was a bit scared and flurried by being asked questions.

June Harvey could give no further information about Miss Kemp, nor about the shop. Her friendship with Gordon Longford had been a trivial affair, and not encouraged by her. Sergeant Welsford did not tell her how extremely valuable it had proved to the police. For the finger-prints found on the Harveys' front room table, and known to be Longford's, were identical not only with some found on a book lying beside Pamela Merston's body, but also with those discovered on the garage door at Dr. Ellis's house in Barton Street.

Only the man himself was missing; otherwise the case was complete. In Pamela Merston's flat alone had been found three of the drug-carrying nightdresses. In the careless, untidy way of addicts she had not taken the precaution of destroying them after extracting their contents. Besides this, one well-known addict had confessed to obtaining supplies through "Lulu." And Longford's latest crime confirmed all the rest. His fury at the failure of his schemes, the stupidity and clumsiness of his associates, the treachery of his mistress and, above all, the blow to his self-conceit, his imagined isolation and immunity from police attack, had led him to this new killing, a brutal, pointless, foolish act, which was nevertheless an inevitable step in the series of murders begun in a jungle camp at the other side of the world.

The rain that had fallen steadily all day cleared off at eight o'clock that night, but the stars were hidden by cloud, and there was no moon.

Captain Harvey, who had gone on duty at six in a light drizzle, prepared for a thoroughly uncomfortable spell, turned back the collar of his coat and shouted down from the bridge to Tom Wild, "Looks like we'll welcome the New Year in in the dry, after all."

Tom climbed up on the bridge: he had the late edition of an evening paper in his hand.

"Mac just give me this," he said. "There's a lot about this 'ere 'Murder in a Mews'; that girl 'oo's friends found 'er strangled late last night. They ain't found the chap as done it, but they've circulated a description of 'im. 'Man the police would like to interrogate. Average 'eight, fair 'air, yellowish-brown eyes.' You don't 'appen to know 'im, I suppose?"

"Sorry to say I 'aven't 'ad the pleasure," replied Captain Harvey. "Me and my family don't mix in 'igh life to that extent."

"You surprise me."

Captain Harvey grinned cheerfully.

"I'm not all that interested in 'orrors," he said. "Read us out something interesting."

Leslie left the Lyceum Theatre in a golden dream.

"We don't 'ave to go 'ome yet, Mum. You promised me we'd go up to Trafalgar Square to see the New Year in. Mum, you promised."

"Oh, all right."

Even Mrs. Harvey was softened by the final pageant; the Palace attendants, the lords and ladies, the King and Queen in comic magnificence, the prince and princess in a blaze of glittering nuptial robes.

Leslie urging her forward, they went slowly up the Strand to join the waiting throng.

June made up the kitchen fire and poked it into a blaze. Her father would not be in until after two in the morning; her mother and Leslie would not be back much before one, if she knew Les. She wanted to go to bed, but though she was tired, she was too unhappy and too anxious to sleep, so she sat on in the warm kitchen, watching the flames spring up and wondering what would become of her now.

For Harry had not come. Even her desperate imploring note had had no effect on his stubborn pride, or was it his indifference? Obviously he had never loved her: he had probably just been amusing himself, taking advantage of their chance encounter over Leslie's accident. Perhaps he was laughing now at her note, showing it to his friends and laughing.

Stung by this thought she got up and turned on the

wireless, then sat down near it to wait for it to come on. Very faintly a dance tune took shape and grew, then stopped. She glanced up at the clock; it was just eleven-thirty.

"That is the end of the programme of dance music by the B.B.C. Dance Orchestra. Before we go on to the next part of the programme, I have a police message to announce. A man whom the police are anxious to interview in connection with the murder of Miss Pamela Merston is believed to have entered a Vauxhall car, registration number G.L.999, in the Car Park at…"

June stared at the wireless, horrified. The newspaper account had haunted her all day. She remembered Miss Merston only too well, her insolence in the shop, her cruelty at the restaurant. But until now she had not remembered that among Miss Merston's men friends, intimate enough to rouse her to jealousy, was Gordon Longford. The voice was still speaking—

"…believed to be still in possession of this car which has not been identified on the road since 2 p.m. to-day. The man is of medium build, about five foot ten inches in height, with fair hair, yellowish-brown eyes…"

June shivered and crouched lower in her chair.

"…last seen was wearing a light fawn raincoat and a brown Tril…"

An arm in a light fawn raincoat reached across June's shoulder and turned the switch of the wireless. In the dead silence that followed the cutting off of the announcer's voice, she forced her paralysed muscles to work and turned her head. Gordon Longford stood before her.

She whispered, "Gordon! How did you?…" and could say no more, for he was strangely altered, and stared at her with a fixed intensity that terrified her into silence.

He dropped into a chair near the fire, holding out his hands to the blaze, and rubbing them together to get them warm. Then at last he spoke.

"Get me some tea." His voice was altered, too, harsh and grating, where before it had always been gentle. She did not dare to disobey him, but got ready some cups and saucers.

"My father will be in any minute now," she said, though she knew that she could not expect him yet. "And Mum and Les too. The pantomime's over at eleven."

"Ah! I concluded that they must be out or in bed when I saw you through the window, alone."

She cursed her stupidity in so betraying her defenceless-ness. Through the window! So that was how he had come in. She saw that he had left it slightly open at the bottom.

"I tell you they'll be in any minute. You'd better not stop till they come. Dad wouldn't like it."

He laughed shortly, showing his teeth in a wide grin. "You think not, my beautiful? How will he feel when he finds you gone?"

"Gone?"

She shrank away from him, edging towards the back door. "Come and sit down, little fool. You can't get away. You aren't going—till you go with me. Sit down. I've a few things to say to you, and time is short."

She crept back to her chair and sat huddled up, trying frantically to subdue her rising hysteria, and to think of some way of getting into touch with the police. He sipped his tea and went on talking.

"Have you ever met a man who was successful and happy and in love with a glorious girl, and then someone strikes him a blow in the back, and he is crippled and ruined? Well, that has happened to me. I trusted my friends, and they betrayed me. But they have got what they deserved, and I am still free, still able to plan and foresee—to carry things through. Why do you think I am here? You heard the police message. But they'll never find that car. Why?... Never mind at present. But I'll tell you something more to the point. I've a rich customer, a careful man—very careful. Even his wife doesn't know yet that he drugs. He flies to the Continent once a week—in his own plane, from his own grounds. At midnight we're going back to the car; the paint on the number-plate will be dry then. At twelve-thirty we'll be on the plane and to-morrow we'll start life all over again—together."

"You're mad!" All June's sturdy common-sense revolted at this fantastic scheme. She forgot that she was dealing with a killer, a hunted man who showed his desperate state in his drawn features and haggard eyes. She remembered only the Gordon Longford she had repeatedly discouraged and refused, and had outwitted in a fog. "If you think I'd go with you, you're vastly mistaken. I'd rather die first."

He moved so quickly that she had no time to escape. One arm was round her, pinning her against him, while the other hand found her throat. The amber eyes were hot and furious. "I wonder if it would not be better to kill you," he whispered savagely. "You know too much. You know too much."

He bent her head back to look into her face. She screamed once, and then his hand moved with lightning swiftness to cover her mouth. Though she struggled and kicked and fought with all her might, she knew that her strength was leaving her. She tried to bite the hand that was crushing her lips. He laughed softly.

"I have always wanted you," he said.

As he spoke the clock on the mantelpiece began to strike the hour. A church clock nearby took up the chime on a deep note, and instantly with ringing bells and answering chimes, the noise grew and deepened. Sirens on land and from every ship on the river, fog-horns, bells, guns, drums, hooters, rockets, combined in wild barbaric sound to welcome in the New Year. The din struck on Gordon Longford's ear with the shock of a sudden blow. In his mind he had removed himself into a place apart where there were only two people, himself the victor and June the vanquished. Now the whole world was about him again, screeching at him, yelling for his blood. Instinctively his grip loosened, for his heart was racing again with the fear that had been on him for over twenty-four hours.

In his confusion, deafened by the rising and falling waves of sound that beat the air, he did not hear the window thrown up as Harry Reed leaped into the room. But he saw the light of recognition and joy spring up in June's eyes, and, throwing her from him, whipped round in time to duck the blow from Harry's right. June saw the murderer's hand flash to his pocket and screamed, "Look out, Harry, he's got a gun!"

The shot went wide, but it checked Harry's attack. He dived for June, pulling her down with him to the floor behind the kitchen table. Longford sprang to the still open window and disappeared through it into the night.

At the Friary Road Police Station Harry explained his late visit to the Harveys' home. His lorry had broken down forty miles out of London, and it had taken several hours to bring a breakdown car to the lonely spot where it had gone out of action, and to repair the fault. He had found June's letter at his own house, and being impressed by the urgency of her appeal he had gone out again at once to make sure that all was well. The front of her house was dark, but a ray of light shining through a gap in the curtains of the kitchen window and falling upon the wall next door showed him that someone was still up. He was on his way to the back door when he heard the sounds of a struggle and June's cry for help.

"But he got away and you don't know which way he went?"

"He had a gun," Harry apologized.

"Oh, I'm not blaming you for not holding him. Don't mistake my meaning. But we've got to be quick. If he gets back to the car he stole and on to that plane we've lost him. He'll be waiting for the local hue and cry to die down, but he'll know he can't keep the plane waiting long. We may trace the plane, but not in time to stop it. He didn't say where he'd got the car hidden, did he, miss?"

"No," answered June. She was still feeling shaken, but with her arm through Harry's and her hand in his she tried her best to be helpful. "Only about the paint on the number-plate."

"Yes, he'd be changing the number," Mitchell frowned. "He's not been back to his own digs, he's not been seen anywhere near the shop, or a pub he used to frequent, or Holman's place at Eltham."

"I should think if he wanted Miss Harvey to go with him the car would be round these parts. He said they would be on the plane at 12.30, didn't he?"

"Yes." June nodded to Welsford. Mitchell's face cleared.

"That's right," he said approvingly, "only we don't know his friends about here."

"Not now that Ellis is dead," agreed Welsford.

The Inspector banged his fist on the table.

"I'm a damned fool!" he cried. "The new doctor isn't sleeping in yet; he only goes down there in the surgery hours. And the housekeeper isn't living there either; she struck at being alone in a suicide's house. She goes in for the day, and does her shopping in the afternoon, leaving after the evening surgery. If Longford had the garage key there'd be nothing to stop him putting his stolen car in there in the afternoon and locking himself in. The chances would be all against Miss Pollen noticing, the doctor himself..."

"Hasn't got a car," said Welsford. "He's one of these young locums. Ellis's relations got him from a medical agency the day after the suicide."

"And anyone else seeing a car go in the garage would think it was the new doctor's," finished Mitchell, springing to his feet. "It's worth trying."

Harry and June were allowed to go in the police car as far as the corner of Barton Street and were there set down and ordered to go home. The police car drove quietly round the corner and stopped opposite Dr. Ellis's garage. Mitchell and Welsford with two uniformed constables crossed the road to the side door.

"Blimey!" whispered Harry to June. "There's a light in the garage. Wot's the odds 'e's just off?"

They waited, breathless and excited, to see what would happen next. It happened very quickly.

As the police crossed the road, their tread echoing in the stillness of the street, the light under the garage door went out. Mitchell gave a few brief orders to his men and, stepping forward, rang the side-door bell. Instantly from behind the garage doors a car engine broke into a roar, and before the constables could move forward, the garage doors, which had already been unlocked, though they looked fast shut, were struck from within and banged open. The rear of a car, forcing the doors wider open, appeared in the gap, and as their resistance was overcome, shot suddenly backwards across the road and crashed into the offside front wing of the waiting police car. Before the surprised Force, who had scattered before the onslaught, could gather themselves to attack, a man leaped from the damaged car and rushed away down the street.

"It's him!" yelled Harry, dashing off in pursuit.

At the corner of Wood Wharf Cottages he was just in time to see Longford take the river steps in a bound. Harry followed, but when he got to the beach it was empty.

"Which way did he go?" panted Mitchell, arriving at the head of his men.

Harry peered into the darkness and ran to the piles holding up Jim Sawyer's landing-stage. By the light of the Inspector's torch he saw that some of the weed was torn off the first post and lay on the shingle.

"Up there," he pointed.

The men scrambled up and Harry with them. He was about to follow them down the landing-stage when June's voice called to him, "Give me a hand up, can't you, you big stiff?" and, looking down, he saw her standing below with both arms raised.

He pulled her up and caught her in his arms.

"Well, if you aren't a little sport!"

"Did you think I was going to stay down there alone at this time of night?"

They moved quietly towards the end of the jetty, where the police were searching the sheds. Harry, fearing a scuffle when the murderer was taken, hung back to avoid endangering June, but she urged him forward.

"Quiet!" ordered Mitchell. In the stillness that followed they heard the sound of oars not far off.

"He's taken a boat. Go and get the river police, Welsford."

The detective-sergeant shot off on his errand, nearly colliding with Jim Sawyer, whose approach had been unheard.

"Lookin' for someone, Inspector?" he asked genially.

"Have you helped a man off here in a boat in the last five minutes?" asked Mitchell sharply.

"Me help...? O' course I 'aven't. I was just turning in when I thought I 'eard a noise."

He looked about him and shook his head.

"There now, 'Arry. I call that downright unfortunate. 'E's bin an' took your boat. It was layin' out 'ere, right under 'is nose, as you might say."

"My boat!" Harry stared: then he felt in his pocket. "God! 'E can't go in my boat. 'E'll sink!"

Inspector Mitchell looked at the bung and listened to Harry's rapid description of his craft. Holding their breath the pursuers listened again. They heard the water lapping against the landing-stage, but no sound of oars.

"Water-logged," said Jim Sawyer. "If 'e 'asn't fell out."

Mitchell's first thought was to commandeer another boat and search the river, but wiser counsel prevailed. It was a dark night with no moon or stars and pitch-dark off the landing-stage where the Saw Mill building cast a long shadow. The river police, summoned by wireless, would soon be there, and with their swift craft, powerful searchlights, and expert knowledge of the river, would certainly find the fugitive if he was still above water.

"He can swim," said June. "He often said he was no end of a good swimmer, like he was a dancer."

"Then he may have swum ashore, if he hasn't drifted there," said the Inspector.

"'E won't 'ave drifted," explained Jim. "Tide's near the bottom of the ebb; current's runnin' straight down-stream, wot there is of it."

"We must wait, then," said Mitchell.

June clung to Harry, content to wait anywhere so long as her head was on his shoulder.

"You'd better take your young lady home," suggested Mitchell. "This is no place for her."

"Before I go, Inspector," said June, "I'd like to thank you. You might have got me into trouble over those nightdresses. Perhaps we ought to tell you—it can't matter now…"

"That's all right, Miss Harvey. I know Kemp was trying to protect herself by making a present of them to you."

"It only goes to show," said Jim Sawyer, with a solemn wink at Harry, "you can't be too careful 'oo you takes presents from."

Inspector Mitchell glanced sharply at the boat-keeper. A secret satisfaction and amusement gleamed in the latter's small eyes. What did he know of this business? There was nothing to connect him with the drug-smugglers save the fact that he had salvaged one broken box of rubber, a box that should have contained nightdresses, and had not. That in its way was typical of Jim; his scavenging seldom brought him much profit through official channels, and yet he prospered unnaturally. A rogue, if ever there was one, and slippery as an eel. It would take some doing to pin anything on to Jim.

But Harry was not listening; he was straining his eyes to catch another glimpse of a dark patch he had seen far off beyond the barges where some shore-lights danced on the water.

"See that?" he cried, pointing it out to the Inspector. "You'll get 'im yet."

"I doubt it," muttered Jim Sawyer beneath his breath, but no-one heard him.

As if in answer to Harry's words a distant hum was heard on the river, and while they gazed in the direction of the sound, two police launches, their powerful searchlights playing ahead, came charging down-stream, throwing up a cloud of foaming spray in their wake. They cut out their engines and slowed down as they neared Sawyer's jetty, so that Mitchell was able to hail them and shout what had happened. Then they nosed forward again, the searchlights moving to and fro, covering every foot of the river from bank to midstream.

The watchers crowded to the edge of the landing-stage, staring at the bright circles of light until their eyes ached.

"There! Look! Now they're on to him. Look!"

The circle widened as the two lights met and fused. In the centre of it lay the dark bulk of Harry's boat, the gunwale level with the water, while clinging to the rudder could just be distinguished the two hands and wet head of a man.

Norris in the foremost launch was able to recognize his features and let out a yell of triumph that carried to the group on the landing-stage. But the cry ended in a shout of warning.

Perhaps Longford was exhausted by his long flight or startled by the sudden illumination that stripped off his cover of darkness. Whichever it was he suddenly lost his grip upon Harry's boat, and in his frantic clutch at her gave her a push that sent her out of his reach.

"He'll have to swim for it now," cried Mitchell. "But they've got him all right, and he deserves it."

"No," said Jim Sawyer. "The eddy's got 'im first, pore devil."

Longford, parted from his water-logged craft at the edge of the first suction-pool, had one thought, and one only, to swim in-shore, away from the searchlight's beam, where he might take cover behind some barge or creep out upon some dark beach or wharf. He took a strong stroke—straight into the centre of the pool.

A nightmare force spun him round, clutching at his legs, drawing him under. He fought his way back to the surface, gasping and terrified, but the unseen enemy gripped him once more, pulling him down. The searchlight was on him again now, the launch was driving at him through the water, men were shouting, poised with ropes and belts to throw to him—to save him for the gallows. And he wanted to be saved.

Norris saw his white imploring face, ghastly in the brilliant light, come up to the surface of the water, then with a scream of despairing rage and terror that rang in the listeners' ears for many days, he flung up his hands and was gone.

So Gordon Longford went down through the muddy water gasping and struggling, to choke out his life in the slime of the river bed. He died there like a rat in a flooded sewer.

But the water of London river spun in the pools and flowed away—as it had flowed past the silent awestruck group on Jim Sawyer's landing-stage, past the launches waiting vainly for the suction to be cut off at the Saw Mill, past the wharfs and the factories, the cranes, the houses, the walls and beaches, the fettered ships at their moorings, the heavy, loaded barges, the docks and warehouses and rubbish dumps and old forgotten workings, past the low banks and the little hills, to the wide, gull-haunted reaches, and the great sands, and the sea.

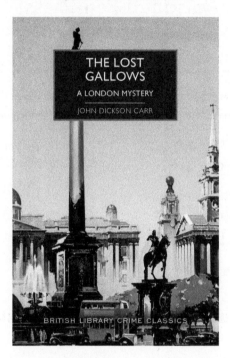